HOMETO

SHIPMENT 5

His Best Friend's Baby by Molly O'Keefe
Caleb's Bride by Wendy Warren
Her Sister's Secret Life by Pamela Toth
Lori's Little Secret by Christine Rimmer
High-Stakes Bride by Fiona Brand
Hometown Honey by Kara Lennox

SHIPMENT 6

Reining in the Rancher by Karen Templeton
A Man to Rely On by Cindi Myers
Your Ranch or Mine? by Cindy Kirk
Mother in Training by Marie Ferrarella
A Baby for the Bachelor by Victoria Pade
The One She Left Behind by Kristi Gold
Her Son's Hero by Vicki Essex

SHIPMENT 7

Once and Again by Brenda Harlen
Her Sister's Fiancé by Teresa Hill
Family at Stake by Molly O'Keefe
Adding Up to Marriage by Karen Templeton
Bachelor Dad by Roxann Delaney
It's That Time of Year by Christine Wenger

SHIPMENT 8

The Rancher's Christmas Princess by Christine Rimmer
Their Baby Miracle by Lillian Darcy
Mad About Max by Penny McCusker
No Ordinary Joe by Michelle Celmer
The Soldier's Baby Bargain by Beth Kery
A Texan Under the Mistletoe by Leah Vale

HOMETOWN HEARTS

Accidental Hero

LORALEE LILLIBRIDGE

HHARLEQUIN® HOMETOWN HEARTS

Recycling programs
for this product may
not exist in your area.

ISBN-13: 978-0-373-21462-4

Accidental Hero

Copyright © 2005 by Loralee Lillibridge

Printed in U.S.A.

Loralee Lillibridge grew up in Texas loving cowboys and rodeos, but relocated to Michigan after her marriage to a handsome Yankee who stole her heart. She still favors country love songs, and seeing a field of Texas bluebonnets can make her cry, but she admits the west Michigan lakeshore has a special beauty all its own. She enjoys writing heartwarming stories about ordinary people and extraordinary love.

Loralee is former president and founding member of the mid-Michigan chapter of Romance Writers of America. You can write to Loralee at PO Box 140095, Walker, MI 49514-0095, or visit her website.

Dedicated to my wonderful husband, children and grandchildren, whose belief in me is amazing. I'm so blessed to have your love and support.

Chapter One

"Bo Ramsey's back."

The shock of her father's words riveted Abby Houston to the spot where she stood at the kitchen sink, up to her elbows in dishwater. It took a minute for the words to sink in. When they did, she gripped the counter with soapy hands and waited for her heart rate to return to normal before she spoke.

"What did you say, Pop?" Surely she'd heard him wrong. That name had been censored from their conversation for almost two years. Hearing it now sent her stomach spiraling in a swirl of unwanted sensations. She hated experiencing symptoms that smacked of weakness; she prided herself on being strong enough to close the door on her past. Now, it seemed her strength was about to be tested again.

She held her breath as Buck Houston crossed the room to stand next to her, sympathy written all over his aged face.

"Just thought you should know, kitten. I ran into Shorty Packer down at the feed mill earlier this morning. Said Bo's staying with him out at his ranch. Been there more'n a week already."

"I… I suppose he has a right to come back. He always did as he pleased." Abby grabbed for a towel and busied her hands, angry because she couldn't stop them from trembling. She was determined to keep that bit of emotion hidden from Pop's scrutiny.

Buck snorted. "If you ask me, he'd be a heap smarter if he stayed away. Nobody in these parts will be too happy to see him again." His arm went around his daughter's shoulder in a comforting embrace.

"Have you seen him?" She couldn't keep her voice steady. Where was the nonchalance she'd been practicing for so long? She blinked away angry tears.

Buck shook his head. "Nope, and I don't

want to, either. Got no use for the likes of him. You stop fretting, Abby-girl. Chances are that cowboy won't be around long enough for your paths to cross. I just didn't want you to be surprised when you heard it in town. You know how Sweet River folks love a good gossip. I'm surprised Shorty's managed to keep the news a secret this long."

Abby leaned against Buck's chest and let him hold her the way he'd done so many times during her growing-up years. There'd been just the two of them ever since she was twelve. Lord knows, he'd done his best to be both mother and father to her. She knew the real reason he fought to hang on to the often unproductive ranch was because of her. She'd watched him struggle to provide for her, often at great expense to himself. She understood his sacrifice and loved him dearly for always being her champion.

Somehow, they'd survived those lean years. How ironic that now, she was the one trying to keep the wolf from the door. There were a dozen students in the equine therapy program she directed, as well as inquiries from interested out-of-town parents. Her determination to ease the load on Pop's shoulders was the motivation behind her drive to succeed. Bo Ramsey and her past were no longer important.

"Don't worry about me, Pop. I'll be fine. I'm sure Bo won't try to see me. Why should he?" Her voice was soft and husky, its quiver hinting at the panic hovering just beneath the surface of her self-control.

"Abby, I wish…."

"Don't, Pop. Don't even start, okay? That was a long time ago and best forgotten." She pulled away and started for the back door, grabbing her hat from the wall hook on her way out. "Let's get the chores done before I go to town. I don't have any students today, but I promised IdaJoy I would help during the lunch rush. Saturdays are the café's busiest days."

Abby was halfway to the barn before Buck caught up with her.

"Bo Ramsey's back."

For the second time that day, the impact of those words slammed Abby's heart against her ribs. With a calmness that was a total sham, she concentrated on making her legs carry her across the room to the nearest stool at the lunch counter.

The Blue Moon Café was empty except for

IdaJoy Sparks, sole owner of the local diner and main information center for the entire community of Sweet River, Texas, population not quite a thousand people on a good day. IdaJoy's announcement, made the minute Abby walked in the door, came as no surprise. Still, Abby was grateful there were no others around to witness her moment of weakness.

She thought she'd prepared herself for this. Knew IdaJoy would confront her with the juicy gossip. Didn't need the questions that were bound to be asked.

"I know," Abby said, as soon as she could breathe normally.

"You do?" IdaJoy's voice screeched up a whole octave at the end of her sentence. She had a unique way of sounding like an angry blue jay when she got excited—which was most of the time.

Abby put a death grip on the cup of coffee the waitress shoved in front of her. Her hands were shaking so hard, she didn't dare try to lift it to her lips yet.

IdaJoy snapped her gum between her back molars loud enough to rattle windows and arched her penciled eyebrows at Abby.

Abby nodded. "Pop told me this morning, but there's no reason for me to—"

"Land sakes, hon," the woman interrupted. She reached across the counter to pat Abby's arm. "Of course, there's reason. Why, everybody in town figured you two as practically married before he up and ran off with that—that Marla person."

She popped her chewing gum again and smoothed her lacquered beehive hairdo. "By the way, how do you like my new color?" She swiveled around to present Abby with the full view. "It's called Bustin' Out Blond. Thought it was time for a change. Life's gettin' way too boring." Without waiting for Abby to comment, IdaJoy grabbed a cup of coffee for herself and came around to sit on the stool next to Abby.

Eager to get on with the gossip session, the woman's chatter never slowed down long enough for Abby to change the subject. IdaJoy could jump from one thought to another without batting a mascaraed eyelash. Sometimes it was hard to keep up.

"I declare, I never thought Bo would do such a thing," she said, her blond beehive wobbling precariously with each shake of her head. "Men! Fickle, fickle, fickle. What that cowboy ever saw in her is beyond me. She was always a troublemaker for her Uncle Shorty, you know, ever since he took her in. Remember…" IdaJoy stopped midsentence and eyed Abby sharply. "You all right, honey? You look a teensy bit peaked. Want some water?"

"I'm fine," Abby assured her with a weak smile.

"You sure you feel like waitin' tables today, hon? You skipped breakfast, didn't you? Now, you stay right where you are and I'll go fix you some toast. Back in a jiffy."

With another motherly pat to Abby's shoulder, the woman sailed away in a swirl of heavy musk perfume, leaving Abby sitting there, staring at the cup still clutched in her hands, too numb to answer. Too weak to stop the flood of memories.

The first time she'd ever seen Bo Ramsey, he was a newly hired hand for the spring roundup on Shorty Packer's ranch and the best-looking cowboy ever to stroll down the streets of Sweet River. His skill with horses and expert riding ability soon gained him the respect of the other Packer ranch hands, but the female population of Sweet River, Texas, admired him for very different reasons. His smoke-black eyes and X-rated smile put fantasies in the minds of every woman in town over the age of sixteen, and Abby was no exception.

Shorty's niece, Marla, lived on the Packer ranch and had wanted Bo right from the beginning, so it was no surprise to see her work her wiles on the good-looking cowboy. Marla always wanted to be first, no matter what the prize. She collected men like most women in Sweet River collected recipes.

The big shocker came several weeks later, when Bo delivered a young steer to Buck Houston's ranch and met Abby face-to-face. *Intense* didn't begin to describe the immediate attraction that caught them both by surprise. Faster than the speed of small-town gossip, their relationship catapulted beyond anything either one had ever imagined or hoped for. By early summer, the entire town, including Abby herself, expected wedding bells to ring in the near future, even though no promises had been spoken. Then Bo had announced he was leaving to make a career in the rodeo circuit. Riding, especially the challenge of bull-riding, had always been in his blood. He knew he was good and had wanted Abby to share in his success. Abby had tried to make Bo understand that her father needed her on the ranch. She couldn't leave. Not with the ranch's finances finally beginning to climb out of the red. She didn't dare leave the bookkeeping to her father's hard-to-follow system. His simple belief that everything would eventually take care of itself was the very thing that got the ranch in trouble in the first place. Buck Houston knew ranching, but was too easygoing to worry about crunching numbers. Besides, she considered rodeo life too risky. She wanted stability in a marriage. And a family. They argued, fought, made love and argued some more. In the end, neither one surrendered. And in the blink of an eye, Abby's whole life changed.

Even now, there was no way to describe the crushing pain Abby felt at Bo's betrayal. He left in late August without saying goodbye, but Marla made sure the whole town knew what a wonderful father Bo was going to make. That bit of information was the final blow that had shattered Abby's heart. Never again would she believe in ever after.

She looked at her shaking hands, dismayed that those bittersweet memories still posed a threat to her carefully monitored emotions.

Anger at herself for allowing such a thing to happen burned deep inside her chest.

"Now, eat up, hon." IdaJoy pushed through the swinging door from the kitchen with well-curved, swaying hips, a plate of wheat toast and homemade strawberry jam in one hand, coffeepot in the other. She placed both in front of Abby, then frowned. "You look like you've seen a ghost."

She leaned across the counter and lowered her voice. "I guess maybe that'd be the case, if you saw Bo again, huh? I hear he looks a whole lot different now. That's what Louie LittleBear told me, and he should know."

Abby forced her thoughts back to the present. "Different? Oh, well, it's been two years, after all. We all look…"

"I'm talking real different, like Louie almost didn't recognize him at first. Saw him when he took some feed out to Shorty's place. Bo was in the barn, but hurried off without so much as a howdy when Louie said 'Hey.' Shorty was the one who told him Bo was staying there. Didn't say why, though." Her eyes widened. "You reckon Marla's there, too…with their kid? Louie said he didn't see 'em. What else did Buck tell you?"

IdaJoy's penchant for gossip was tempered by her honest concern for the people she loved, and Abby knew the older woman cared about her. It was just so awkward, being the object of sympathetic looks and whispers in a town the size of Sweet River. Everybody knew everything about everyone and nothing was sacred. She should be used to it by now, but it still stung a bit.

"Only that Bo is staying at the ranch for a while. Shorty didn't offer any other information." Abby was proud of the way she managed to keep her voice from faltering. With IdaJoy hanging on her every word, the woman would no doubt latch on to the very first sign of nerves and blow it all out of proportion. Good thing she couldn't hear the *rat-a-tat-tat* of Abby's heartbeat right then.

IdaJoy hugged Abby's shoulder right before she rose. "Well, hon, you just make sure you hold your head up and don't you be feeling bad. No sir. You've done all right for yourself, even without a man."

And that's supposed to make me feel better? Abby stood and made her wobbly way to the kitchen, right behind IdaJoy. Work—that's what she needed to take her mind off the past. She yanked a blue denim apron from the shelf and tied it around her waist, then grabbed an order book and pencil. Shoulders squared and chin jutting, she prepared to forget about Bo Ramsey one more time.

The Saturday noon crowd at the Blue Moon was a noisy, hungry bunch of locals. Most of them were ranchers and every last one of them knew Abby. They remembered Bo, too, and the majority of them already knew he was back in town. One out of every three old-timers managed to make some pointed comment about him to Abby. Not that she was counting or anything.

When the last of the diners left, Abby heaved a sigh of relief. *Finally.* Her face ached from keeping a false smile pasted on it for the last two hours. Maintaining a *who cares* attitude while she dodged all the probing questions had strained her self-control to the limit. Hadn't anyone in town forgotten that humiliating episode in her life?

She was clearing off the last table when the growl of a truck slewing into the graveled parking lot caught her attention. Through the slatted blinds of the front window, she saw Shorty Packer heading for the café. Abby's pulse stuttered. Behind Shorty another cowboy followed, his hesitant gait somewhat unnatural and one-sided, the set of his shoulders much too familiar. Abby watched him yank his hat low, obscuring his face, but she knew…oh, God, she knew.

With her hands pressed to her chest, she felt her heart take off in a marathon race. Her mouth went dry. Her face grew hot. She closed her eyes and imparted a silent prayer. *Lord, please don't let me make a fool of myself.*

For the first time in two years, the man who had loved her and left her was almost close enough to touch. She didn't know whether to laugh, cry or call 9-1-1.

With a nod, Shorty said "Howdy" and headed for the lunch counter, but Bo remained motionless in the middle of the room, his face shadowed beneath his wide-brimmed hat. Abby knew he'd recognized her by the sharp intake of his breath. Not being able to see his eyes didn't keep the heat of his gaze from igniting a high-voltage intimacy that sizzled straight into her raw-edged senses. His very presence caused her breath to catch in her throat and created a weakness in her knees and that produced an acute longing that both terrified and dismayed her.

Her own gaze drank in his shape swiftly. His body was thinner, harder than she recalled, yet every bit as seductive as it had always been. A missing button caused his wash-softened denim shirt to gap just enough to reveal the white T-shirt stretched taut across his chest. Hard-muscled arms, so achingly familiar in rolled-up sleeves, evoked images she tried desperately to push away. Everything about him tore at her heart. Those low-slung, faded jeans hugging his hips and long legs. The same well-worn boots that had—just once—been hastily discarded by the side of her bed.

A tiny gasp escaped her lips as bittersweet memories flashed in instant replay. She didn't need to see Bo's face to remember. Dark, smoky eyes. A mouth that could pleasure her with slow, burning kisses and coax her body into a hot, pliable mass of desire. Midnight-black hair she could almost feel sliding between her fingers, grasping it as the final shudder of ecstacy claimed her. Oh, God, why was she doing this? Why couldn't she make herself forget?

She licked her lips and searched for something to say. Before she could find words, he turned. She heard him swear when he bumped the corner of a table, nearly falling in his rush for the door. She watched him limp away, shoving chairs aside and slamming the door behind him. How ironic that after all this time, Bo Ramsey was still in a hurry to leave her. And the pain in her heart was still the same.

Gravel spit and gears groaned as the pickup spun out of the parking lot. Shorty just watched the dust settle, then eased himself onto a red vinyl-covered stool at the end of the counter.

"Damn fool ain't supposed to be driving yet." He shrugged. "Guess I shoulda' told him you might be here."

Abby wondered if her heart would ever return to normal. With shaking hands, she concentrated on pouring Shorty's coffee into a thick, white mug. She managed to get most of it where it belonged. The rest she wiped up with a cloth.

Shorty looked at her over the rim of his half-full cup. "You knew he was back, didn't you?"

She nodded, trying to ignore the way her pulse was thrumming. She didn't trust her voice enough to speak just yet.

"Well, hell's bells, girl, ain't you gonna say something?" He plunked his cup back on the counter, skewered her with his gaze.

Abby swallowed around the lump in her

throat. Her eyes stung and she blinked hard to hold back the tears.

"What do you want me to say, Shorty?" She could barely squeak out a whisper. "That was a rotten thing to do," she said, swiping at an invisible stain on the already spotless counter one more time.

"I wasn't talking about that," the old cowboy said. "Ain't you got nothin' to say about how he looked?"

"Looked? He was in such a hurry to get out of here, I barely saw him." *Oh, my heart saw him, though.*

"Aw, girl, that boy's had a terrible time of it. He's come back to stay with me at the ranch until he's done healing. Had a run-in with a nasty bull at a rodeo back in February. Lucky to be alive and walking. Only thing is, he ain't used to people lookin' at his face yet. I'm surprised you didn't notice the scars."

Abby sucked in her breath when a pain sharper than a razor's cut sliced through her heart. *So that's the reason for the low-tipped hat.* She gripped the edge of the counter, leaned against it for support. "Tell me what happened."

Shorty took a swallow of what was left of his coffee and dug around in his pocket for a cigarette. Abby frowned at him hard enough to make him put it back. He fished out a wooden toothpick instead and tongued it to the side of his mouth, set his hat on the stool beside him and rested his elbows on the counter.

"Bo was in Dallas when I got a call from one of his rodeo buddies that he'd been busted up pretty good and was in the hospital there. I figured Marla was with him, but his friend said she'd already been there and gone, so I drove up there to see what the hell was goin' on."

He set his toothpick aside and blew on his already cold coffee, sipping it so slowly, Abby thought her hair would turn gray before he ever finished the story. When he lifted the plastic cover of the pastry display, she gave an impatient sigh and slapped her hand over his. "Shorty, please. Tell me the rest."

He withdrew his hand with a shrug, picked up his toothpick and tapped it on the counter. "You know, the people at the hospital told me the doctors did all they could in surgery. Bo's leg and face were the worst off. Had some busted ribs, too. A messed-up cowboy but lucky to be alive, even if he don't walk so good. I couldn't stay with him no longer, so I came on back here and kept in touch by phone, ya' know." He lifted his cup, drained it noisily before he continued.

"He stayed in the hospital a long time before he was transferred to some kind of therapy clinic. When he got done with the treatment there, he phoned me. Said he didn't have no place to go and asked if I could come and get him." Shorty heaved a sigh and closed his eyes as if remembering. "I wasn't about to let him down."

Abby fought the tremors coursing through her body. Hearing about the accident made her blood run cold. Even though she had just seen Bo with her own eyes, it was hard to believe he'd survived what Shorty had just described.

"You mentioned his face. I wasn't able to see it when he came in. What's wrong with his face?" A sudden urge to grab Shorty by the collar and insist he talk faster forced Abby to grab her own hands instead and clasp them tight.

"Well, he's got some powerful scars," Shorty drawled. "That bull made a mess of his face. The doc did what he could. Hell, he was the best plastic surgeon around, but he couldn't give Bo back his good looks. He don't look so awful, though. Just, uh, different."

Abby caught Shorty watching her with a cautious eye while he kept on reciting his tale.

"That's what Bo can't accept, ya' see. People stare at him and he can't stand their pity. That's why I brought him back here. Figured he could stay out at the ranch with me until he decides what he's gonna do with the rest of his life. Truth is, Abby, he says he ain't gonna ride the circuit again because of his crooked leg. And besides, he's broke. Somebody's gotta take care of him."

"Well, where's that high-falutin' niece of yours…and their kid?" IdaJoy never minced words. "Why isn't she here takin' care of her man?"

Abby was relieved when IdaJoy asked what she hadn't dared.

"Well now, I'm thinking that's Bo's business," Shorty said.

"Nothin' good ever comes from hiding the truth," IdaJoy pointed out. She waggled her finger at Shorty.

Shorty shrugged. "Maybe so, but that's Bo's tale to tell, not mine. Right now, I'd be much obliged for a big bowl of your five-alarm chili. Oh, and how about puttin' some in one of those take-along cartons? For Bo.

Then I've got to find me a ride home." He shot a hopeful glance toward Abby.

She hesitated when IdaJoy shot a disapproving look her way, knowing if she offered, she'd risk seeing Bo again. But then again if she didn't, she would regret it later.

"I'll be finished here in about half an hour. If you want to wait, I'll take you back to the ranch." Abby turned to head for the kitchen and bumped smack into IdaJoy, who stood there with her hands on her hips, snapping her gum and shaking her beehive hairdo.

"Oh, you are so asking for it, Abby Houston."

Abby frowned. "Yeah, you're probably right, but…" *But what?* her conscience asked innocently, as her heart danced a Texas two-step.

Shorty grinned like he'd just won the lottery.

Chapter Two

Abby's pulse raced much too fast as she sped down the farm-to-market road with Shorty in the passenger side of her car. Her entire nervous system had been scrambled ever since Bo showed up at the café. Had it really been only a little over an hour since she'd seen him? Felt his presence? Nearly let her heart be bruised again? She took deep breaths and tried to concentrate on driving, even though the way to the Packer ranch was so familiar she didn't need to watch the road. Some things you never forgot. Even when you tried.

Her damp palms were slick on the steering wheel and she swiped them across the front of her cotton shirt, one at a time. She had to swallow hard to keep the uneasy churning in the pit of her stomach from bringing her lunch back for reruns. The stifling afternoon heat kept her on the edge of nervous nausea. One of these days, she'd have enough money saved to repair the car's broken air conditioner. Even with the windows lowered, the interior of the six-year-old Taurus was frying-pan hot. Right now, she had other things to think about.

When they'd left the Blue Moon twenty minutes earlier, Abby had made up her mind to stop when they reached the ranch, let Shorty out of the car and head right on home. She didn't need to get out. Didn't need to see Bo or anyone else that might be around. No need at all. Oh, right. Like that was going to keep her mind from slipping back to times and places best left undisturbed.

But undisturbed memories are like treasures stored away in dusty attics—often uncovered by accident and brought out to linger over. To cherish once again. So Abby blew the dust off her memories and drifted back to the time when Bo was the center of her universe—her reason for being.

Glorious. That's what the time with him

had been. He'd made her feel cherished. Special in a way she'd never felt before. She'd been swept off her feet and had fallen hopelessly in love. She'd believed he felt the same. Then he'd left without saying goodbye, and her world suddenly had become a black hole.

When she finally emerged from the darkness of heartbreak, anger took its place with an intensity that had almost destroyed her. Desperate to forget, but with a stubborn Texas pride too strong to let her give up, she'd focused on survival, facing the sympathetic looks of the community with her head held high. She'd believed her heartache had faded. Until now.

Her foot mashed harder on the gas pedal and the ribbon of highway blurred beneath tires she should've replaced last month.

"You tryin' to get a speeding ticket or what?" Shorty snapped, his bushy eyebrows knit together in a gray scowl.

Abby checked the numbers on the speedometer and jerked her foot from its rigid position. "Sorry, guess I wasn't watching."

The old rancher stuck his toothpick back in his shirt pocket and drummed his fingers on his knee. He crossed and uncrossed his stubby legs, squirming around in the seat like a toddler with a bladder problem.

Finally, he cleared his throat. "Yeah, well, guess you've got reason enough to have a wandering mind, seein' Bo again and all."

"Ramsey's return is no concern of mine." Abby shot him a sideways glance just in time to catch the flicker of distress in the older man's eyes. "Shorty, is something wrong?"

"Uh, no." He hesitated, then exhaled loudly. "That is… I reckon this might not be the right time to bring it up, Abby, but I was thinkin'…uh, just wonderin' if you could use some extra help at that riding school of yours? You know, something a cowboy with a bum leg could do."

Abby hit the brakes. The car lurched, swerved and with a cough, chugged to a halt on the side of the road.

Shorty peeled the safety belt away from his throat and pushed back in the seat, his eyes wide.

"Gawdamighty, woman! Didja' forget how to drive?"

Ignoring his colorful roar, Abby slammed the heel of her hand on the steering wheel, counted to ten under her breath, then whipped around in the seat to stare at him in disbelief.

"Did I hear you right? You want me to let Bo Ramsey work with *my* students? With *my* horses? Not in this lifetime, Shorty." She shook her head so vigorously, the scrunchy holding her thick ponytail flipped off and landed on Shorty's knee. She didn't even bother to retrieve it.

When he blanched visibly, Abby was pretty sure he got the message. A fleeting stab of remorse snagged her conscience. Verbal attacks were not her usual style, but Shorty's ludicrous suggestion was anything but usual.

For heaven's sake, she didn't need any more problems to deal with, especially one as provoking and personal as Bo Ramsey. So why was she even considering Shorty's request? She wasn't, was she? No, of course not.

"I ain't said nothin' to him about your riding program yet, Abby." Shorty gingerly retrieved the ponytail holder with two fingers and deposited it on the dashboard. "He's powerful depressed, though, and I just thought… maybe…"

He scratched his chin, ducked his head in that sheepish way of his that made Abby grind her teeth.

She leaned her head against the back of the seat. Why, oh why had Bo come back now, just when she was getting her life in order? Finally learning to live without him. She didn't want to feel sympathy toward him. She didn't want to feel anything at all. She owed him absolutely nothing. She would *not* feel guilty.

Shorty kept right on talking. "You know, Buck mentioned that you were sorta' hard up for helpers since you got a few more kids this spring. Bo'd be mighty helpful with the horses, even if he can't ride right now. Just seeing the spunk those youngsters have and how they deal with their handicaps might show Bo a thing or two. There's lots of things…"

Abby bristled. "They're not handicapped, they're physically and emotionally chal- lenged, but they work hard for every goal they reach. And for the record, we're doing just fine, thanks. Some of the volunteers have already offered to work two classes. We can't afford salaried helpers yet."

She turned the key in the ignition, revved the behind-schedule-for-a-tune-up engine and eased the vehicle back onto the black- top. Shorty was right. Her students had spunk to spare and she was so proud of them. There was no denying the inspiration they gave to anyone who observed them in the arena.

"The program isn't all that large, anyway," she added, trying to soften her sharp refusal. "There's only a dozen students so far. I don't need any extra help."

Shorty leaned back in his seat and released such a mournful, Oscar-worthy sigh, Abby was tempted to applaud. She would have, if the situation had involved anyone but Bo Ramsey.

"Well, that may be," he drawled, giving her a beseeching look, "but Bo's sure needing your help now."

He needs me? Oh, that is so unfair. Abby could barely see the road for the sudden tears blurring her eyes.

In all his thirty years, Bo Ramsey had never expected to return to Sweet River, especially like this, but with a body busted up from the wear-and-tear of riding rodeo bulls, and less than five dollars in the pocket of his jeans, he'd hit the bottom of the barrel with a loud thud. Shoot, he'd been down there so long, he had a personal relationship with every damned slat in it. And now, his pride had to take a backseat to being practical. Talk about bitter pills. The feeling of failure still stuck in his craw. He wondered if he'd ever be able to swallow around it.

He shifted his position in the vintage porch chair for the hundredth time, easing his left leg around to find a more comfortable angle. One that wouldn't send those knifelike pains shooting clear to his eyeballs. He refused to give in and swallow any more of those damned pain pills. He reached for a longneck instead, knowing that wasn't the answer either, but not really caring.

He'd been sitting there long enough to indulge in more beer and self-pity than was probably good for him, his only excuse being that the unexpected sight of Abby at the Blue Moon had blindsided him. Temporarily robbed him of his good sense. And, just like last time, he'd taken the coward's way out.

Old memories he'd buried a long time ago crept out from their hiding place in the dark recesses of his heart. Persistent cusses, those memories, poking at him like cactus needles, paining him almost as much as the physical injuries to his body. Maybe more. He rubbed his hand over the scarred side of his face. Maybe not.

This wealth of land and cattle that made up Shorty's ranch had been Bo's home longer than any place he'd ever lived. Taking in the familiar view, Bo acknowledged that everything was pretty much the same as when he'd left. Everything but his own life. That was a mess of his own making.

His chest ached with deep regret for all he'd left behind. All he could never have. Bitterness crawled down inside his soul and lodged—a familiar, yet unwelcome tenant.

Bo shifted his leg again, his groan harmonizing off-key with a mournful groan coming from the far side of the porch. Shorty's old yellow dog slowly made his way to Bo's side and gave his hand a slobbery greeting.

With sad eyes nearly hidden in the folds of its loose-skinned face, and long ears drooping past bony shoulders, the mongrel looked like somebody'd smacked him with an ugly stick. Twice.

"Hey, Ditch." Bo scratched the old dog behind the ears.

Ditch dog. That's what Shorty'd called him, ever since he'd found the injured pup lying on the side of the road years ago. The pooch had to be as old as Shorty's truck by now, because Bo had heard the rescue story at least a hundred times in the past.

Ditch dog. Bo felt like something of a ditch

dog himself ever since Shorty'd fetched him back home from the hospital. Patched him up, too. Just like ol' Ditch. Only difference was, the dog had become Shorty's best friend. Bo wasn't sure he could even lay claim to that anymore.

He tipped the longneck back, drank deep, then set the empty bottle aside. He left the porch to seek the solitude of his room. Hell, could life get any worse?

He'd gotten as far as the front room when he heard the car come up the gravel road. Bo knew in his gut who Shorty had persuaded to give him a lift home. Crossing the room, he stood by the window and moved the curtain aside just enough to sneak a look without revealing himself.

He watched as Shorty climbed out of the car. Ditch loped off the porch to greet his banty rooster-sized friend, wet nose nudging hopefully against the rancher's hand for a pat on the head.

They make quite a pair, Bo mused, as a twinge of envy snuck past his good sense. The dog had gotten older, but the man hadn't changed much. The Willie Nelson-style braid that dangled down his back was the same, except the gray hairs were beginning to outnumber the black ones. A few wrinkles creased Shorty's leathery face, but the denim work shirt and faded jeans looked like the same ones he'd been wearing the day Bo had said goodbye.

On the backside of fifty, Shorty Packer had always cottoned to the belief that unless something was broken, you kept your hands off of it. Still, he'd give you his last biscuit and tell you he'd just eaten, if he thought you were hungrier than he was. He was generous to a fault if you were his friend, and meaner than a rattlesnake if you were his enemy. But he was fair. Bo respected him for that, and was shamed to the point of disgust, thinking maybe he'd lost the respect of this man who'd done so much for him.

Deep in thought, Bo didn't notice the driver get out of the car until the door slammed shut. She stood by the car and looked toward the house. The instant thudding of his heart startled him. Damn. Sweat beaded his upper lip. He swiped at it, his fingers brushing across the raised seam of scars crisscrossing his face.

Cursing the clumsiness that prevented him from hurrying, he was almost within the safety of his bedroom when the front door opened and Shorty shouted.

"Bo, you in here?"

Where else would I be? He kept silent, listening. No other voice accompanied Shorty's. Was that disappointment he felt? Hell, no. He was glad she hadn't come inside.

"I'm here," he answered.

When the other man's footsteps echoed on the planked floor, Bo slowly, carefully, retraced his own. Guilt for taking off with the truck pricked at him unmercifully. Might as well apologize now and get it over with. He was halfway down the hall when he saw her.

Abby stood behind Shorty, taller only by a few inches, just enough to be visible. Shorty moved farther into the room, giving Bo an unobstructed view of her. His insides dipped on a wild roller-coaster ride.

There she was, standing in the doorway holding a big yellow bowl. She was totally unaware that the early afternoon brightness illuminated her with a halo of sunshine. Bo half expected a heavenly choir to break into song at any moment.

Instead, vivid memories flashed before him in living color. The softness of her sun-gilded skin pressed against his and the way it went all hot and damp when they made love; the curve of her rosy smile, the sweetness of her lips and the way her mouth melted beneath his when they kissed; the scent of honeysuckle that always clung to her and the way she glowed, all dewy and golden after he'd thoroughly loved her. Those memories were so intense, the pain of leaving her still crowded his chest. Restricted his breathing.

"Hello, Bo." Her husky whisper trailed an erotic path across his skin as if she had physically touched him.

As soon as she spoke, the familiar tightening in his groin made his head swim. He ought to leave the room before he made a total ass of himself. He turned his head, ducking it slightly to avoid giving her a full view of his face. Damn, he'd gone and left his hat on the porch. He needed to get the hell out of here.

"Your hearin' gone bad as well as your manners, boy?" Shorty scowled like an irritated parent. "Abby's brought you some of IdaJoy's mighty good chili. Least you could do is say thanks."

Bo stared at the plastic-covered container clutched in Abby's hands. She never gave him a chance to back away. Just marched up to him before he could turn his face. His heart flipped upside down when her unflinching gaze raked him up and down.

Dark blue eyes flashed undeniable disgust. Her summer-blond hair whipped around her face when she shook her head in apparent disapproval of what—or was it, who—she saw. He didn't blame her for despising him.

"You smell like a brewery, Ramsey. Maybe this chili will burn off the excess alcohol. Enjoy." With one swift move, she shoved the dish into his stomach so hard he had to grab it or end up wearing the contents.

She ran from the room and out to her car without another word. Bo heard the crunch of gravel as she drove away.

He turned to Shorty. "What the hell was that all about?"

Shorty gave him a look sour enough to curdle milk. "You ought to know, boy."

Bo carried the dish to the table, wishing he'd never made that phone call asking Shorty for help. He hated being a damn charity case.

"You shouldn't have brought her here," he grumbled. He uncovered the yellow bowl and inhaled deeply. His mouth watered at the tantalizing aroma of fiery spices. He'd always been a sucker for IdaJoy's chili.

"Brought her here?" Shorty's voice rose and two shaggy eyebrows peaked over dead-serious eyes that bored straight through Bo.

"The way I see it, she brought me here. You took my truck and left me stranded, remember? And that's a whole 'nother matter. Who said you were fit to drive yet?"

"I got back here okay, didn't I?"

"Maybe," Shorty conceded, "but don't try it again."

"Hhmmph." Bo hated being treated like a ten-year-old. He pulled out the chair to sit down. Before he could blink, Shorty was right there, spoon in one hand and a glass of water in the other. His explanation was typically Shorty—gruff and to the point.

"Get used to it, boy. From now on, water or milk's the drink around here. The choice is yours."

The older man's no-nonsense tone drew a tight smile from Bo. It had been a helluva long time since he'd been handed an ultimatum like that. A long time since anyone even cared. Well, he'd deal with Shorty and his rules just as soon as he finished eating. Right now, all he wanted was the chili. He picked up the spoon and dug in.

A volcano erupted inside his mouth the instant the first bite hit his tongue, lava-hot and scalding a path clear through to his unsuspecting stomach.

Bo let loose with a bellow and a string of colorful cusswords, sending Ditch scurrying out of the room. His chair toppled backward and his water glass went flying in his haste to reach the kitchen sink. Angling his head under the faucet, mouth wide open and swallowing frantically, he almost cried with relief as the gush of cold water tumbled down his scorched throat.

When the fire in his gut finally subsided, Bo shook his wet head, spit, sputtered and glared at Shorty through watery eyes. He was helpless to form his question into words. His tongue—shoot, his whole damn mouth—was numb.

"Oh, yeah," Shorty said, poker-faced, as he bent to retrieve Bo's water glass from the floor. "I think Abby might've added a few extra chili peppers."

Twilight pulled the sun below the horizon, leaving behind a rosy haze that promised another hot night. The air hung like a wet curtain, heavy and unmoving. Mosquitos, buzzing lazily alongside an occasional lightning bug, flitted past the two men sitting on the long, covered porch. The tension between them was as thick as the air.

Bo slumped back in his chair, a glass of milk, compliments of guess-who, in one hand. Some nightcap. At least, it wasn't flavored with chili peppers. Granted, he'd never been much of a drinker until the accident.

For the past two weeks, the two men had done nothing but argue about his newly acquired habit. Shorty nagged and Bo ignored. He wasn't even sure why. It wasn't like he thought the beer tasted good. He stretched out his legs and got ready for the argument he knew was sure to come. He wasn't disappointed.

"I just cain't figure you out, boy," the old rancher began. "Ain't like you to look to a bottle for answers. That never solved a problem yet."

Bo grunted. "Save your sermons for the Sunday congregation, okay?" The sarcastic words spilling out of his mouth of their own accord tasted sour on his tongue, but he couldn't pull them back for the life of him. Didn't try. What the hell difference did it make anymore?

He hated being so damned dependent, but who would hire the likes of him now? He was about as useless as a bucket of warm spit. Until he could manage to walk without tottering like an old man, there wasn't much he could do but sit on his backside and complain. He was getting to be an expert at that.

But Shorty wasn't about to cut him any slack, it seemed.

"You've been back here nigh on two weeks now and so far, the only thing getting better is your leg, 'cause your attitude sure ain't improving. It's time you stopped wallowing in self-pity. I don't aim to be wet-nursin' you no more. Time for you to play the hand you been dealt, and get on with the game. Plain and simple."

Bo muttered under his breath. Shorty was right, as usual. He knew his attitude sucked. He knew why, too. He just wasn't ready to tell his friend the whole story. Not yet. There'd been a lot of things he'd meant to say the day Shorty picked him up from the therapy clinic, but the words had stuck in his throat. Hell, what do you say to the man who has just bailed you out of the hospital, chased the bill collectors from your door, and offered you a home without asking a single thing in return? "Thanks" just didn't seem to cut it. And Shorty hadn't even asked about Marla yet.

Marla. Shorty's niece and the reason Bo had left Sweet River. The reason he'd left

Abby Houston with a broken heart. Not to mention the damage he'd done to his own.

Ditch snored softly, his big head resting on Shorty's boots, seemingly oblivious to any danger as his long tail darted back and forth underneath the chair's wooden rocker. Every time Shorty rocked forward, the dog's tail swished under and back, under and back, like a metronome with a mysterious timing device, never missing a beat.

Bo had been watching the dog's laid-back attitude for the last half hour. "You ever catch his tail with that rocker?" he finally asked, pointing to Ditch.

"Nope." Shorty kept on rocking. "Dog's got more sense than most of us humans. Knows how to stay out of trouble, don't back talk, and is a heap more grateful for small favors than most folks."

Bo pushed out of his chair and shoved his hat back without giving a thought to the way it bared his face.

"Dammit, Shorty, I *am* grateful," he said, plunking his glass so hard on the nearby wobbly metal table that Ditch thought it best to slink off to the other end of the porch. "There's not a minute goes by that I don't remember I'm in debt up to my eyeballs to you. Don't you think I'm ashamed of the mess I made of things? You can't begin to know how it really was."

Shorty raised a shaggy eyebrow. "Then maybe it's time you told me, son."

The word *son* sucker punched him right in the gut. He couldn't avoid the truth any longer. Especially not with the only man who had ever called him son.

Chapter Three

Pale morning light filtered through the open barn door, haloing the clock on the wall with dust motes. Abby glanced up wearily. Almost six o'clock and already the barn was hotter than a mouthful of jalapeños. The air hung heavy with the pungent smell of the horses. Hay, feed and freshly hauled manure combined in a uniquely familiar odor that Abby barely noticed.

She'd been out in the barn since four-thirty. At this rate, she'd have all the chores finished before Pop even woke up. Monday's chores always seemed to take longer. She mopped her damp forehead with a frayed bandana and readjusted her baseball cap before tackling the last of the stalls.

Well, that's what she wanted, wasn't it? Dirty work. Hot, hard work. Any diversion to take her mind off last Saturday's confrontation with Bo. Well, hot and hard wasn't going to do it. Oh, yes, it would.

Knock it off with the fantasies. What on earth had she been thinking when she shoved that kicked-up chili at him? She'd reacted like a child in the throes of a temper tantrum. *Nice going, girl. Real maturity.*

She stabbed a forkful of new bedding straw and shook it over the clean floor, then made sure the last water trough was full. If she concentrated really hard, maybe she could keep her thoughts where they belonged—on the students that would be showing up in a few hours and not on the rush of emotions that kept her insides churning.

Since it was too soon to put the horses in the arena, Abby made her way to the large room at the back of the barn where the tack was kept. She smiled as she passed the horses. The animals' objections had been very clear when she'd entered their stalls earlier. Her intrusion at such an early hour had definitely not been appreciated, but fresh oats and clean bedding quickly appeased their grumpiness.

"You are such sweeties," she crooned, giving them each a loving caress as, one by one, they stuck their heads over the stall doors to greet her. Their whinnies and nickers made her heart swell with love. These docile creatures were her pride and joy. As senior citizens in Abby's small equine community, the horses were patient beyond belief when it came to the students. Loving the attention they received, the animals were always eager to please and quick to respond to the sometimes timid commands of the novice riders. Somehow, they sensed their importance to the children. The uncanny communication between horse and student never ceased to amaze Abby, so she made pampering and indulging them a priority because—aside from the children—the horses were the most important part of her riding program.

Some had been donated by area ranchers. She had managed to convince a few local ranch owners that, even though the horses were too old to be of much use on a working ranch, they were invaluable to the special children who attended the Sweet River Riders group. Abby loved every one of the horses dearly and so did the few volunteers who showed up each day to complete her staff. The children adored the animals without reservation, and most of them had bonded quickly with a favorite.

In the long room where the tack was stored, Abby counted blankets, straightened the bump pads and lined up the helmets. While she sorted halters, reins, saddles and lead ropes, she thought back to when she had first begun her training to become a director of this worthwhile program.

She'd been drifting through the days in a zombielike state for those first few months after Bo had left Sweet River, nursing her hurt like a wounded animal. Humiliation kept her from leaving the ranch for anything other than business until a friend in Austin called her and urged her to volunteer at an equine therapy school. After two weeks, Abby knew she wanted to be an active participant, and that she wanted to direct a program of her own. The intensity of the instruction and the enormity of such an undertaking were welcome challenges, enabling her to focus her energies on something besides her shattered heart. The children needed her. And Abby sorely needed them.

Now, ironically, Shorty was insisting that Bo needed her. Well, she didn't want to hear that and wasn't about to be roped into feeling sorry for him. He had a wife. Let her do the honors. Hadn't he chosen Marla over Abby and left Abby to face the sympathetic looks and whispers of the community all alone? Old anger reared its head again, triggered by the painful memory of rejection.

A sob tore from her lips and she swore under her breath at her inability to conquer the past. Disgusted, she lugged a box containing plastic spray bottles of waterless cleaner from the storage closet, slammed it down on the table, and counted out a dozen of them. With her eyes squeezed tight against the intruding sting of tears, she made a silent demand. *Get out of my head, Bo, and stay away from my heart.*

She plopped a stack of paper towels alongside the box and stepped back to make a quick visual check. Everything was in order and ready for the arrival of the twelve boys and girls. With six in each class, she could manage just fine. She was in control and darn well didn't need Bo Ramsey around to complicate her life. Not now—not ever. But, bitterness still left a nasty aftertaste.

She slid the barn door shut and headed for the house, blocking out her heart's cry of panic. Salty tears tracked her cheeks and she licked them from her lips. The man from her past might be back in Sweet River, but she refused to acknowledge the possibility that she might feel something besides sympathy for him. Absolutely not. She dashed the back of her hand across her eyes before she reached the kitchen door. Crying was so stupid!

"Breakfast is all ready, kitten." Buck shoved a hot mat under the coffeepot and set it on the table. "You were already in the barn when I got up, so I figured you'd have chores done before I could get out there. Why didn't you wake me?"

The delicious aroma of Buck's dark roast coffee brewing, along with the sizzle of bacon and hotcakes on the griddle, met Abby as she entered the kitchen. The screen door slammed behind her.

"I woke up way too early, Pop. Besides, the hard work was good for me." She gave him a good-morning kiss on his unshaven cheek and hurried to the bathroom to wash away the grime.

"Mmmmm, the pancakes smell delicious," she called with forced cheerfulness. "Blueberry's my favorite." Hurriedly, she splashed cold water on her face, then pressed a wet washcloth on her eyes to eliminate the tell-tale redness and hopefully, to relieve her escalating headache.

By the time she returned to the kitchen, all evidence of her sudden, out-of-the-blue crying jag had been washed away. It would never do for Pop to know just how upset she was over Bo's return. Pop's health was her number one priority now, right along with keeping the school running in the black. Upsetting him would only add stress, and the doctor had warned her about that. His last checkup had shown a rise in his blood pressure, which surprised Abby, given her father's even-tempered disposition.

"By the way," her father said after he sat down. "Marsha called. She can't help out today. Caleb's got a tooth that needs to be pulled. With Jan gone to that quarter horse show in San Antonio, we'll be two helpers short." He poured syrup over his pancakes.

Abby frowned. "Darn, I hoped with you filling in for Jan, we wouldn't have a problem. I don't know who else I can ask on such short notice." Would there ever be a time when she *didn't* have some sort of crisis in her life?

Lately it seemed she had to carry her share and everyone else's, too. Shoot, she was turning into a first-class whiner.

She finished her coffee and pushed away from the table. "I'll have to start calling around, but I don't think it will be any use. The first group of kids will be here at nine. It's after seven now."

Buck rose and carried his plate to the sink. "What about that Kelly boy? He's been hanging around the feed store since school got out, looking for work."

"Does he know anything about horses?" Abby rinsed and stacked the dishes to put in the dishwasher later.

"One way to find out," Buck said. "Pick up the phone."

Abby's headache grew from bitty-sized to mega-magnitude when Karl Kelly said, yep, he could sure use the work, and nope, he didn't know much about horses but he reckoned he could learn.

She'd felt awful when she told him it was a nonpaying job and even worse when he sighed and said "Oh well, it don't matter, Miss Abby. Pa'll get a job one of these days."

"Well," Abby said thoughtfully, "I guess we could manage to pay you something."

The amount she mentioned had Karl bubbling over with gratitude. When she hung up the phone, Abby knew she'd done the right thing. Replacing the dishwasher could wait a while longer. So could her car's air conditioner.

"Teddie, good morning," Abby called later from where she waited near the gate to the arena for the morning's first arrivals. The youngster being led across the yard made no response. "Hello, Caroline." She acknowledged the child's mother with a wave.

The young woman returned the wave but the boy hung back, pulling against his mother's hand. He was shaking his head, clearly not wanting to come any closer. His reluctance tugged at Abby's heart. Six-year-old Teddie North was one of the first students signed up for the therapeutic riding program, yet his progress was much slower than the other students in his class. Abby was still trying to break through the barrier of his shyness. Trying to win his trust. With both legs recently out of heavy casts, Teddie struggled with his limitations. So far, the only one he trusted besides his mother was the little mare,

Star—the one he loved to pet, but refused to ride.

Out of the corner of her eye, Abby saw Buck leading Star out of her stall. She smiled. Pop could always be counted on. Her heart swelled with love and admiration. Without him, her school would still be only a dream. Buck had supported and encouraged her through all the tough times. She would be forever grateful. The children and their needs had pulled her through the loneliness—after Bo. Somehow, Pop had known they would. She'd never blamed her father for their financial problems.

Star whickered and bobbed her head. Buck let her trot to the fence where Teddie and his mother stood on the opposite side. Blowing softly, the little mare pushed at the fence until Teddie poked his hand between the rails. Immediately, Star nudged it, lipping his small finger in a gentle welcome. Teddie's face lit up, and his childish giggle made Abby smile.

She approached him hesitantly, speaking softly. "Do you think you'd like to try riding her today, Teddie?"

The look of panic on the boy's face was so pronounced, Abby quickly turned away to hide her disappointment. Every day she hoped for a breakthrough to reach the youngster. Today wasn't going to be the day, but she refused to give up hope.

She dug in her pocket for a carrot and handed it to Teddie. "Here, why don't you give her this, instead? She likes it when you give her a treat."

Teddie took the carrot and timidly stuck it through the fence, a cherubic grin appearing when Star nibbled out of his hand.

"I don't know why he won't try to ride," Teddie's mother said, keeping her voice low. "All he talks about all week is Star. He loves her, really he does." She reached out to caress her son's tiny shoulder, then moved her hand to tousle his hair.

Abby spoke reassuringly. "Star loves him, too, and someday he'll ride. You'll see." She gave the little mare a pat on the rump, then excused herself to check on the arrival of the other students.

Thankfully, the Kelly boy had turned out to be a fast learner and a tremendous hit with all the students. Even Teddie seemed to trust him although he was still afraid of the horses and never went beyond the gate. Abby decided that Karl's help was well worth giving up a new dishwasher.

After everyone had gone, Abby massaged the back of her neck, and fell into step beside Buck. "Why are Mondays always so long, Pop? Karl did all right, don't you think? Are tuna sandwiches okay for lunch?"

Buck shortened his stride and put his arm around his daughter's shoulder. "Which question do you want me to answer first?" His warm chuckle was as comforting as his embrace.

Abby gave him a tired smile. Her habit of asking more than two questions in a row was an old joke between them. Pop's answer never varied. She leaned her head against his arm and sighed. "I guess I know the answers to two of them. Mondays are long because they just are, and Karl definitely did all right. I think he likes working with the students as well as the horses."

Buck nodded. "And a tuna sandwich is fine. Yeah, Karl's a good kid. I wish there was some way we could give him a regular salary to help out with chores. His folks are having a tough time getting by since his dad got laid off."

"I decided to take some out of the money I'd been saving to fix the dishwasher, Pop. It's not much but maybe we can have him come a few more times."

"Well now, that's just fine. I knew you'd figure something out."

"But, we still have the veterinarian's regular visit coming up, plus the bill at the feed mill is due by the end of the month." Abby couldn't help feeling overwhelmed at the increasing debts.

"Something'll turn up," Buck said, his optimism sincere. "It always does." He gave her a reassuring squeeze, then moved to open the gate. They walked in silence across the yard toward the house.

The growl of a pickup interrupted their thoughts. "Looks like it already has," she said.

Shorty's ancient truck clattered across the cattle guard at the ranch entrance and bounced up the drive, stopping right next to where Buck and Abby stood.

Abby's heart hiccuped and stuck in her throat the minute she caught sight of Bo sitting on the passenger side. She heard his familiar voice as she hurried past, but didn't stop until she reached the porch.

"Of all the damned tricks…" Bo sputtered at the man behind the wheel when they stopped in front of the house. He'd figured out where Shorty was headed as soon as the truck veered off the main road and headed west on the farm-to-market route.

By the time they'd skirted town, Bo's protests had escalated right along with his blood pressure, but his stubborn friend ignored him with a possum-like smirk and kept on driving. That irritated the hell out of him, too.

"I'm not getting out," he declared, crossing his arms over his chest and settling back in the seat. He glared at Shorty.

When he spied Abby coming from the corral, he yanked his hat down. He could almost feel the daggers shooting at him from Buck Houston's angry eyes. He should've been suspicious when Shorty told him he'd found something for Bo to do. No way was he taking charity from the Houstons. Besides, the horses he glimpsed as they drove in looked like geriatric throwaways. They sure couldn't require much more than a green pasture and a clean stall. Any kid could do that.

"Quit being a jackass," was all Shorty had time to say before Buck walked around to the driver's side and stuck his hand through the window.

"Hey, Shorty, good to see you."

"You, too, Buck," the older man said as they shook hands.

"Bo," Buck muttered with a slight nod. He withdrew his hand.

"Houston," Bo replied, curling his fingers in a tight fist. *Well, damned if I need your handshake.*

"Something special bring you out this way, Shorty?"

Buck still stood at the side of the truck, but Bo knew the man's gaze was focused on him. Abby stood on the porch steps, obviously waiting to see what would happen next. He wasn't quite sure what Shorty's plans were, but he was positive no one around here was going to like them. Especially him.

"I got something I'd like to talk to you about, Buck." Shorty moved to open the truck door.

"Sure," Buck said. He jerked his thumb toward the porch. "Come on up. I'll have Abby bring us something cold to drink."

"Well…" Shorty hesitated. "I was thinking maybe somewhere more private."

"Oh. Well, all right." Buck started toward the barn. "We'll be out of the sun in here."

Shorty slammed the door to the truck and started to follow. "Back in a few, Bo. You ought to go and thank Abby for the chili." He tossed the comment over his shoulder with a don't argue tone that Bo couldn't have missed even if he tried.

Bo slid a little further down in the seat. Banged his knee on the dash. Ow! Geez! He shot a glance toward the house...and Abby. *Well, hell, now what do I do?*

While he was wrestling with that question, Abby descended the steps and slowly made her way to the truck. The temptation to watch was more than he could resist.

The way she swung her hips in that sweet, seductive sway jump-started his pulse, and his temperature shot skyward. She'd always had the power to incite a riot in his body. He remembered how astonished she'd been when he'd revealed that very personal phenomenon to her. Surprised and delighted. Yes, and he'd been more than surprised at the way she'd enthusiastically proved her delight. *Knock it off, Ramsey. That was a long time ago, before you turned into the world's biggest fool.*

As she walked toward him, Bo was reminded again of the reason he left Sweet River and what his reckless decision back then had cost him. He should have tried harder to understand Abby's reasons for refusing to go with him. Maybe if he'd listened to her instead of stubbornly refusing to compromise, he and Abby would be a happy married couple by now.

And that thought, along with other notions crossing his mind as she approached the truck caused sensations he'd rather not acknowledge. But his physical reaction was impossible to ignore. He was only human, after all. And his jeans were suddenly unable to accommodate his uncomfortable response. Thankfully, he was still in the truck since a cold shower wasn't an option right then.

Abby stopped and rested her hand on the open window, her eyes bright, questioning. He remembered those bewitching blue depths. Deep enough for a man to get lost in. Perceptive enough to find the hidden truth beneath his scarred exterior if he wasn't careful. The very reason he didn't want to be here. He lived every day with the painful knowledge that he'd never stopped loving her, but there was no way he could tell her that now. No everlasting way.

Abby wasn't quite sure what made her decide to approach the truck and its occupant. Maybe she was just a glutton for punishment. Then again, maybe it was because Bo looked so uncomfortable in the noonday heat, and she felt obligated to offer him the hospitality of her shaded porch. Oh, who was she kidding? She just plain wanted to see him again. No excuses, no sane reason. Just wanted to. And maybe if she talked to him like a responsible adult, she could put a final closure on the crack in her heart, instead of the temporary bandage she'd been using.

With her heart in her throat, she greeted him. "Hello, Bo. I wasn't expecting to see you again."

"You can blame Shorty for that," he grumbled. "I didn't know he was headed here, or I wouldn't have come with him." He turned to stare out the opposite window.

"Oh, really?" Like he didn't know the way to her place. Did he think she was stupid? Well, she'd show him it didn't really matter to her one way or the other. She would treat him the same as she would anyone else who happened to stop by. Courteous and no more.

"Since you're here, you might as well get out of the heat." Trying to be cordial while talking to the back of his head challenged her genuine inclination to be polite. And Bo wasn't helping matters by refusing to look her way. He kept his face turned and his darn hat pulled so low, she wondered how he could even see anything but the underside of the brim.

"No thanks, I'll just wait here," he said. "Don't know what Shorty wanted to see Buck about. He told me somebody had some horses to take care of, but guess he made a mistake. Doesn't look like you need help around here. Not with those worn-out nags in your pasture. You'd be further ahead to sell them instead of paying out good money for feed."

"That's all you know, Ramsey." Abby bristled at his condemning observation of her wonderful four-legged friends. "Those horses are a vital part of a very important riding program. Don't criticize before you understand what you're talking about."

"A riding program?" He turned to her, and she realized she'd piqued his interest enough to make him forget his scars, at least for the moment. Then it dawned on her—a sneaking suspicion of why Shorty had brought him here. If anyone knew horses, it was Bo, but that didn't mean she wanted him here. She wasn't sure she was strong enough to face the possibility of having him around on a day-to-day basis and not be tempted to hash over old memories. Did she even want to?

Looking at him, she could understand his reluctance to expose himself to public scrutiny, yet the scars didn't keep her legs from going goofy or her pulse from singing karaoke at the sound of his voice. His crooked leg and awkward gait didn't detract from his seductive Texas charm. No, there was nothing scary about Bo except the fact that he still had the power to hurt her. Deep in her heart, she acknowledged that secret and vowed to keep those longings and desires to herself. After all, he was a married man.

Still, his experience around horses would be a tremendous help and relieve Pop of some of his workload. To do or not to do? Was it worth the chance? Pop could sure use the extra pair of hands.

"Have you ever heard of using horses to help children with physical and emotional problems, Bo?" Her question slid out on the deep end of a sigh as she grabbed the door handle. "Come over to the porch where it's cooler, and I'll tell you about it."

Without waiting for him to object, or for the chance to change her own mind, Abby opened the door, squinting against the noon brightness. "It's too hot to stand out here in the sun. I won't offer you a beer, but I've got cold, sweet tea already made."

She started to help him out of the truck, then thought better of it, remembering how he'd shot out of the café parking lot on Saturday. She stepped aside to give his male pride a wide berth. Holding her breath might not help, but she did it anyway.

He reached for the sunglasses in his shirt pocket and settled them on his nose.

"You're right, it is too hot to sit out here," he said, surprising her with his swift agreement. "And I haven't had honest-to-God sweet tea in a helluva long time."

He eased out one leg, then the other, until he was standing outside the truck. After a moment's hesitation when he hung on to the door for balance, he followed her to the shaded porch.

The shuffle of his uneven stride as he dragged his leg along the walk made her slow her own pace. But when his labored breathing sent a warm puff of air to tickle the back of her neck, it was all she could do to keep from breaking into a run.

Chapter Four

By the time she returned from the kitchen, Bo was lounging in a wicker chair near the porch steps. The sight of him sitting there looking right at home made her insides turn as cold as the ice cubes in the frosted glass she handed him. If only her hand would stop shaking. Her nerves were giving her fits lately.

"Much obliged," Bo said and reached for the glass.

His fingers brushed hers. Warm, callused fingers. Sensual fingers. Abby abruptly hurried away to sit on the steps. *Why, oh, why did I do this?*

An awkward silence, broken only by the sound of ice clinking on the sides of their glasses, hung between them.

Abby fidgeted.

Mosquitos buzzed.

Bo inspected his drink. Cleared his throat. "So, what's this horse therapy thing you've got going?"

Abby's head snapped around. He was watching her through those damned dark glasses, and she stifled the urge to reach over and yank them right off his face. She hated being unable to see his eyes.

"Not therapy for horses, Bo. Therapy for anyone with special needs. Children, mostly, but there are a couple of young adults, also." Slowly, deliberately, she emphasized each word. "It's designed to give a sense of accomplishment and strength to the students. To make them proud of their achievement. Some have never walked, some have emotional as well as physical difficulties to overcome, but here with the horses, they're no different from anyone else. Riding puts them on an equal basis. It helps them focus and learn to concentrate, not to mention that it builds self-confidence. There are numerous advantages to the program."

She paused to catch her breath, realizing she must sound like an evangelist for the cause. "Sorry, sometimes I get carried away."

Bo inclined his head. "And you accomplish all that by letting them ride horses?"

She struggled to keep her voice calm against the veiled pessimism in his question. She'd learned a long time ago that arguing with him never accomplished a darn thing.

"It's more than just the riding. They learn about responsibility by taking part in the care of the animals, by remembering to put the tack away after their ride, by learning to give commands as well as follow them." She looked at him straight on. "Even the students who can't walk find a way to interact with the horses. It's called trust." She paused to let her words sink in. "Communication, Ramsey. A vital part of life. Something necessary in any type of relationship."

When she saw him flinch, Abby was satisfied she'd made her point. She reached up to push a wayward strand of hair out of her face and tuck it back under her baseball cap. "Until you see one of the classes in progress, I suppose it's difficult to understand."

She wished he'd take those darned sunglasses off. Didn't he know she could see his face anyway? The dark lens only hid his eyes, a fact that kept her on the edge of anxiety. She started to ask about Marla, but changed her mind when she realized Bo was actually listening to her.

His rapt attention pleased her. Satisfied an empty spot in her heart that longed for his approval, yet filled a need to prove to him she had survived their unexpected breakup, thank you very much. She had her self-esteem in place and her emotions carefully tucked away.

He removed his dark glasses as if he'd read her mind. His gaze zeroed in on her face. "You've done this all alone?"

Her cheeks warmed under his scrutiny. Almost as if he dared her to look at the jagged scar that snaked from his hairline to his chin, narrowly missing his left eye. But nothing could make her forget the way those sultry eyes could seduce with a suggestive flicker. The way they shuttered lazily when they darkened with desire. With raw need. How many times had she felt the heat of his gaze caress her naked body? How many times had he touched…?

"Abby?"

Bo's soft drawl and hypnotic gaze held her captive. Kept her from rational thought for only a fraction of a second, but a millennium passed before she found her voice.

"Yes, alone... I mean no, I have Pop's help. And volunteers. Lots of them. They're invaluable. Without them, I wouldn't be able to continue. There's even a group of retired ranchers who come around once a week to help with repairs. And they bring feed when they can. It all helps." Darn, she was babbling.

"I still don't see how—" Bo was interrupted by a shout from Shorty before he could finish.

"Okay, Ramsey, let's hit the road." The rancher climbed in the truck and revved the motor. "See ya, Abby," Shorty called over the engine noise.

Abby jumped to her feet, accompanied by a rush of disappointment. The unexpected sensation astonished her, but she was even more surprised at her next words.

"I have another class later this afternoon. Spectators are always welcome."

Bo gulped a last swallow of tea and set his glass down. "No way," he said so abruptly Abby cringed and stepped back. "But thanks for leaving the chili peppers out of the tea."

She thought one corner of his mouth

twitched right before he turned and carefully took the steps one at a time.

The X-rated way his hips swivelled in jeans so tight they should have been banned set off a meteor shower of white-hot desire zinging through her body as his uneven gait carried him to the truck. She took one final, greedy look before she bolted for the house.

The screen door banged shut behind her at the same time the raucous blare of a horn assaulted her ears. Swinging around, Abby saw a dusty black Tahoe pulling in the drive behind Shorty's truck. The words Stuart C. Wilcox, DVM painted on the side of the vehicle in bold red letters reminded her that Buck had called the veterinarian earlier this morning about Jo-Jo's swollen eye. She really didn't feel up to dealing with the good-looking, totally nice, Dr. Stuart Wilcox right now. Especially with Bo still around.

Not that it mattered. In fact, if Stuart asked her out again, she might just say yes. Why not? Their last date had been enjoyable enough. Dinner at a charming little restaurant, a quiet drive through the hill country in Stuart's sleek silver Lexus, followed by a nice, though somewhat uninspiring, goodnight kiss at her door. No stress, no pressure.

Nice was what she was looking for, right? And being with Stuart didn't threaten her heart, a safety factor she rated right up there with smoke detectors and seat belts.

The Tahoe blocked Shorty's truck, and from the shouts and honks coming from that direction, neither driver wanted to move. Abby put her hands on her hips. Now what? There was plenty of room out there to park a couple of semis. You'd think a decrepit, old vintage pickup and a shiny, uptown SUV could manage to share the space. Abby left the porch to referee, feeling a little like a pre-school teacher in the middle of a playground squabble. Where the heck was Pop? She could use some help here.

"Looks like someone forgot his manners," she said, marching over to give Shorty her best "shame on you" look. "Dr. Wilcox needs to get on over to the barn. Can you pull up a little and let him go around you?"

Shorty shrugged, rolled his eyes and inched the truck forward.

Bo stood next to the truck, and Abby wondered if he was having difficulty getting in, or if he was just waiting while Shorty argued over the right-of-way. Something must have changed his mind, because the next thing she knew, he was standing in front of her, generating heat from his body like a kicked-up furnace. Would she ever stop reacting to him?

Bo jerked a thumb in the direction of the Tahoe. "He's the vet? What happened to Doc Barnes?" The dark glasses were back in place, but there was no doubt his gaze was leveled at the latest visitor to the Houston ranch.

The challenging question made her frown. "He retired a year ago and Stu... I mean, Dr. Wilcox, took over his practice."

"Stu, huh?" Bo shoved his hands in his pockets, cocked his head to one side. "Looks mighty citified for a country vet. He ever work with anything bigger than fancy poodles and cats with an attitude?"

Abby crossed her arms over her chest. "Of course. He's worked with horses. Cattle, too, for crying out loud. He's been helping the ranchers around here for quite some time. Ask Shorty. He uses the doctor's services, too."

Bo hesitated just long enough to take off his sunglasses.

"And you? Do you use his services?"

She bristled when he looked at her straight on. No hat hiding his face. No dark glasses concealing those soot-black eyes.

Her chin lifted. His subtle, double-edged question ticked her off, big-time. The defiant side of her nature wanted to punch his lights out. The practical side stifled that urge, but only after a struggle.

"If I do, Ramsey, it's no concern of yours." She kept her voice low, every word carefully measured. "My horses need the best care available. They're old. One of them is nearly blind, and they all have aches and pains, just like a lot of people. Dr. Wilcox gives them excellent care."

"Hey, I'm sorry." Bo touched her arm. "I was out of line. Wilcox is probably quite capable of doing his job." He turned to go, then said over his shoulder, "But if you ever need a gimpy cowboy to muck stalls, I know one who might be interested." He climbed in the truck, jerked his hat down and slammed the door shut—hard.

"Let's go," she heard him tell Shorty.

The rancher swung the pickup around the Tahoe and made a new track down the drive.

Abby stared after them. Well, what brought that on? Certainly not jealousy on Bo's part. He was a family man now. His sudden marriage to Marla had provided enough fodder for the town gossips. She certainly wasn't going to give them any more by becoming the other woman. She'd been their object of pity long enough.

Heading for the barn, and Jo-Jo's stall, she pretended not to see the inquisitive glint in Pop's eyes as she passed him on his way to the house. She wasn't going to answer his questions, either. She just wanted to be left alone.

"Looks like it's only a minor infection, Abby," the doctor said, looking up from where he'd been working when she entered the stall. His examination of Jo-Jo's eye finished, Stuart set out a vial of antibiotic and readied the horse for an injection.

"This, along with the drops I'm leaving, should take care of it, but I'll stop by at the end of the week to check it again, just to be on the safe side."

Abby walked over and stroked the horse's neck, trying to divert its attention—and hers—from the shot. She would never get used to the size of the needles necessary for the animals' injections.

"I appreciate it, Stuart. I know I'm probably overly cautious about my horses, but it's important for me to keep them as healthy as possible. They're not exactly youngsters."

"You know I'll do what I can." He finished with Jo-Jo, packed up his implements and headed for the clean-up area to wash his hands.

Abby leaned against the wall outside Jo-Jo's stall and mentally added the cost of today's visit to the balance she still owed the vet. Trying to figure out just how she was going to pay the mounting bill was keeping her awake too many nights lately. The more she delved into the mishmash of Pop's on-again-off-again bookkeeping system, the more she realized she should've gotten involved sooner. Should've focused her attention on the business of the ranch instead of selfishly wallowing in the condition of her humiliated heart. How pitiful was that?

Lost in her disturbing thoughts, she didn't hear Stuart's approach. When he touched her arm, she spun around. He stood close enough for her to read the eagerness in his expressive face. Close enough for her to anticipate what he was about to suggest. She waited and tried to feel a measure of excitement.

"How about dinner tonight?" His cultured, calm voice didn't threaten or demand, even as his thumb caressed the inside of her elbow. "There's a new place on the outskirts of Austin I'd like to take you. I hear the chef does wonders with stuffed trout."

Abby studied him—the sexy cleft chin, silver-gray eyes and thick, cropped hair that was neither blond nor brown, but shades of both. Even his physique was a photographer's joy. He would be right at home on the cover of any top magazine. Smooth, polished, intelligent. A definite candidate for Texas's most eligible bachelor list.

So, why didn't she feel something here? Tingling nerve ends or goose-bumpy shivers? What kind of problem did she have, anyway? Why couldn't she work up some good, old-fashioned lust? He'd made it clear on their previous date that he'd like to pursue their relationship, even though he didn't push the issue. Were her hormones totally nonfunctioning? He was Mr. Nice Guy, for crying out loud. The type she'd convinced herself she wanted—deserved, even. The type that wouldn't give her heart any reason to cry.

"Tonight? Well, I…" Abby took a step backward. Stuart slid his hand down her arm, entwining his fingers through hers.

"I know it's Monday," he said, "but we'll make it an early evening, I promise. What do you say, Abby? Pick you up at six?"

There was nothing subtle about the desire in his voice or the admiration in his eyes, but he never overstepped the boundaries of good conduct. Stuart Wilcox was as honest and forthright as he was good-looking. She knew he wanted her.

"All right, six is fine." Abby forced a smile and untangled her hand from his. "Now, I really need to fix Pop's lunch and get ready for the afternoon class." She hesitated. "I'd ask you to join us, but I'm afraid it's only tuna sandwiches."

His polite refusal nearly had her shouting with relief. The way he'd wrinkled his nose at the mention of tuna, she was pretty sure it wasn't his favorite item on the menu. That little bit of information she tucked away for future reference and hurried on to the house. A quick glance at her watch reminded her of everything she had to do, and prompted her to contemplate how she could add a few more hours to the day. Instead of daylight saving time, she could call it sanity saving time. Specifically hers.

All afternoon, concentration eluded her as she struggled to get through the rest of the day. The hour-long classes were a blur, her attention scattered by mental arguments in

Stuart's favor and counterarguments from Bo's intruding image. She really needed some alone time to sort out the disturbing thoughts that were making her unusually impatient and antsy. Not her normal self. By the end of the last session, she wondered if she had actually done any supervising at all. Thank goodness for the volunteers. She needed someone around here to stay sane.

And Pop. Bless him, he hadn't even questioned her when she told him about accepting the dinner date with Stuart. Just raised his eyebrows in that way he had of silently asking if she wanted to talk. But when she hadn't, he'd given her a hug and told her tomorrow would be better. The eternal optimist, her Pop. If only she could believe him.

She was ready when Stuart arrived exactly at six o'clock. He looked handsome in his charcoal slacks and gray silk shirt. Not at all like the man who had grubbed around in her horse barn that same morning.

"You look lovely, Abby," he said. He opened the car door for her and she slid in.

She thanked him and wished she'd worn something a little snazzier than her navy silk shift.

"I hope you like this restaurant. It has a five-star rating," he said when they reached the highway and sped toward Austin.

"I'm sure I will." Abby leaned back against the leather seat and ordered herself to relax. She needed the break and Stuart was wonderful company. Wasn't he?

"Tired?" He reached for her hand. "I wish there was more I could help you with."

"It has been pretty hectic, what with the new students and all, but things are slowly coming together. Pop and I appreciate the care you've given our animals." She let her hand remain in his. The feeling was nice, but there weren't any of those delicious shivers tickling her spine. No rapid heartbeat, either. She sighed.

"I'd do a lot more if you'd let me." Stuart's attention briefly left the road. His sincere smile should've lifted her spirits. It didn't.

"Thanks, Stuart, I appreciate the offer." She eased her hand away, smoothed her skirt.

"Well, put your problems aside for a few hours tonight and leave everything to me."

He exited the main highway and by the time he pulled the Lexus into the inn's valet parking area, Abby had made up her mind to stop making comparisons between Stuart and Bo. She'd concentrate on having a good time. How difficult could that be?

Dinner passed comfortably. Stuart had been right—the food *was* delicious. "More wine?" Stuart said later, as he poised the bottle over her glass, when they had finished their meal.

Abby shook her head. "No more, thanks," she said. "Two glasses are my limit." She didn't need any more of a buzz than she already had.

Wine was not her drink of choice, but Stuart had made such a to-do over the wine selection, she didn't have the heart to tell him she'd rather have tea. Especially after her obvious dismay when the waiter served their stuffed trout entrée. Well, how was she to know the thing would be served with its whole face staring right at her? Give her a nice blackened catfish dinner with fries any day. She was relieved when the meal was over and they left the inn. She just wasn't cut out for gourmet dining.

The moon cast a pale light on the ribbon of road leading back to Sweet River. Replete with the fine wine and the meal, Abby fought to keep her eyelids from drooping.

She heard Stuart slide a CD into the slot.

Soon, Andrea Bocelli's thrilling tenor voice filled the car with romantic Italian love songs. Abby couldn't understand a single word, but the beauty of his music touched her heart.

"He's blind you know," Stuart said.

"That has nothing to do with his musical ability," Abby answered. "A voice like his is a God-given talent. I'm sure it took courage to share it with others." She looked out at the stars twinkling in the night-blue sky and wondered if Bo would ever find his courage again. "We all have some special talent to give. It's not always clear what our talent is. That's where courage comes in."

"I agree," Stuart said. "Those kids in your classes are evidence of what real courage is."

He stopped the car and Abby realized they were home. Stuart came around to open the door for her. Her hand was on the handle before she remembered he was a gentleman. Not too many of them left in this do-it-yourself world. She relaxed and waited for him to help her out of the car. Sometimes, being a woman was truly enjoyable.

They walked to the door, his hand lightly holding her arm. A delicate breeze swept across the porch in an effort to chase away the day's heat.

Abby stood very still. She wasn't sure if Stuart intended to kiss her good-night or not, but their last date had ended with one, so she tried to appear composed.

"I've had a wonderful time, Stuart. Thank you for inviting me."

"My pleasure," Stuart said and moved closer. He placed his hands on either side of the door and gazed down at her.

She was caught between his arms with only a little space between them. A whiff of his aftershave drifted past her nose as he bent his head.

The kiss was perfectly executed. Flawless. And that really bothered her. She should have felt something besides this sense of remorse. Guilt. Inability to respond. She certainly shouldn't be thinking about Bo while Stuart was kissing her.

Guilt still tormented her after they had said good-night and she reached the quiet solitude of her bedroom. The splitting headache that had been lying in wait all day mushroomed into her full-fledged enemy.

She traded her simple navy silk dress for the comfort of her faded University of Texas nightshirt, took two Tylenol tablets and slapped a cold, wet cloth across her forehead.

Neither treatment was winning her war of nerves.

Lying in bed with her eyes squeezed shut, Abby tried not to think about Bo. There were numerous reasons why she ought to consider a serious relationship with Stuart. One was… Stuart was very nice. That was a good reason. And committing to Stuart definitely would help the program financially. *Oh, who am I kidding?*

She jumped up, hustled to the bathroom to rewet the cloth, then flopped back on the bed. She tried harder than ever to come up with a better reason. Stuart was trustworthy. Bo wasn't. Excellent reason. Bo was married. Well, hello! That was the best reason yet.

But, something didn't add up. Where was Marla? And wasn't it strange that Shorty and Bo had both refrained from mentioning her? What was it Shorty had said? Something about that being Bo's tale to tell? Maybe it was time to find out what that tale was.

She flipped over on her stomach and buried her head under the pillow. No, she absolutely would *not* be that vulnerable again. Once before she had given in to passion alone, ignoring the warning signs that had almost cost them the ranch. She'd offered her heart only to have it tossed aside, but her priorities were in place now. Pop and the ranch came first.

She had to stop thinking about the past. Stop remembering. *Right. And that will happen about the same time "The Eyes of Texas" becomes the national anthem.*

When the hall clock struck three, Abby was still wrestling with the enemies of her heart. She finally fell asleep, not quite certain if she'd won the match.

Chapter Five

For the first time in the three weeks since his return, Bo awoke at first light to hear a whole different set of early morning noises than he was accustomed to. Right now, a rooster rivaled the brightness of the sun for attention, newly weaned calves bawled for their mothers and horses whinnied in the corral, ready to run with the wind. Funny how easy it was to forget when you'd been gone awhile.

He'd left the window open on purpose last night to invite the cool breeze, and now the earthy smells of the barn and the animals wafted in on the light, sunshiny zephyrs that stirred the plain white curtains. The scent of cedar trees mingled with the perfume of the thick honeysuckle vines covering the trellis near the porch. God, he'd missed all this. Missed the familiar smells and sounds of ordinary things that could soothe the soul.

Stretching his long body, he lifted his injured leg up and down to test its flexibility. Definitely not the best-looking leg he'd ever seen, but hell, it matched the rest of his body. He propped his hands behind his head and listened to a mockingbird in the oak tree outside his bedroom window try out its entire repertoire of tunes. His mind wandered back over the events that had eventually brought him back to Sweet River. Full circle and alone.

His predicament with Abby was his own fault—he owned up to that. He remembered the night of their big fight and subsequent breakup. They'd been watching the local Fourth of July fireworks display. He'd assumed, since their relationship had become serious, that Abby would be willing to accompany him when he decided to hit the rodeo circuit. Hadn't she understood that his job on the Packer ranch was only a temporary stop on his way to something bigger than being just a ranch hand? If he succeeded in the rodeo, he could give her all the things she deserved.

What followed was the worst day of Bo's life. He had taken Abby's refusal to leave the ranch and her father as final. He hadn't really listened to her reasons. Selfishly, he hadn't wanted to.

Deeply hurt, and full of anger and self-pity, he took his frustrations to the beer tent, where most of the town, including Marla, was celebrating. His boss's niece was more than willing to help him forget his problems. Two pitchers of beer later, he'd grabbed what she had offered without a thought to the consequences. Under the circumstances, he'd believed that marrying Marla was the responsible thing to do. When he discovered that she was lying to him about being pregnant, he'd made things worse by not telling Abby. The whole mess had culminated with the bone-shattering accident that had cost him his career. Now he was thirty years old with about as much future as a gravel road to nowhere. End of story.

Bo eased his bare legs over the side of the bed and stepped around the jeans heaped on the floor, right where he'd dropped them the night before. Yawning, he headed for the bathroom, hoping the hot shower would ease his nagging aches and pains. The ones that never seemed to fade. To hope those painful memories could be washed away completely was probably too much to ask, so he didn't.

He avoided the mirror when he passed the sink and carefully stepped into the tiled shower stall. With the water turned on full force, he stood there absorbing the heat while the stinging spray pelted his body. *Ahhh.* He rolled his shoulders, grateful the aches and pains were slowly beginning to disappear and his bones were healing. If only the damned limp and crooked leg weren't constant reminders of the accident.

There had been a time, not so long ago, when he feared he'd never stand on these two legs again. But sheer Texas stubbornness had brought him this far, and Shorty seemed determined to drag him the rest of the way. God only knew why, since there was no way he'd ever sit in a saddle again.

He lathered up, then tipped his head back to let the water work its magic. Shorty had reminded him that his muleheadedness was the very thing that helped shove him out of the hospital bed sooner than the doctors expected. Stubbornness must be good for something, after all.

He turned the water off, stepped out and grabbed a towel from the towel bar. When his scarred reflection stared back from the steamy mirror, he growled a curse and spun around to look the other way. In that brief instant, his mood soured. How could he have forgotten *that* nasty reminder? Damn.

The damp towel fell to the floor, and he stomped clumsily out of the room, wet feet and slick tiles nearly upending him. He teetered and grasped the door frame. Hell, he couldn't even manage to stay upright. What made him think things would be any different here in Sweet River?

The seed of hope that Abby might care enough to forgive him struggled against the knowledge that what he'd done was unforgivable. Not only did she have every right to hate him for walking out on her, but how would she react if she knew that his noble gesture in marrying Marla had turned into a joke? On him. He'd been a fool to come back.

And a bigger fool to finally agree to Shorty's harebrained idea, he decided an hour later, as he hung on to the seat of the old truck while his friend made the drive to

Buck Houston's ranch rival a NASCAR event. Yesterday, Abby hadn't exactly jumped on his halfhearted offer to muck out stalls.

Shorty swerved the vehicle sharply to the left, then whipped it back again, barely missing an armadillo roadkill. In the bed of the truck, Ditch's toenails clicked and scratched on the metal surface as he scrambled to stay upright. In Bo's estimation, the hound's complaining howl was more than justified. The bone-jarring torture chamber masquerading as Shorty's pickup rattled Bo's thoughts as well as his battered body.

Admittedly, he knew a lot about horses, but he didn't know jack about special-needs kids. Okay, he'd take a quick look at the setup to satisfy Shorty, but one scared cry from them—just one—and he was out of there. Fast.

He fingered his sunglasses to make certain they were in place, then tugged his hat lower. He was pretty sure he'd lost his everlovin' mind. Self-inflicted pain was something he usually tried to avoid. Yeah, right. So, why was he doing this?

He spied the answer to his question as soon as Shorty stopped the pickup in front of the barn. She was in the arena working with her students. His heart kicked up a notch the minute he saw her. He had to tamp down his eagerness, as well as his growing arousal, since Shorty was eyeing him like a duck fixin' to peck a June bug. Bo still wasn't convinced this was a good idea, but after he'd finally explained about Marla, Shorty had issued him a nonrefundable ticket on a huge guilt trip. There was no way to avoid the long, rough ride.

Learning of Abby's financial trouble had been a jolt. He'd always assumed Buck Houston to be a fairly wealthy man. It sure wasn't in Bo's realm of power to help them out. Lord knew, he had nothing to offer except his experience with horses. And that was only if he wasn't expected to ride them. So right now he'd have to settle for just being an unpaid stable hand, whatever that was worth. If she'd have him.

He hunched his shoulders defensively. That was about all a busted-up, scar-faced cowboy could expect, anyway.

In the arena, a young girl on a sway-backed gray horse rocked awkwardly back and forth in an English-style saddle. Bo gave his silent approval to the use of a bump pad between the blanket and saddle, knowing it helped balance the rider as well as giving added protection to the older horse. The girl eagerly waved to the group of onlookers standing nearby, but when she suddenly jerked back on the reins, he heard Abby call from the other side.

"Remember, Evie, use quiet hands. Old Cloud has a tender mouth."

The volunteer walking alongside, holding Cloud's lead rope, helped Evie adjust her grip on the reins. The girl straightened her riding helmet and gave Abby an enthusiastic thumbs-up salute. A sunny smile lit up her round face, sending a bright beam of courage, of pride and accomplishment.

Bo's gaze never left the action in the arena. As soon as Shorty headed over to the corral in search of Buck, Bo left the truck and quietly made his way to the opposite side, where he had an unobstructed view of Abby. If she knew he was there, she didn't acknowledge it. Never even looked his way. Her entire focus was centered on the children and the horses.

A hot fist of desire clenched deep in his gut. She was more beautiful than he remembered. No one but Abby could make a pair of jeans look like a second layer of skin. No one had that sweet hip-swaying walk, either. Or legs that stretched clear up to Trouble. The curvy fit of her bright red tank top dared him to look, its crimson hue snagging his attention like a matador's cape taunting a bull.

He watched her tuck her thick blond hair under her cap, pull it through the back opening and yank the visor down against the glare of the sun. Her skin was tanned to a soft summer gold, and he remembered, even without seeing her face, those freckles marching across her pert, tilted nose. Lips so soft and rosy they needed no extra enhancement and eyes the darkest blue of a perfect sapphire—oh, yeah, Bo knew her features by heart.

Every inch of his skin prickled, every nerve in his body snapped to full alert. This woman had the power to reduce him to dust, and she didn't even know it. But dust was about the sum total of his worth. She *had* to know *that*. He surely did.

How long has he been watching me? Abby glanced up from where she was standing next to the mounting block, and her heart slammed against her ribs almost before her brain registered what was happening. *Damn you, Ramsey, you said you weren't going to show up.* She should have known he'd never follow through with his word. Nothing new there.

The dark sunglasses and low-tipped Stetson were predictably in place, as were the jeans barely hanging on his narrow hips. Today he wore a midnight blue T-shirt at least one size too small. The way it shrink-wrapped his chest revealed every muscle and bone like an X-ray. Abby was clear across the arena from him, but not far enough to avoid the blitz of heat caused simply by looking at him.

Shorty and Pop stood by the gate, heads together like two conspirators. That alone was enough to make Abby's nervous system shore up in self-defense. Couple that with Bo's unexpected arrival, and she felt like she'd been blindsided—twice. When her constant companion, Headache Number Nine—or was it Ten?—resumed hammering against the inside of her skull at the exact minute Bo opened the gate and ambled toward her, her brain taunted, *Coincidence?* Not likely.

Only Ramsey could make a one-sided, slow-motion shuffle with an injured leg look like a sexy invitation to tango. Actually, *tangle* was a more appropriate word, because the closer he got, the more her emotions tied knots around her common sense.

And then he was right in front of her, temptation in blue jeans. Every buried memory of their time together resurrected itself and slammed into her with the force of a Gulf Coast hurricane. With knees like water and heart rate escalating, Abby's awareness of the world around her narrowed until all she saw was the man. And all she felt was the intensity of those smoky, seductive eyes as he lowered his glasses to lock his gaze with hers. She was conscious only of the sudden heat coursing through her veins. Her erratic breathing heaved her chest. Made her words stumble.

"I thought… What changed your—?"

"Just show me what you want me to do," Bo interrupted before she could finish, as if he'd anticipated her question.

Abby chewed her lip. She needed time to put her emotions back together, to get control of the situation again. Dammit, this time she wanted things to be on *her* terms. She'd only issued the invitation as a matter of pride. To prove she was capable of moving on with her life without him. She never thought he'd accept.

Backing away slowly, she put much-needed space between them. "I wasn't expecting you. Class isn't over yet."

"I'll wait. Unless you have something better for me to do."

"No, nothing." She couldn't think straight, let alone put a sentence together. She hated that weakness in herself.

"I can't pay you," she blurted to his retreating back, after he'd turned and headed over to where Shorty and Buck were standing. The dishwasher money would barely cover Karl's salary. There wasn't any more in the savings.

Bo didn't answer or look around, just shrugged his shoulders. Kept walking that one-sided walk.

Abby couldn't believe he actually wanted to work here. Couldn't believe it earlier that day when Pop had urged her to find some sort of job for Bo to do. What had Shorty confided to him yesterday in the barn that changed his mind?

Since her breakup with Bo, her father had been extremely vocal about his disapproval of the cowboy's actions, but this morning when she'd asked, Pop only shook his head and said, "Wait and see." Well, fine. She didn't care about Bo or his problems. Wouldn't care. Not anymore. If Bo wanted work, she'd give him work, no holds barred. She'd have him mucking out stalls, repairing fences and answering to her until he wished he'd never left Dallas. Or wherever.

A margin of satisfaction that felt a whole lot like sweet revenge curved her mouth into a half-smile. Her sympathy was in short supply. She didn't care if he had one good leg or three. If it would benefit her kids, she'd bargain with the devil himself. With a deep sigh, she wondered if maybe this time she had.

Whatever had prompted Abby's anger, Bo knew that he would feel the brunt of it before the day was over. Knew he deserved it, too, but that didn't make him like it. When he approached Buck and Shorty, he wasn't too pleased with the smirks on their faces, either. What the hell else were those two old codgers planning? He'd agreed to the stable hand thing, for crying out loud. For free. Wasn't that enough?

"Well…?" Shorty's cryptic comment left no room for Bo to hedge an answer.

"I reckon she'll make up her mind after class," Bo said, setting his dark glasses back in place. He pointed to where four timbers lay several feet apart in the center of the ring. "What are those poles for?" He hoped the quick change of subject would discourage further prying.

"The kids learn to walk the horses over them. Balance in a half seat when they do.

And they have to give the right command or the animals won't move." Buck's explanation was followed by a shout of encouragement to the riders in the arena. "See that little guy?" He pointed to a child of about six sitting on a small taffy-colored pony. "He's legally blind, only sees shadows. Bravest little kid you ever saw. Watch him."

Bo's attention riveted on the boy and pony. The child whooped and laughed as he bounced up and down in the saddle. The pony clip-clopped in a rhythmic trot, guided by a volunteer jogging alongside. The child's enthusiasm was contagious. Bo envied his excitement. He'd felt that same adrenaline rush in the arena when he had pitted his own strength against an angry bull. The desire to experience that feeling again was so intense, Bo was almost tempted to try. If only he could find that courage. Deep down in his gut, he knew he wanted to try.

He watched the pair finish circling the arena and come to a halt in front of the mounting block where Abby waited. When the boy pushed one hand in the air, Abby clapped it with hers in an enthusiastic high five. Rider, helper and instructor all sported matching grins.

"Walk on," the child commanded softly, and Bo watched the pony line up next to the others waiting in a half circle. When the last rider was in place, each child who was able dismounted with the help of a volunteer. Others were lifted from their saddles by parents.

The horses were then tied to various hitching posts inside the fence, and the workers helped the students put away the tack and brush their mounts. Everything was done in a timely, though often awkward, fashion. Abby walked among the group checking each child's progress, offering a smile, a hug, an encouraging word. Bo saw pride shine in her eyes. The children's faces reflected that pride.

It took some time for all the tack to be returned to its proper place and the pads and blankets put away. All the riders were responsible for taking care of their own equipment, to the best of their ability. Helmets were lined up on a low, easy-to-reach shelf and hands were washed with waterless cleaner before the students left the tack room. The cookie of the day was chocolate-chip, an obvious favorite. Bo couldn't help smiling at the jubilant youngsters' squeals and shouts as one of the helpers doled them out.

Abby made certain the students were safely

out of the barn and returned to their parents before she met with her volunteers for a quick run-through of the next day's class. Satisfied that everything was in order, she joined the three men leaning on the fence rail, watching her. Bo's eyes were hidden by dark glasses, yet their uncanny ability to make her insides quiver was much too familiar.

"Those kids sure are somethin'," Shorty said, breaking the awkward silence that Abby noticed was absent until she approached.

"Actually, Shorty, I'd call them something *special*," she said. "These six are the youngest class, but I think they're the most determined. All except Teddie. I just can't seem to reach him."

"Which one was he?" Shorty glanced around.

"He wasn't riding." She tugged off her work gloves and stuck them in the back pocket of her jeans, then resettled her baseball cap. "You probably couldn't see him from here, but he's usually watching from the observation area with his mom. He hasn't had the casts off his legs for long and doesn't feel safe on the horses yet. But his mom brings him to almost every class. We keep hoping that in time, he'll gain confidence. Anyway…" She looked at Bo, then jerked her head toward the barn. "If you're serious about working here, Ramsey, you can start by cleaning the stalls. And, when you've finished with that, there's a section of fence to be repaired, too."

She pointed to an old stake truck backed up next to a smaller building. "And those bags of grain need to be unloaded. I'll show you where they go. Think you can handle it? I've got a lot of chores to get done before dark."

"I'll manage," Bo muttered, with a scowl.

Abby planted a kiss on Buck's cheek, lingered there long enough to whisper in his ear, "I don't know what you're up to, Pop, but you'd better have a good explanation by suppertime."

The uneven shuffle of Bo's boots on the gravel followed her as she headed for the barn. She kept looking straight ahead, forcing herself not to slow her pace. She had no time to waste on sympathy where Bo Ramsey was concerned.

Two hours later, smelling strongly of the barn he'd been cleaning, Bo filled the final bucket of grain and closed the door to the last stall. The physical exertion of the everyday chores had him huffing and puffing harder than any therapy he'd been through at the hospital. Earlier, when he was unloading the sacks of grain in the sweltering heat, he'd peeled out of his shirt. Now, he pulled a blue bandana from his back pocket and mopped his face.

He was tempted to find a shade tree and rest a spell. If Abby was determined to make him suffer, she was doing a great job. He hadn't realized how much his body had weakened since the accident. Even his aches had aches, but wonder of wonders, he almost felt human again. Or would when he had a chance to catch his breath. He still had some fences to mend, literally as well as figuratively. Since he sure as hell didn't know how to fix the emotional stuff, he figured he'd better get started on the physical job. He damn well didn't want Abby catching him standing idle.

She'd gone out of her way to make herself scarce after giving him a few terse instructions. Like he'd never mucked out a barn, for cryin' out loud. He'd kept an eye out for her, just in case she decided to do a spot-check on his performance. Made him feel like he was on probation or something. Still, he was pleased with the job he'd done, in spite of his complaining body.

Now he just needed to find the section of broken fence and get started on that job. The sooner he finished, the sooner he could leave. Halfway to the house in search of Abby, he remembered his shirt and sunglasses. Grumbling, he backtracked to retrieve them.

"Giving up already?" Abby stood just inside the barn door, hands spread at the curve of her hips and a saucy tilt to her head.

Where'd she come from? Damn. Her ability to appear out of nowhere like that irritated him like a bad case of prickly heat. If she'd been in the building while he was working, why the devil hadn't she said anything? *Does she think a busted-up cowboy like me can't do a few simple chores?* Ah, hell, he didn't have reason to expect anything else.

"Nope, just fetching my shirt. If you'll show me which fence needs fixing, I'll get started on it. I'm all finished in here."

He brushed past her, recovered his shirt and jerked it on. The dark glasses were in place before he turned around.

"I thought you'd be ready to call it quits by now," she said as she walked toward him, stopping so close she left him no breathing room.

Even in the smelly confines of the barn, Bo caught the scent of the familiar honeysuckle fragrance she wore and it all but buckled his knees. *Get over it, Ramsey. The woman despises you.*

She reached up to steal his glasses. "Why do you keep hiding behind these?" Her breath swirled across his face, warm and sweet.

He snagged her wrist, imprisoned it and drew her against him, making it impossible for her to avoid looking into his eyes. "Look at these damned scars, Abby." Reaching down, he took her other hand. Slowly, deliberately, he moved her fingers over the trail of scars that angled from his hairline to his chin, dividing his cheek and catching the corner of his lower lip. "Does this answer your question?"

He waited for her to flinch. To turn away in disgust. Instead, she surprised him by doing neither one. Only the slight tremor in her hand hinted that the sight of his face had any effect on her at all.

"I see the scars, Ramsey, but if you're looking for sympathy, I'm not offering any. I see kids every day with bigger challenges to deal with than a few lines on their faces. Let your wife supply the pity you're obviously looking for. You won't find any here. I have better things to do with my time."

Of course, she did. He'd forgotten about the veterinarian. He grasped her shoulders with both hands before she could leave. A chunk of raw anger stuck in his throat. He wished he could shout at her, deny her accusation, but what she said was painfully close to the truth. He *did* want her sympathy—in a twisted sort of way that only reminded him of his weakness. But more than that, he simply wanted her. Wanted his mouth on hers, wanted the taste of her on his tongue, wanted… But he'd never have that right again. He dropped his hands as quickly as he'd grabbed her and stepped back awkwardly.

"Yeah, I guess you do, namely with your doctor, what's-his-name." His clumsy attempt to retreat with dignity pissed him off. Oh, man, he had to get out of here. He headed for the door.

"For your information, his name is Wilcox." Her words slammed into his retreating back. "And he's not *my* doctor," she shouted.

Bo stopped, moving his feet carefully this time as he turned to face her, fists clenched at his sides. A rough whisper came from his throat. "Well, for *your* information, Abby, there's no wife, either."

Chapter Six

Grinding his teeth against the spasm of pain in his leg that was making a dignified exit impossible, Bo walked through the barn door stiff-legged. He didn't have a clue where to find the broken fence, didn't have anything to fix it with anyway. Besides that, Abby still held his sunglasses. Might as well quit and go home. This whole idea of Shorty's was a first-class disaster.

He'd only gotten a few feet away when a barrage of sudden, sharp pokes between his shoulder blades stopped him dead in his tracks. His balance tilted and he staggered.

Abby's angry outburst accompanied the next

pointed jab. "Hold it, Ramsey. You can't make a statement like that and just walk away."

Bo turned around just as her fist plowed into the center of his chest. "What the…?" His gaze narrowed at the sight of her flushed face and stormy eyes.

Her hand splayed out across his midsection on impact. Stayed there just long enough to generate a hot spot before she jerked it away.

"I said—"

"I heard what the hell you said." Bo rubbed his chest where the heat from her touch still lingered. Desperate for time to organize the crazy thoughts spinning around in his brain, he took two measured breaths to steady himself. He needed to find a way to dispel the censure in her eyes. Knew he could never atone for the hurt he'd caused her. Regret firmly anchored itself in his heart, but he was afraid Abby would never believe him. Why should she? Still, he owed her an explanation because the whole damned community would know the details if Marla ever decided to come back to Sweet River.

He dragged in another deep breath, slowly expelled it. "Like I said, Marla's not my wife. It didn't work out." He half expected Abby to laugh in his face. When she didn't, he waited for the next explosion.

Abby's insides started to crumble. A shiver cat-pawed its way up her spine in spite of the heat. She'd been balancing on the edge of an emotional precipice ever since he'd made her touch his scars—something she'd wanted to do from that very first day when she'd looked him square in the face and shoved the bowl of chili at him.

She hadn't dared, of course. Not because she was repulsed, but because she knew if she touched him, it would be harder to keep her anger alive. And anger was her only defense. At first, she'd used it to keep from falling apart in public. Somewhere along the way, she'd become dependent on it to get her through the endless nights alone. She didn't dare let go of it now. And she darned well wouldn't feel sorry for his failed marriage. She absolutely would not.

But a corner of her heart still held questions. What about the child? She didn't even know whether they'd had a boy or a girl. Funny, now that she thought about it, Shorty had never mentioned the baby's arrival. Never even talked about it. Did the child look like Bo? A little boy with flashing, dark eyes and black hair, or maybe a beautiful little girl with long curls. She ached at the thought.

"Well, life isn't always what we expect, is it?" Even knowing her caustic words sounded mean and spiteful, Abby still couldn't bring herself to offer sympathy. *She* deserved the sympathy. *She* was the one who'd been dumped.

"You got that right." Bo bent to retrieve the glasses lying on the ground between them, straightened, then settled them on his nose. "What about you, Abby? Is your life better or worse than you expected?"

Her tightly held self-control rushed to the surface on a tidal wave of anger. "How can you even ask such a question, Ramsey?" She put both hands on his shoulders and shoved him back a step. He staggered. She didn't care.

"My expectations were blown to hell and back when you walked out on me." Another shove. Another backward step.

"You humiliated me in front of the entire town." Two more shoves and she had him backed up against the side of the barn.

She puffed a wayward strand of hair out of her face and shoved him one more time for good measure. "I don't give a flying fig whether your marriage worked out or not."

She fought against the urge to scream—to

hammer at him with both fists, to hurt him—anything to get rid of the internal demon that was battering her heart with unbearable pain. It wasn't fair. Dear God, it wasn't fair.

Hot, stinging tears filled her eyes. She blinked hard to keep them from spilling down her cheeks. Dammit! The last thing she wanted was for Bo to see her cry. Her pride was hanging on by a straggly thread as it was. It was so hard not to give in.

A sudden move tipped her forward and she leaned into him, molded against his hard angles. Heat flared at every place where their bodies touched. She gripped his shoulders for balance and his hands went around her waist in a flash, holding her immobile. The burst of emotions robbed her of all common sense. She tried to pull away. Needed to escape what was happening. Didn't really want to.

"Abby, please don't cry. Let me explain."

His words nicked a corner of her heart's hiding place and his eyes seemed to search her face for something, but what? Permission to break her heart again?

The sincerity of his quiet plea had her choking back the already threatening sobs burning her throat. The temptation to stay right where she was, tucked in the familiar circle of his arms, overwhelmed her. Confused her. Made her foot-stomping mad, for cripes sake.

"Damn you, Bo, you made me look like a fool. I trusted you. Believed you. Don't expect me to listen to your excuses now. It's too late. I don't care anymore."

Heart pounding and pulse racing, she pulled away from his embrace and ran for the safety of the house. Broken fences were the last thing on her mind.

Bo passed the next half hour leaning against the trunk of a gnarled pecan tree at the end of the lane. He'd been trying to figure out what the hell had happened back there in the barn. When Abby took off after his attempt to explain about Marla, he'd retreated to the barn to try and get a grip on his emotions. When that hadn't worked, he'd said to hell with it and made his way down the driveway to wait for Shorty.

The sun had already scorched his hide to cinders and his rear end was getting numb from sitting on the hard ground. Besides, the way his stomach was growling, he figured it must be close to suppertime and for a change, he was hungry.

The whole situation with Abby made him see things about himself that he'd just as soon ignore. Too much thinking was bad for his frame of mind.

If his leg hadn't acted up again after he'd unloaded those fifty-pound bags of grain, he might have been tempted to try walking home. *Yeah, right, cowboy. You couldn't walk one-tenth of the way. Better stop dreaming. Dreams are for kids.*

He took off his wide-brimmed hat and mopped his face with his bandana. Kids, he thought, remembering the exuberant smiles on the faces of Abby's students. Remembering their joy, their pride when they managed even the smallest accomplishment. Their unswerving determination to do their best against odds that would've had most kids whining and hollering for help, had earned Bo's admiration, yet reinforced his own feeling of uselessness.

How he'd envied those kids when Abby bestowed them with that heart-stopping smile, that assurance of total love and admiration. He knew her words of encouragement would never be given to him. Not as long as he kept the truth from her. And how could he tell her if she wasn't willing to listen?

The unmistakable sound of a pickup roared off in the distance, and Bo struggled to his feet.

"About time," he muttered. He'd probably catch hell when his friend discovered he'd copped out before finishing the job expected of him.

Well, so much for good intentions. It was better for everyone this way. He couldn't work near Abby knowing how she felt about him. He didn't blame her—just didn't want to spend his days watching her and that damned vet getting cozy right under his nose. The sooner he got back to Shorty's, the sooner he'd be able to get Abby out of his mind.

AH-OOO-GAH!

The ear-shattering noise momentarily stunned him. Hell, Shorty's truck didn't have an air horn. Who was this? When the cloud of dust cleared enough for him to see, his mouth dropped open at the sight of a tired, old farm truck barreling straight at him. He ate dust when it slewed to a stop in front of him.

"What the...?"

Abby stuck her head out the window. "Just shut up and get in the truck, Ramsey."

Well, shoot, he wasn't about to argue. He climbed in, one arm braced on the seat for leverage, while he pulled his body up with a groan.

He was debating what to say when Abby saved him the trouble of deciding.

"If you're planning to volunteer around here, you'd better get used to finishing a job before you take off." She thwacked a pair of leather work gloves into his lap. He thanked his lucky stars it wasn't a pair of bricks. Her aim was right on target.

"Fences don't mend themselves." She gunned the motor and executed a perfect U-turn in the middle of the gravel road.

Bo couldn't decide whether to laugh or not. Abby was acting like he was her hired hand, when just a few hours ago, she'd made certain he understood the job was strictly voluntary and she didn't care whether he was there or not. She'd always been as changeable as Texas weather, blowing hot and cold in the space of a minute. But he was grateful for the chance to be with her again. Maybe he could persuade her to listen to him.

Her unpredictable nature was one of the first things that he'd noticed about her when they'd met back then. He'd been wrangling for Shorty at the time—a footloose cowboy with little to worry about except his next paycheck and finding a pretty woman to keep him company. Shorty obliged him with a weekly paycheck. He'd had no trouble finding willing company. Then he'd met Abby.

She hadn't been impressed with him the first time he'd hauled a breeding bull over to the Houston ranch. When the bull had stubbornly balked at leaving the cattle hauler, she'd started right in giving him advice on how to handle the obstinate animal. Even offered to take over when it looked like Bo and the bull had reached a standoff.

When he had turned down her offer of help, she'd flounced off mad as a rained-on rooster. Fuming silently, she'd watched from a distance, obviously enjoying his predicament. That only made him work harder at impressing her. No such luck.

If she hadn't been so distracting, leaning on the fence rail in jeans too tight to be legal, he might've been able to concentrate on what he was doing. But no, he'd snuck another look at her just as the ornery bull decided to lumber out of the trailer into the pen. Then his arm got in the way of a razor-sharp horn. Abby had flown to his side in a heartbeat. Careful to lock the gate behind them, she'd hurried Bo into the house, insisting on bandaging the cut herself. That had been the beginning of the best time in his life. The end came months later, after their big blowup and his stupid, irresponsible night with Shorty's niece. Then, Marla dropped her bombshell, and life as he knew it simply stopped. Down the toilet. Hell on earth.

Looking at Abby now, Bo wondered how he could ever have believed Marla's lie about being pregnant. Why hadn't he asked for proof? He also knew he wasn't the only one she'd slept with. But no, he'd fancied himself as the good old boy—thought he was doing the big, noble thing, her being Shorty's niece and all. Obviously, he hadn't known the first thing about being noble or he wouldn't have left without talking to Abby, no matter what the cost to his pride.

Noble, my ass. He'd acted like a selfish SOB. A damn coward, not wanting to see the hurt in her eyes—the condemnation. Now he was paying for it. The whole nine yards. Marla's lie, the accident, this ice-cold fear in his gut of ever getting on a horse again. Paybacks were hell.

After two miles of silence down the south fence line, Abby stopped the truck and opened her door.

"There's a roll of fencing in the back," she said over her shoulder as she jumped out. "I'll get the rest of the tools while you unload it."

She's going to help? Well, he wasn't surprised. He'd screwed up before, so now she expected it of him. Probably didn't think he was capable of repairing a common fence. She'd depended on him before, and he'd failed. He'd do well to remember that. She wasn't about to cut him any slack, and he sure as hell wouldn't ask for any. He'd fix her damned fence even if it took him all night.

His good intentions vanished in a heartbeat at the sight of the massive roll of barbed wire stowed in the back of the truck. Looked like enough to repair five miles of fence, at least. Hellfire, they'd be out here until midnight.

Grumbling under his breath, he tugged on the leather gloves and got to work. He'd be damned if she'd hear him complain, even though his leg and shoulder ached like a son-of-a-gun.

Abby had just made a quick inspection of the downed wires, then turned back in time to see Bo struggling with the roll of fencing. She heard the choice words he muttered as he fought for balance, staggering when the unwieldy load shifted in his arms.

"Need help with that, Ramsey?"

"Does it look like I do?"

Abby bristled at the sharp retort delivered with a dark scowl that dared her to act on her offer. "Well, excuse me."

She remained where she was and tried not to give in to the wave of guilt chipping away at her conscience. Instead, she picked up the wire cutters and started removing the broken strands of fence from the posts. Bo Ramsey could fall on his face. She didn't care. But he'd better get his act together pretty soon. He had a long way to go before she'd believe in his dependability again. A very long way. Miles.

Two long, hot hours later, Abby leaned against the front fender of the truck and filled a plastic cup with cool water from a thermos. She looked down the fencerow and squinted, barely able to make out Bo's figure.

He was tightening the last strand of barbed wire and would be heading back to the truck soon. Cutting away the broken fence and pulling the staples out hadn't taken her as long as his job of stringing the new wire. She'd come back to the truck a half hour ago after Bo had rejected her repeated offer to help. Well, good. She was tired and hungry, anyway.

She should have taken some water to him, but after his last brush-off that was not going to happen. The job was almost finished anyway. She could've driven the truck out to meet him, too, but a resurrected streak of stubbornness made her decide against it. She pulled the last granola bar from her pocket and ate the whole thing.

When she saw him struggling to keep his balance while he fumbled with the bucket of tools and dragged the roll of fence toward the truck, it was impossible for her not to have a change of heart. In fact, her conscience scolded her big-time. What on earth had she been thinking? She wasn't a mean person, yet she was deliberately making an injured man perform chores that obviously caused him tremendous pain.

As Bo drew closer, Abby had a clear view of his entire face. His hat was pushed back on his head and his sunglasses were pocketed.

She studied the scars he so diligently tried to conceal. They were exposed almost as if he'd forgotten about them. If he turned slightly, she could see traces of the face she had known before—the face of the man she'd loved.

But this was a different man, she reminded

herself. Physically and emotionally. She'd picked up on that right away. After all, her students were challenged in both areas, too. She felt capable of helping them, even in small ways, with her riding program. Bo's problem was different. She wasn't sure if she could deal with his negative attitude. Didn't even know if she wanted to. After all, she hadn't figured out her own state of emotions yet. Why on earth would she want to tackle his?

Bo reached the truck, and Abby pushed away from the fender to take the tool bucket from him and hoist it in the back. Tugging on gloves, she climbed up, grabbed one end of the roll of fence, and helped him load it into the back. Without a word, Bo accepted her help then dropped, rubber-legged, to sit on the ground.

Abby jumped down, retrieved the thermos from the truck's cab and offered it. "Here, the water is still cool."

He snatched it and tipped it up, chug-a-lugging until it was empty. "Thanks." He swiped his mouth with the back of his hand.

"Sure. You earned it." She capped the empty container and tossed it in the front seat. "Guess we'd better hit the road. I expect Shorty's waiting for you at the house. It's way past suppertime." She drew a deep breath and mumbled, "Thanks for the help." The lingering taste of granola in her mouth had the distinct flavor of guilt.

Bo leaned forward from where he sat, arms resting on his bent knees. He pulled up a blade of grass and worried it between his fingers.

When he looked up, his gaze settled on her face, locked on her mouth. "If I didn't know better, I'd guess this was your idea of some kind of endurance test."

Her mouth dropped open. "Me? Why would I do that?"

"C'mon, you know you have every right." He reached for his dark glasses.

"Leave them off."

His eyes flickered in puzzlement. "Why?" He tugged at his hat.

"I told you before, they don't hide anything but your eyes."

"Are you saying the sight of my face doesn't bother you?" He stared at her with dark intensity.

Her heart tripped. How could she answer that? His scars were deep and his face no longer the same, but she didn't dare tell him that the irregular seams and rough-hewn planes created by his encounter with a bull only added to his irresistible male magnetism. She couldn't—absolutely wouldn't—admit his face intrigued her more now than the one from his past.

Hadn't he known she'd fallen for the man he was inside, not the packaging? His dark, sensual good looks had been easy to accept, but did he think she was so shallow that appearance was her only priority? Maybe he'd never really gotten to know her, after all, in the months they were together. That would've made it easier for him to leave her.

"Well?" He struggled to his feet and faced her, arms crossed over his chest, obviously waiting for her answer.

"Are you saying it should?" Stalling for more time, she walked around the truck to the driver's side. This was one conversation she didn't want to have. Not now. "C'mon, it's time we got back to the house."

For someone with a bum leg, he moved surprisingly fast. In an instant, he was behind her. He reached for her arm, missed and caught her hand instead. She stumbled when he tugged to turn her around.

"I'm not saying another word until you look

at me." He cupped her chin, tipped her face up and skewered her with onyx eyes. "If you want to know the whole story, you've got to give me a chance to tell you."

Lightning fast, he jerked the keys from the ignition. Her eyes widened in surprise. Bo read it as fear, and the tightly coiled self-control he'd been trying to contain all day long immediately unleashed.

"You and I need to talk." He pushed away from her then, took her hand and led her to the back of the truck. None too gently, he gripped her waist, lifted her up and planted her rear on the tailgate. "Now, it's my turn to explain and your turn to listen."

He kept his hands around her waist, partly because he feared she'd try to escape, but mostly because he wanted to feel her warmth. Needed to touch her. Thought about kissing her. But not now. Not as long as her eyes held that look of fear. Or was it pity?

"I should've done this a long time ago, Abby, but I didn't. Now I want to tell you why...if you'll let me."

Her lips tightened and, Lord help him, Bo thought she was going to haul off and deck him. Instead, her body went rigid beneath his hands, and he felt a shudder ripple through her as she spoke.

"Is this what you call a captive audience?" Like shards of ice, her cold words knifed into him, but at least she didn't try to pull away.

He dared to relax his hands a bit, hoping to ease her tenseness. He had to be careful not to make her feel sorry for him. It was important that she understood the reason he'd left. Even if it had been a stupid-ass mistake on his part. Even if she could never forgive him, he needed to tell her the truth.

Her intense, navy blue gaze skimmed over and past his messed-up face like she didn't even see the scars. How the devil did she do that? Most people instantly recoiled on seeing the puckered, red slash across his face. Hell, Marla had practically gagged. But not Abby. Her reaction was almost emotionless. A cold wash of regret settled in the pit of his stomach when the realization for her indifference hit him. She no longer cared.

"Are we going to stay here all night, Ramsey? I'd like to get home before Buck sends out a search party."

"We'll leave when I'm through talking." He cleared his throat, swallowed hard and tried again. Somehow, he had to get past the urge to haul her up against him and kiss the living daylights out of her until she kissed him back. *Might as well wait for Hell to freeze.*

He struggled for composure. "Some things aren't easy for me to admit, Abby. Won't be easy for you to hear, either."

She leaned back against her braced arms, swinging her legs off the back of the truck. "Get on with it, then. The sooner you talk, the sooner we can leave." She looked past him, around him, everywhere but directly at him.

Hell, he sure didn't have to worry about any sympathy coming from her. His insides tightened. This was harder than he'd expected. He hadn't been this nervous when he'd ridden his first bull. Should he stand in front of her or hitch himself up on the tailgate to sit beside her? Did it matter?

He opted for standing right where he was, and the fact that her legs were curved on either side of his hips like a sexy pair of parentheses had nothing to do with his decision. *Ramsey, you liar.* Suddenly, his tongue was three sizes too big for his dry-as-dust mouth.

"I want you to know that I married Marla only because I thought the child deserved to have a father, as well as a mother."

He waited for her to say something—

anything—to give him a thread of hope that he was getting through to her. Making her understand. She said nothing, but he could've sworn he heard her swift intake of breath.

He barged ahead, knowing he had to spit the words out fast or he'd chicken out again. "I realize now that I should have explained but I was so damned ashamed, I couldn't face you."

Abby sat up straighter. "And that's supposed to make it easy for me to forgive you? To forget how you hurt me and humiliated me? Never in a million years, Ramsey."

"I…no, that's not what I mean." He was making a bigger mess of things now. Digging a deeper hole. "I only meant that I take full responsibility for everything. For the pain I caused you and Shorty and Buck—hell, I hurt everyone I ever cared for. I thought I was doing the right thing. Honest."

With his hands still circling her waist, he felt her body stiffen with every word he said. He knew as sure as bluebonnets grew in Texas that Abby wasn't about to forgive him, but he had to finish telling her. Everything. How else would she ever trust him again?

Chapter Seven

"Call me a jerk or dumb jackass or whatever you want, but I truly believed Marla when she said I got her pregnant. There was only one time—the night of our fight. She never meant a thing to me. I know it was a foolish thing to do, but she was there and, well… I thought it was over between us." He looked down at his boots, then back up at Abby. The disappointment in her eyes hurt more than any injury he'd ever had. "I realize that's no excuse."

"Nobody is that naive, Ramsey, especially a cowboy like you. Safe sex isn't exactly a brand-new discovery."

Abby's voice was level and calm, but sharp

enough to carve a hole in his heart the size of a crater. *A cowboy like you.* She couldn't have made it any plainer. He'd been totally irresponsible and careless, believing Marla when she told him she was on the Pill, instead of using protection like he should have. He'd fallen for every hokey trick in the book, thinking with his lower anatomy instead of his brain. He deserved everything he'd gotten.

He dropped his hands, backed away and felt his world come to an end for the second time in his life. "For the record, she lied about the child. She was never pregnant. Never."

Bo took his hat off, ran nervous fingers through his hair and resettled the Stetson. He drew a deep breath, releasing it with a sigh. "When I found out, I couldn't bring myself to tell Shorty the truth, so I filed for divorce and left. I traveled all over the country and stayed away from Sweet River. Marla contested the divorce and for the next year all I did was ride bulls and pay lawyer fees."

Abby remained silent, and Bo could see the doubt in her eyes. Bo waited a minute before continuing.

"Anyway, after the accident, while I was still in the hospital looking like so much chewed meat, Marla showed up and said she didn't want to be tied to a cripple. She finally agreed to the divorce when she realized I wouldn't be a moneymaker any longer. Spending big bucks was all she'd ever been interested in, anyhow, and she cleaned me out but good. Reckon by now she's already got her hooks in another cowboy eager to part with his winnings."

Abby cocked her head, lifted one eyebrow. "That story sounds like an amateur's version of 'Sex and the Cowboy.' Do you honestly think I believe that? And why would I want to?"

"Because it's—"

Abby clapped her hands over her ears. "Stop. Just stop it. I don't want to hear anymore."

She jumped down off the tailgate and started for the front of the truck. "I've got things to do, Ramsey. Let's go."

His hand snaked out and captured her arm with one swoop, drawing her back. "It's the honest-to-God truth, Abby. Why would I invent something that only makes me look like a damn fool? If I'd wanted to make up a story, I sure as hell wouldn't cast myself as the villain."

When she hesitated, Bo pulled her closer.

A soft gasp escaped from her lips. The temptation to taste them sizzled through him as if his body'd been hot-wired. The look she gave him was full of questions and probably a wagonload of doubts, too, but he was positive he could feel her heart thudding in sync with his.

If he was smart, he'd back off. Knew he ought to. But smart was something he'd never considered as a personal asset. Besides, he couldn't stop the direction of his thoughts, even though his better judgment kept hammering alarm signals against his skull.

Just when he thought he had his rampant desire under control enough to make an intelligent attempt to explain, Abby reached up and placed her fingers on his face, against his scars, this time without any prompting on his part. He could barely feel the butterfly-soft touch of her caress, but his heart leaped when her hand drifted lower to spread open-palmed across his chest. Moved up…and down…then inched under his shirt. Could she feel his skin quiver? Her hand stopped right over his pebbled nipples. That did it.

With a low, hungry growl, he grabbed her hand and forced it back to his face. Restraint, good judgment, rational thought—hell, everything sensible—collapsed and he was hit by a longing so acute, the intensity of it staggered him. Sent his mind spinning in Technicolor whorls of desire.

God help him, he had to kiss her. Just once. He turned his head, angled his mouth into the palm of her hand, nipped the pad of soft flesh between his teeth, then lowered her hands to his hips.

There is a God in Heaven. Bo wanted to fall to his knees in gratitude when he felt Abby's body soften against his. Instead, he simply dipped his head and settled his mouth over hers, hungry for her taste—greedy for more than a single kiss could provide. His tongue flicked against the curve of her lips—rubbing, teasing, darting back and forth until she parted them to let him in. So sweet. Oh, yeah, he remembered how sweet. Remembered how soft. Remembered everything.

Deepening the kiss, he sipped, tasted, stroked until he felt the tip of her tongue meet his, hesitantly at first, then bolder, faster, hungrier.

He fumbled, tugged at the buttons of her blouse until it fell open. With needy fingers, he fought with the clasp of her bra. When he won, her pillow-soft breasts spilled into his hands. Her nipples peaked and hardened instantly when his hands claimed them. His mouth followed to kiss, to suckle, to lave with his tongue. He paid homage to both, then urgently returned to cover her mouth with hot, hungry kisses again. And again. He couldn't get enough of her.

He moaned when her hands crept beneath his shirt to circle his waist. Sighed when she stroked his back, and her fingers found their way inside the waistband of his jeans.

"Oh… Abby." His voice thickened, filled his throat. He could feel his own breath warm her cheek as he kissed his way up the slender column of her neck to the tiny curve of her ear, lingered long enough to trace the delicate circle there with his tongue, then nibbled a return path to delve deep into the magic sweetness of her mouth. Tongues tangled, stroked. She whimpered into the moistness of their kisses.

His ears roared as his blood surged with every wild and crazy beat of his revved-up heart. His hands roamed her body, eager to reacquaint themselves with the sweet curve of her hips, the smoothness of her skin, the total magnificence of her woman's form. Heat and desire and all things good and wonderful pooled in his groin. He was granite hard.

Abby felt like she'd slipped back in time. *This can't be happening.* The sensations were exactly the same, and her body responded as if nothing had ever changed. Bo's magic mouth and wild, fevered kisses were enough to call back every pleasure they'd shared in the past—every intimate, whispered request they'd eagerly fulfilled for each other.

His hot, hard body pressed against hers— angle to curve, hardness to softness. Need feeding on need. The friction of their bodies rubbing together created a heat-index reading right off the charts.

She opened her mouth wider for him, dug her fingers harder into his back as his kiss went on and on and her belly filled with liquid fire. Her tongue went wild in his mouth. She answered his frustrated moan with one of her own. She couldn't get close enough. She was flying out of her skin.

The need to cry out in sheer ecstasy gathered in her throat, a painful knot of urgency. It had always been like this. Bo's kisses held the power to render her helpless. There was nothing like it on the face of the Earth, and oh, how she still wanted him—needed him like the air she breathed and the water that quenched her thirst. Had never stopped wanting him, even when she'd known it was hopeless. Even when she couldn't forgive him. And now…now he was here, kissing her, telling her he was free. Telling her…

If lightning had struck her right then, Abby couldn't have reacted any differently. The realization of what Bo had just told her slowly began to register in her hormone-driven brain. How stupid could she be? She tore loose from his arms and shoved him away, swallowing great big gulps of air to clear her head.

He'd said something about a mistake—then kissed her so deliciously crazy, she'd spun into instant brain lapse. *Way to go, girl. Let him know you're needy,* she reproached herself. All she needed was a little air. Just enough to switch her system back to reality mode.

"That was quite a move, Ramsey. And quite a story." She was still having trouble with the breathing thing. Her heart thundered, and her chest ached from somewhere deep inside. Her pride was totally wrecked.

"You almost had me convinced," she said. *And on my back, too.* She winced at the startling realization. She was so not ready to admit that weakness. Evidently, the past two years had not been enough time to mend her broken dreams.

She looked down. The twisted strap of her undone bra drooped over one wrist. When had that happened? Her exposed breasts were still wet, hard peaks, and the sight of their lingering arousal sent another shock wave of heat zigzagging between her thighs. Her blouse clung haphazardly to one shoulder. She was the picture of lust unfulfilled. Mortified, she yanked her bra back in place, her shaky fingers doing their best to connect the clasp.

Okay, so she was way past convinced. Her good sense had been momentarily short-circuited. That's all. And the warm, heavy feeling in her belly was probably a prelude to her period. Sure, it was. Just because she'd already crossed that week off her calendar this month made no difference.

Oh, girl, you need professional help, she thought to herself.

More angry than embarrassed by her lack of willpower, she groped for the buttonholes on her blouse, shoving buttons through them willy-nilly, not caring whether they lined up or not.

She shot a glance toward Bo. He was stuffing his shirt back in his jeans, the evidence of his frustration still vividly apparent. A fine sheen of perspiration highlighted his face. He wore a look of total bewilderment. Terrific.

She looked at the repaired length of fence— the culprit that had brought them out here in the first place, and realized she should've known better. Being alone with Bo Ramsey was courting disaster. Listening to his fabricated tale of woe was even more dangerous because she caught herself wanting to believe it. More to her chagrin, he had used his injuries to garner her sympathy—a low-down, dirty trick that had almost worked. He knew her so well.

"All I intended to do was tell you the truth about why I left Sweet River, I swear." He took a hesitant step toward her, hands outstretched, then stopped and shoved them in his pockets. The imploring look he gave her went straight to her heart, and it took every bit of her wavering self-restraint not to fling herself back into his incredible embrace.

But she couldn't—wouldn't—until she sorted through his words for something that she could believe, something that made sense.

There was nothing left to do but climb in the truck and pray he wouldn't say another word. It was all too bizarre. No baby? No wife?

"I'm going back to the house. Get in or walk, it doesn't matter a bit to me, Ramsey." Abby climbed in the truck. The engine roared to life with a loud bang and a snarling growl.

Bo hefted himself in and slammed the door. She wasn't going to give him an inch. He slid down in the seat, angled his bad leg across the floor and covered his face with his hat. As soon as he got back to Shorty's place, he was going to stay there. The hell with this volunteer stuff. Doing the right thing only got him deeper in cow piles, so he might as well be the bad guy everyone thought he was.

The silence on the ride back to the house was interrupted only by the occasional chug of the truck's decrepit engine and the clatter of the equipment bouncing around in the back. Abby kept her foot mashed against the gas pedal, convincing him she purposely aimed for every rock and pothole in the two-track, just out of spite. He couldn't wait to get the hell away from her. There was enough sexually charged current inside the cab of the truck right then to rocket it straight to the moon—and he was about to fly with it. As soon as he got to Shorty's, he was heading for a cold shower.

"Thank God," Bo muttered when he caught sight of Shorty's pickup waiting in the drive by the barn. He'd been trying to figure out just what he would do in case Shorty wasn't waiting to take him home. He could hardly put one foot in front of the other, that's how tired he was, but he'd be damned if he'd spend another minute in the company of this woman. Still, walking the fifteen miles or whatever back to the Packer ranch was about as appealing as hiking the Himalayas right now. He couldn't do either one and live to tell about it.

As soon as Abby stopped the truck, Bo slid out, caught the heel of his boot on the rusty running board and pitched forward, nearly kissing the ground in front of him.

Good ol' Ditch saved him from that embarrassment by pouncing on him with a welcoming bark and planting two huge paws on his chest. Thrust back against the seat, Bo was eye to muzzle with the mutt, the victim of an over-enthusiastic, slobbery greeting.

"Thanks, dog, you're one in a million," Bo said, wiping off drool from the exuberant smooch. He gave Ditch a grateful scratch behind the ears, hoping his shaky effort to steady himself had gone undetected. *Not very damn likely.*

The dog's long tail wagged excitedly back and forth as the two headed for Shorty, the pickup and Bo's escape. He didn't wait to see if Abby watched or not. He would've run, if he'd been able.

Abby stared out the kitchen window. Twilight shadows played across the corral, creating a fantasy of light and dark, but she was oblivious to it all. Her mind relived—and regretted—her recent lapse of sanity with Bo.

She'd gone over every touch, every kiss, and had come to the painful conclusion that she was no better than Marla had been. Hadn't she practically begged for Bo to take her right there in the pasture? Talk about the farmer's daughter. Obviously, she didn't have a shred of decency in her entire body. Or pride.

"You don't have to pound those potatoes to death." Buck's admonishment broke through her fog of disturbing thoughts.

She stared down at the pan of mashed potatoes she was holding. They clearly didn't need further mutilation. She quickly spooned them into a stoneware bowl.

"They had more lumps than usual." That excuse was weaker than water, but she wasn't about to admit to her wandering thoughts.

Avoiding Buck's eyes, she set the bowl on the table, then turned back to the stove to pour gravy into a small tureen. Pop had too much insight into her actions as it was. Lately it seemed he was always one step ahead of her, when it came to certain matters. Bo Ramsey, to be exact.

After pouring the gravy, she dished up the butter beans, put a bowl of okra in front of Buck and took the pan of corn bread out of the oven. Her mind definitely hadn't been on the supper she'd managed to put together, but she hoped any further conversation with Pop would be about the riding program and not about how much time she'd spent fixing fences with Bo.

After she filled their glasses with iced tea from a tall pitcher, she sat down opposite her father, determined to avoid any questions he might have about the last few hours of her day. No way was she ready to talk about Bo, about what he'd told her concerning his marriage and the shocking revelation about the baby that never was. It was just too much to digest. Too preposterous to believe. There would be time later to retreat to her room and try to put the events into perspective.

Oh God, she sounded like some kind of prissy old maid. Let's face it, the *events* had been hot and heavy sexual foreplay that had almost ended in the ultimate passion-in-a-pickup scene. She gave herself a mental shake. It was pure sex, and no fancy words were going to change that. Bo's kisses were like fire in her blood. A forbidden fruit so tempting she wanted it all. She'd been with no one since him. Wanted no one since him. And she'd been ready to surrender without thinking of the consequences. Was physical need the only thing between them now? The fork she held dropped from her hand with a clatter.

Buck set his half-empty plate aside, plunked his elbows on the table and eyed her with concern. "And just where have you been the last ten minutes, kitten? Some other planet? You've barely touched your supper, staring into space like a zombie ever since you sat down."

If only he'd let the matter drop. But when Pop got a notion in his head, he was like a hound dog on the trail of a rabbit, chasing it for as long as it took to get what he wanted.

Trouble was, Abby didn't have any answers. What she *did* have was more questions.

"Sorry, Pop, I guess I'm just tired. It's been a long day." She picked up her fork and pushed the food around on her plate, her throat too full of her aching heart to even think of eating. Concentrating on basic things like nourishment for the body wasn't easy. Food simply didn't satisfy the type of hunger her body craved.

"Seems to me this day had the same amount of hours as yesterday." Buck picked up his glass and swirled the last of the tea around the ice cubes before he finished it. "How come you and Bo took so long out there? There was only a small section of fence needing repair. Shouldn't have taken two hours to do that. Shorty was getting mighty tired of waiting. Hungry, too. You should've asked them to stay for supper."

No way was that going to happen. "Bo doesn't work very fast. You know, his leg and all."

She lowered her head and tried to look fascinated by the half-dozen butter beans she'd been rearranging on her plate. Pop's steady gaze had a way of ferreting out the truth from her, and right now, she didn't want to talk about what had occurred out there in the south field. Especially with her father.

Buck snorted. "Mmm-hmm." He raised his eyebrows. "And since when does that…"

Abby felt the heat rise to her cheeks. She grabbed her plate and left the table. "Just let it go, Pop. Okay?"

Buck's parting remark followed her as she set the dish on the counter and hurried from the room. "Seems to me I'm not the one who needs to let go." He picked up his own plate to carry to the sink. "And by the way, how about fixing some meat with our supper next time? A man's gotta have something besides okra and butter beans. I ain't no vegetarian."

The bedroom door slammed behind her. She threw herself across the bed and groaned. How could she have forgotten to cook the steaks?

Buck left the table grumbling, thinking it might be a good idea if he started learning to cook.

Chapter Eight

Later that week, Abby walked into the den and tossed a stack of invoices on Pop's desk. "There just isn't enough money to pay all of these this month," she said.

The morning sun streaming through the open window made the red PAST DUE lettering stamped on every one of the bills glow even brighter. She flopped down in the old leather chair near the window.

Normally, the panoramic view from the study never failed to lift her spirits. This morning, however, the beauty of the sun-dappled wildflowers and verdant pastures escaped her. There was nothing beautiful in the stack of overdue bills she'd been wrestling with for the past hour.

With a sigh, she leaned her head against the back of the chair, waiting while Buck shuffled through the bills. The scowl on his lined face deepened with each invoice he inspected. Not surprising, considering the monumental totals. She'd tried her best to juggle the figures, to stretch the dollars a little further. No miracle was going to happen, she was certain. And having to confront Pop with the problem was the last thing she wanted to do.

"How did we get so far behind?" He looked up, clearly puzzled.

"Pop, we've been in the red for several months now. I just didn't want to mention it until I'd exhausted all the other possibilities. But unless we can come up with at least four thousand dollars by the end of the month, I'm afraid the program will have to close. Five thousand would be even better. The veterinarian's bill is enormous, to say nothing of the bill at the feed mill."

Abby hugged her arms to her chest. She'd been so careful about their spending, yet it still hadn't been enough to put them in the black. She needed more students, but that would involve finding more horses, more volunteers and more equipment, feed, veterinarian services. More, more, more. It was a never-ending circle—a merry-go-round with no place to get off.

Maybe starting the program on her own had been a bad idea. If only she hadn't been so impulsive. So stubborn. Hadn't her friends advised her to look for a partner? But no, she had to prove to the entire town that she didn't need anyone. Prove that she didn't need Bo Ramsey. Not a very impressive reason for jumping in over her head.

Buck got up and rounded the desk to give her a hug. "Oh, I'm sure we can get an extension on the loan. I'll talk to Ben Cross down at the bank."

Her father was the epitome of optimism with his wide smile and twinkling eyes. Abby wondered if he ever really worried about anything. That was all she ever did lately.

"You do that, Pop. Maybe Mr. Cross will listen to you." She didn't intend to reveal that she'd already approached the banker, practically begging, but to no avail. Pop didn't need to know that.

"Well, something will turn up. It always does." He gave her another hearty hug. "Say, isn't it about time for the first class to start? I'll help you get things ready."

"Never mind. Karl came over early, and we've got everything under control. That kid is a real treasure, you know. For someone who didn't know much about horses, he's learned fast. I'm glad you suggested him," Abby said.

"He sure seems to enjoy being around the horses. And the children like him, too," Buck said.

Abby nodded her head in agreement. Replacing the dishwasher would have to wait. Keeping Karl on was more important. She just wished she could pay him more.

"Now, see, didn't I tell you things always work out?" Grinning, Buck retrieved his hat from the rack on the wall.

"C'mon," he said, hurrying Abby out of the room.

"What's the rush?"

She'd never known her father to stay worried for any length of time, but she'd hoped their current financial problem would snag his attention long enough for them to discuss a solution. Now he was dismissing the issue almost as if he'd never heard her.

Buck looked at her with practiced innocence. "Oh, no hurry. I just thought I heard

Shorty's truck coming down the drive. Isn't Bo supposed to help out again today?"

Abby stopped at the front door. "I don't know what Bo's plans are. He may not be able to handle any more strenuous chores. He didn't say one way or another." After yesterday's disastrous scenario, she highly doubted Bo would return—hoped he wouldn't, in fact—but that was information she didn't plan to share with her father.

She walked out onto the porch, looked down the drive and groaned. "Oh, no." Stuart Wilcox's black SUV was headed toward them.

"I thought the doc wasn't coming back until the end of the week," Buck said, annoyance slightly coloring his tone. "Must have something mighty important on his mind, the way he's driving that thing. Sure can't be checking on Jo-Jo so soon. There wasn't that much of an infection."

"I'm as surprised to see him as you are," Abby said, taking Buck's arm and continuing down the path to the barn.

Buck touched the brim of his hat when the vehicle came to a stop and the doctor got out.

"Good to see you two this morning," Wilcox said.

His greeting was obviously meant for both of them but his gaze lingered on Abby.

"What brings you out this way again so soon, Doc?" Buck stood at the entrance to the barn and watched the doctor unload a huge cardboard box from the rear of the Tahoe.

"Stuart, what on earth…?"

Abby looked at the container, then at the man. Sometimes Stuart was overzealous in his efforts to be helpful. His last benevolent deed had been to order the fancy sign that hung by the gate to the corral. He'd even chosen the name without consulting her. She'd resented his interference, at first. After all, this was *her* program, *her* kids. But when she saw how excited the students were over the sign, she'd given in and kept it. The name Sweet River Riders hadn't been her choice, but later, she grudgingly admitted it was better than Houston Therapy Riding School.

Stuart flashed her his million-dollar smile and carried the box into the tack room. "Look, more riding helmets. I brought several sizes. I hope they'll do. Tomorrow I'll bring the saddles and blankets."

Abby watched him unpack the expensive items. "Good grief, Stuart, where did all this come from?" Something told her she wasn't going to like the answer.

"You mentioned you needed more equipment. Here it is." He stood, holding the box and smiling expectantly. Was he waiting for praise? Or was that smug satisfaction in his grin? Abby suspected what he was trying to do, but gifts for her program weren't going to buy her affection. Darn him, why couldn't he just be the vet and quit trying to turn their friendship into something else? The relationship wasn't going to work. The reason why flashed across her mind in a larger-than-life image. She sucked in her breath. Darn it, Bo Ramsey was interrupting her life—again.

"I don't know what to say. I...*we* can't accept all this, Stuart." She looked longingly at the shiny new hard hats. They were exactly what the students needed. "Our account with you is already past due. Accepting gifts isn't an option."

"I don't know why the hell not," Buck said, stepping forward and peering into the box. "Looks to me like it's just what you need, and the doctor'll write it off as a charitable donation, anyway. Right, Doc?"

Stuart covered his mouth and coughed

politely. "Why, yes, that's how it works, but that's not the reason I brought them."

He looked mildly embarrassed. Had his motive been something other than a philanthropic gesture? Or was he simply being the considerate person Abby knew he was? He could certainly afford to be generous, and the program definitely needed a boost, but the thought of accepting Stuart's pricey contributions gave Abby an unsettling feeling. Like she was being bribed.

"Abby?" Stuart stopped taking any more helmets out of the box.

Darn it, why am I always caught in these sticky situations?

"Oh, all right," she said, giving in much against her better judgement. The children came first. She was damned if she did and damned if she didn't, anyway. Pop's wide grin told her he heartily approved.

"We appreciate your generosity, Stuart," she said.

"Great." The doctor smiled warmly. "When I bring the other equipment out tomorrow, I'll help you get your tack room organized."

Was he questioning her ability, or was it really kindness and concern on his part? She'd never had these doubts about Stuart before.

What brought them to mind now? She'd been considering a serious relationship with him, for heaven's sake.

But that was all before Bo had come back into her life. That intrusion brought so many unanswered questions—so much to think about. Not only questions regarding Bo's physical condition, but about the whole situation developing between them. That was definitely *not* a figment of her imagination. She was certain of that. Still, she needed time to sort matters out in her own mind. And heart.

"Why don't I just put these back," Stuart said, "until I bring the rest of the things tomorrow." He started returning the helmets to the carton. "It will be much easier to organize when we know just what we're working with."

We? Surely he didn't expect to play an actual part in her program, other than as the vet-on-call. "Oh, that's all right. I know how busy you are, Stuart. I'm sure Pop and I will manage just fine, thanks. And now, excuse me, but I really do need to finish preparations for class."

What was she getting herself into? She turned to her father, hoping he'd bail her out.

No such luck. He chuckled instead and said, "Here comes the troops."

Abby thought he meant the students until she saw Shorty's truck bouncing along the drive. *Please let him be alone.* With a swift goodbye to Stuart, she scurried out of the tack room, leaving Pop to deal with the doctor and his costly contributions.

By the time Abby neared Shorty's truck, she could see he was alone in the cab. Relieved, she waved a greeting and continued on to the arena.

"Wait up, Abby," Shorty called. "I need to talk to you a minute."

Abby stopped and turned. Shorty hurried toward her with Ditch loping alongside. She smiled at the pair and wished she had time to visit. "I'm really pushed for time, Shorty. Can Pop help you?"

"Nope. Gotta talk to you." He paused to catch his breath. "Whew, this old man is out of shape."

Abby laughed. "Oh, I'd bet on you in a three-legged sack race anytime." Her laughter stopped when she saw the frown on Shorty's face. "What is it? What's wrong?"

"It's Bo. He said he told you about Marla and the baby. Right?"

She nodded. "Yes, he told me a wild story about Marla never being pregnant and then leaving with all his money. I have to wonder why he waited so long to tell that tale." She pushed a stray lock of hair behind her ear and studied Shorty's wizened face. "Don't tell me you believe him?"

Shorty hung his head. "Bo's telling the truth. And now he's got a load of guilt that's eatin' him up. Says he's gonna leave Sweet River, but hellfire, Abby, he ain't got nowhere to go. I told him he could move over to my empty manager's cabin for as long as he needs, but he says he won't stay now because of you."

Abby put her hands out in protest. "Oh, no. He's not blaming me for his bad luck. I've got enough problems of my own. I don't need his. You can tell him for me that he'd better face up to reality. Life doesn't come with guarantees. Thanks to him, I found that out the hard way. Besides, he needs to get on with his life. I have." She swallowed hard around the lie crowding her throat.

"I didn't think you'd be so hard-hearted." Shorty shrugged his shoulders. "Thought maybe there was still some feelings between you two. Bo said—"

"Never mind what Bo said." She planted her fists on her hips, stuck out her chin. "And for the record, I'm not as hard-hearted as you think. He simply waited too long to explain." She couldn't control the slight hitch in her voice. "He walked away—I didn't."

She looked beyond Shorty's shoulder, avoiding his scrutiny. The children were lining up at the gate to the corral. Just in time to save her from further questioning.

Shorty's efforts to open up the past made her edgy and irritable—a feeling she didn't like at all. She'd never been uncomfortable around their family friend before and being bitchy wasn't her nature, but she couldn't seem to soften her sharp retort. She needed a major attitude adjustment, thanks to Bo.

"Why don't you stop by the barn and say hello to Pop? I've got to check on the students now. I'm sorry you made the trip over here for nothing."

"I'm sorry too, Abby. Sorry you can't forgive him."

The disappointment in Shorty's eyes made Abby's stomach lurch. *Well, that's just dandy. How did I get to be the bad guy here? Had everyone forgotten who left who?*

To add to her stress, Stuart came striding

toward her, all smiles and perfection. Terrific. Why couldn't her heart flutter for him instead of sagging like a wet tea bag? That would solve all her problems.

But the heart that drooped at the sight of Stuart Wilcox knew full well there was only one man who could make it soar. And he wasn't willing to give what she wanted—total honesty. Or what she needed—unconditional love.

By the time Abby convinced Stuart she would be busy all day and had finished with her morning class, the volunteers broke for lunch, the temperature was prodding ninety-five and everyone was ready for a siesta. Especially the horses. Most of them were already rubbed down and stood contentedly under the trees in the pasture. The animals that worked the morning class wouldn't be used again that day. Horses their age deserved a daily rest. Some of them received more than one.

Teddie and his mom had missed the last two classes. Abby hoped he wasn't ill. She desperately wanted him to ride Star before the summer ended. Accomplishing that would be just the boost the boy's self-confidence needed. One more thing to add to her "worry" list.

After she turned the last horse out of the corral, Abby swiped her face with her bandana. She envied the animals their place in the shade. A nap under a tree sounded tempting, but she had exactly one hour to put a meal on the table. She closed the gate behind her and hurried off.

Pop wasn't going to be happy with the salad she'd planned to fix for lunch instead of the heavy meal he always wanted. He needed to eat healthier. Why did everything depend on her? She wondered if this was the way things would always be. Still, with Pop and the wonderful kids in her program to look after—and love—her life could be a lot worse, couldn't it? Hard as she tried, she couldn't come up with an honest answer.

Chapter Nine

Abby set an oversized glass of iced tea down in front of Buck with a promise to have their lunch ready in a jiffy. She stuck her head in the refrigerator, quickly rifled through its contents while she took advantage of the cool interior and pulled out several assorted containers and plastic bags. Whoever invented prepackaged convenience foods definitely deserved a merit badge.

Since most of the ingredients were already washed, chopped or precooked, she set them on the counter and proceeded to make like Martha Stewart. Crisp curly endive and Bibb lettuce went into a garlic-rubbed wooden bowl along with tender baby spinach and fresh romaine leaves. Thinly sliced strips of red and green peppers, diced celery and shredded carrots followed and, finally, circles of the last Texas 1015 sweet onion she'd been saving.

She added tiny buttons of fresh mushrooms for garnish as an afterthought. The entire creation was topped with slices of grilled chicken breasts from a ready-to-eat pack. Satisfied, Abby placed it on the table in front of her father with a mock bow and a wide smile.

"Here you go, Pop. Healthy as well as tasty."

Abby sat down and reached for her napkin. "By the way, did Shorty find you this morning?"

Knowing full well that he had, she wondered why her father hadn't mentioned it while they were working with the children. Pop didn't usually keep things from her. At least, he hadn't until now. Lately, he'd been strangely reticent. Not at all like his usual outspoken self.

Scowling at the salad, Buck answered without looking at her. "Yep. Didn't I mention it to you?" He picked up the bowl, turned it around in his hands and plunked it down again. "This looks fine for rabbits. Where's the rest of the meal?"

Abby couldn't stop her smile. She'd expected his protest to be louder. Pop was a meat and potatoes man from the get-go, but she was determined to give him heart-healthy food. She wanted him to be around for a long time to come.

"This *is* the meal, Pop. There's everything you need right there. Meat, vegetables…" She pointed. "And here's some wheat crackers to go with it." She slid a plateful across the table.

"Huh," Buck muttered. "When I asked for meat the other night, I sorta had in mind chicken-fried steak or maybe some barbecued ribs, not itty-bitty strips of dry white meat. I don't see any potatoes, either."

"I promise you'll have a baked potato tonight." She ducked her head and put a forkful of salad in her mouth.

They ate in silence after Buck grumbled at fat-free dressing on the salad. Abby was wise enough not to comment when she noticed he finished every bite right down to the last lettuce leaf and wheat cracker.

When he pushed his plate back, wiped his mouth with the paper napkin and shot Abby a look she couldn't quite read, she squirmed uncomfortably.

"What?" She needn't have asked because she knew full well Pop would get around to whatever was on his mind in his own good time.

He cleared his throat. "What do you know about the story Bo told Shorty?"

Abby tried to look confused. "What story, Pop?" *As if I didn't know.*

Buck's face grew stern. His eyebrows crawled together in one long gray scowl. "Hmmph. Don't play dumb with me. I'm talking about Marla and the way she tricked Bo into a marriage he didn't want. Shorty told me the whole mess, and I'm betting you know it, too."

"What's got you so upset, Pop? The part about Bo being tricked, or the fact that he's back in Sweet River? Neither one is important to me." Abby hoped beyond hope that she sounded convincing. With her head lowered, she concentrated on the last bit of salad on her plate.

"If I didn't know you better, young lady, I'd say you were fibbing."

Darn it, he knew her like the back of his hand. She took a deep breath and looked him straight in the eye. When she was younger, Pop's uncanny ability to catch her in a fib had made her wary of telling anything but the truth. What made her think she could fool him now?

"Okay, so I knew about it. Bo told me while we were fixing the fences yesterday afternoon. Pretty ridiculous, huh?"

She picked up her glass and drank deeply of the sweet tea. Stalling for time didn't work, either, because Pop's scrutiny just intensified.

"What makes you think Bo isn't telling the truth?" Buck wagged his finger at her.

She hated when he did that. "What makes you think he is?" she countered. "Your opinion of him certainly has changed since he's come back. What else do *you* know?"

Her father was clearly uncomfortable, but Abby wasn't about to let the matter drop now. "You started this, so let's finish it, Pop. We've got a little time before the afternoon class starts." She carried their empty plates to the sink. "Well?"

She leaned back against the counter, crossed her arms and waited for Pop to continue. Something in his expression hinted that he knew a lot more than the sketchy information Bo had revealed to her. Of course, she'd been rather distracted at the time. She bit the inside of her cheek to keep from smiling at that particular memory.

Buck scooted his chair away from the table, cleared his throat and leaned back. "Well, the way Shorty figures, Bo didn't have any reason not to believe Marla when she said she was expectin' his baby. Marla's reputation wasn't exactly lily-white. I always felt a little sorry for Shorty when he wound up having to raise that gal after his sister died. Marla made his life miserable from day one, for sure."

Buck paused just long enough to try Abby's patience. She could swear her father talked slow just to aggravate her.

"If that was so, then why didn't Shorty question Marla's accusation? Why was he so quick to believe the worst of Bo?" She needed something more convincing than the preposterous tale Pop had told her so far. A lot more.

Buck shook his head. "Shoot, everybody knew about the big fight you two had at the fireworks that night. And Bo sure didn't put up much argument when Marla came on to him at the beer tent. Don't forget that half the town saw 'em leave together, too. That gal was bound for trouble long before Shorty ever got her. His sister, Frannie, couldn't control her, either." Buck tapped his fork on the table as he spoke, the nervous staccato beat increasing Abby's impatience.

"Anyhow," Buck continued, "Bo said Marla swore she was on the Pill. Don't matter. He was careless and he knew it. So to keep from giving Shorty any more grief, he agreed to marry her and leave Sweet River. He'd planned on heading for the rodeo in New Mexico, anyway. Thought that would be best for everyone. Especially since you refused to go with him." The tapping fork slipped through Buck's fingers and hit the floor.

"Oh, that's a joke." Abby threw up her hands. "If he'd cared at all about my feelings, he would have explained. Given me a chance to decide for myself." Her face grew warm as her irritation rose. If only Bo had…

She bent to pick up the fork, tossed it back on the table. "Well, anyway," Buck interrupted the direction of her thoughts, "Bo thought he was doing the right thing at the time. That counts for something, I reckon. Shorty said they'd already split by the time Bo got hurt and Marla only showed up when she needed money. That gal put a whole new slant to the word 'gold digger,' believe me. Sucked Bo's bank account dry."

"So just like that, you've changed your opinion of Bo?"

"Well," Buck drawled, "I may have been a bit hasty back then. I only wanted the best for you, you know. Wanted you to be happy." He rubbed his chin. "But, it's plain to see he's having a rough time of it lately. Makes me think he's paying through the nose for his foolish decisions. Hell, Abby, the man nearly got killed trying to make enough money to convince Marla to agree to a divorce. Shorty's positive of that. Now all Bo's got left of his career is a racked-up body and a scarred face. I know he hurt you bad when he left, but I've been thinking maybe we oughta give him a chance to make amends."

"Amends? Well, this is a surprise," Abby said. The hurtful realization that Pop might be right felt like heartburn in her chest. "Looks like everyone is on Bo's side now. When did he get to be the hero here?"

Buck rose and went to his daughter's side. His burly arms circled around her, hugged her close. For a split second Abby wanted to turn away and ignore him. Wanted to be a pouty child again, hiding in the barn. How could Pop forget her misery so easily?

"I'm not taking any sides here," her father

assured her. "You're the only one who matters to me. You know that, don't you? It's not like you to hold a grudge. Besides, I've seen the way you act when Bo's around. You never were good at hiding your feelings for him, even after he left. And that soft heart of yours won't let you turn away anyone who needs help. Just look at the terrific job you're doing with the kids who come here every day."

Abby shrugged and moved away. She knew she was being stubborn. Right now, she didn't care. She didn't have any idea what to do with the raw-edged ache in her heart.

"The program has absolutely nothing to do with Bo," she said. "He doesn't need my help like the children do. He can take care of himself."

She loaded the dishwasher with more vigor than necessary, chiding herself when she whacked a plate against a bowl. This conversation was going absolutely nowhere. Pop and Shorty obviously had their minds made up when it came to what Bo needed. Her pulse tripped at the thought of Bo's needs— thoughts that triggered an unbelievably vivid description of her own needs. That was dangerous territory to be avoided at all costs.

"Speaking of the kids, it's nearly time for

class." She hit the start button on the dish-washer, praying it would work one more time, then wiped off the counter and hung up the dish towel. "Let's go."

Buck grabbed his hat and followed her out the door. "Did you ever stop to think that maybe Bo's having a hard time accepting help, too?"

Abby walked faster and pretended she didn't hear the question. Clearly, Pop wasn't ready to let the subject drop. She wasn't looking forward to the long afternoon.

Five volunteers—two men and three women—bustled about the tack room in-structing, encouraging, even dispelling a few fears, while the children tried to remember what to do with the gear they needed to pre-pare for their ride. If patience was a virtue, then Abby was certain all her volunteers were earning extra stars in their crowns.

Quietly, she observed the group and knew she'd chosen the right direction for her career. And if giving joy and some measure of con-fidence to these special kids was within her own capabilities, she was confident that any sacrifice on her part was worth it.

She was humbled and deeply moved by the

dedication of these people who came every day to give their time to the children. They asked nothing in return for their efforts but gave unlimited love and attention to each and every student. There was no monetary compensation, but Abby knew from her own experience that a dollar value couldn't be placed on the tremendous rewards of the heart. The children weren't the only ones to benefit from the program, and if things worked out the way she hoped, before long she'd have the whole town involved. But that was another dream for another time.

"Hey, Abby." IdaJoy Sparks hurried toward her, and Abby could barely contain the chuckle that bubbled up from her throat when she caught a glimpse of the colorful outfit her friend had donned for her first attempt at volunteering.

IdaJoy's enthusiasm for life—along with a dedicated interest in everyone else's business—was only exceeded by her penchant for flamboyant clothes. *Extreme* wasn't a word the forty-something café owner was familiar with. Neither was *gaudy,* as proven by the formfitting leather pants that, oddly enough, looked perfectly normal on the brassy blonde. Abby knew the revealing spangled top hid a heart as big as the entire state of Texas, but she made a mental note to tactfully suggest something a little less eye-popping for future classes.

"Hi, IdaJoy. I see you're right on time and ready to ride." Abby motioned for her to follow and the two entered the busy tack room together. Since everyone there knew each other, it quickly became as noisy as a coffee break at the Blue Moon.

By the time Abby gave IdaJoy instructions on her duties and paired her up with Laura, a shy seventeen-year-old with a prosthetic leg, the rest of the group was vigorously brushing their mounts and getting them saddled. Shouts of excitement and words of encouragement rang out when Abby called for the first horse and rider to come to the mounting block.

"All right, Rory." She motioned to the teenaged boy standing rigid next to an aging gray horse. "Bring Mick over. Remember to tell him what you want him to do. He won't move until you give him the command."

"Walk on," the boy said softly and gripped the reins with hands that were oddly curled, the effects of crippling arthritis.

With the help of his volunteer, Rory laboriously walked alongside Mick to the mounting block and struggled into the saddle. He pumped his fist in the air when his efforts met with success. "Look, Miss Abby, I did it," he shouted.

"Good job, Rory." Abby's praise, along with the helper's, rang out at the same time.

Each attempt to learn was a major accomplishment and high praise was given in large doses every time a student achieved a goal. Large or small, no endeavor was overlooked. Abby made certain of that.

Rory and Mick progressed around the arena, practicing the turns and the stops and starts. When they were finished, Abby called for the next rider. Each one went through the exercises—some easily, others struggling— but no one gave up. No one wanted to.

Abby called for the last rider and helper to begin and watched IdaJoy and Laura advance. It was a toss-up as to who was more nervous, the child or the adult, but Abby noted with pride that Laura sat the horse like a pro. Lucky was the perfect match for the girl, since he wasn't easily startled and could perform the exercises blindfolded.

IdaJoy was another matter. Abby didn't want her newest volunteer's nervousness to transfer to the horse and rider, so she watched them closely as they executed the turns. When they reached the long poles laid out in the middle of the arena, Abby called to them.

"Don't forget to lift up in the saddle, Laura. Lean forward a bit. Half-seat, that's right. Let Lucky do the work. Trust him."

When IdaJoy glanced Abby's way and grinned, Abby knew she had nothing to worry about. Despite her outrageous taste in clothes and flamboyant personality, IdaJoy loved kids. She wanted nothing more than to have a family of her own. She'd confided her dream to Abby last year, and also her fear that the dream would never come to pass. Abby was saddened by the fact that, so far, IdaJoy was right. The town of Sweet River didn't hold many prospects for matrimony. Maybe volunteering would help fill the void in Ida-Joy's otherwise solitary life. Abby hoped so.

As Laura urged her horse around the last barrel in the course, a flicker of movement by the gate caught Abby's attention. She turned, and her heart *ka-thumped*.

He was leaning against the fence, one booted foot snagged on the bottom rail, arms crossed in a lazy loop over the top one. From a distance, Bo looked like just another ordinary cowboy. Abby knew better.

His hat dipped low, almost touching the top of those familiar dark glasses. His scars weren't visible from where Abby stood. Even his stance concealed the extent of the injuries to his leg. She gripped the side of the mounting block and willed her heart to stop doing cartwheels. The unexpected shock of seeing him again made focusing on her students a major problem.

She was just about to wave Laura and Ida-Joy on, when a small flurry of blue shorts and white T-shirt shot across the arena. Abby cried out. Teddie darted straight into the path of Laura and her horse. His thin legs wobbled as he struggled to reach the other side.

"Star, Star," the boy called to the little mare standing in the far corner of the fenced area.

"Watch out!" IdaJoy's yell startled Laura and she jerked back on the reins. Lucky whinnied and bolted at the sudden harsh pressure of the bit in his mouth.

IdaJoy pulled on the lead rope. "Whoa! Whoa, boy!"

Laura hung on to the reins with both hands. IdaJoy had the horse under control by the time Abby reached them.

In an instant, Bo was there, snatching Teddie out of the way. It all happened in a matter of seconds, but later, Abby swore it had lasted an eternity.

"Are you all right?" she asked IdaJoy and Laura, after Lucky finally stopped prancing and dancing around. The wide-eyed look on their faces told Abby the two were still pumping adrenaline, but a quick perusal assured her they weren't hurt in any way.

"Why don't you lead them over by the rest of the class, IdaJoy? Try to calm Lucky down. I'll be there shortly. Class is finished for today. The others will show you what to do."

She waited until the pair was under the watchful care of one of the veteran volunteers, then turned her attention to Teddie and—reluctantly—to the man holding him. Teddie had the bewildered look of a child who didn't know exactly what he'd done wrong, but was sure he was going to be in trouble for it anyway.

Bo's white face could have been from fear for the boy's safety, or from the pain of exerting his leg. Abby couldn't be certain. Either way, his plight tugged at her sympathetic nature, and she experienced a brief encounter with emotion versus logic. She didn't like the way it made her world tilt.

"Why wasn't someone watching this kid?"

His ground-out question through clenched teeth, and the raw edge of it, set Abby's own jaw in a rigid lock. Was he questioning her ability to provide a safe environment for her students? She took her responsibility seriously. She would never deliberately place any child in jeopardy. Never.

He'd removed his glasses, pocketed them. Accusation glinted sharply in his eyes, and she met his hard gaze with one of her own.

"I didn't know Teddie was here. He usually stays in the observing area with his mother." She glanced around, truly surprised when she didn't see Caroline anywhere. Something was definitely not right.

"Teddie, honey, where's your mom?" She reached to take the boy from Bo's arms, but Teddie turned away and latched on to Bo's neck, burrowing his face against the rock-hard shoulder of his rescuer.

"Is that her over there?" Bo pointed to a harried-looking young woman rushing toward them from behind a parked car. Her frantic shouts carried across the dusty arena as she ran.

Abby nodded and waved her arms over her head. "He's here, Caroline. He's okay."

"Oh, thank God. I just went to get the cooler from the trunk of the car, and he disappeared." With tears in her eyes, Caroline thanked Bo and tried to take her son but was rejected the same as Abby had been.

"No, no, no. Wanna stay with the cowboy." Teddie was adamant as only a six-year-old can be. He kept his face shoved tight against Bo's shoulder.

"Uh, look, kiddo, I think you'd better let your momma take you now. She's pretty worried, you know." Bo loosened Teddie's grip on his neck, set the child down and would have left the scene, but two small arms held his leg captive.

Caroline North knelt beside her child, soothing his anxiety while she quietly peeled him from Bo's leg. With kisses, hugs and murmured words of love, she assured her boy that his world was safe. That she would always be there to take care of him. Finally, Teddie nestled in her arms, content and secure.

The tiny corner of her heart that Abby kept reserved for all her special dreams, wobbled, then tipped precariously as she watched the tender scene. The resulting ache snatched her breath for one brief moment. This was what she wanted. This love, this mother-child bond.

She had dreamed—foolishly, she realized now—that she and Bo would eventually complete their circle of love with a child. Maybe two. There was so much love to share stored up inside her. To her, a family was the ultimate tribute to the unconditional love between a man and a woman. A no-holds-barred, forever kind of love.

But that dream wasn't to be. Those longings had been pushed aside, but not forgotten. She'd refused to let the pain of the past keep her from building some sort of life that included children. Hadn't allowed it to rob her of sharing her love with those who truly cared about her. She chanced a glance at Bo.

He still had that drawn appearance, even though the pallor no longer robbed his face of color. A tightness pulled his mouth in a determined slash, cast a rigid set to his jaw. But it was the almost frightened glaze in his dark eyes that puzzled her. He'd jammed his hands in his pockets as soon as he'd put Teddie down, but not before Abby noticed how they'd trembled. What was that all about?

Chapter Ten

"Wanna stay here with the cowboy," Teddie begged from the circle of his mother's embrace. "Puh-leeeeze."

"Oh, honey, you know that's not possible," Caroline said, smoothing the child's hair back away from his face. "Besides, he only works here. He doesn't live here." She looked at Bo and lifted her shoulders in a plea for help.

Bo awkwardly knelt beside the boy. His sharp intake of breath as he lowered himself to the child's level caught Abby's concerned attention. He hurt more than she'd realized.

"Uh, Teddie, think how your mom would miss you if you stayed with me," he said. Uneasiness roughened his voice, reduced it to a husky growl. "And your mom is right, I don't live here…besides, I'm not a real cowboy anymore."

Bo's effort to communicate with Teddie was clumsy, but admirable. Abby sensed an affection for the child that made him jumpy, and ill at ease.

"Why aren't you a real cowboy?" Teddie squirmed out of his mother's embrace to tug on Bo's hand. "And if you work here, how come you don't live with Mr. Buck and Miss Abby? Is she afraid of your scars?" He tossed a wide smile right up at Bo's openly astonished face and declared, "I'm not."

Abby's gaze connected with Bo's. Her cheeks burned with embarrassment. "Neither am I, Teddie," she whispered to the boy, though she couldn't drag her gaze from Bo. "Neither am I."

A lifetime passed while she waited for Bo's response, afraid to breathe—afraid to hope. It was simply an innocent remark from a child, but she wanted—no, she needed—to hear his answer. Her heart held its beat. Her pulse stilled.

Bo's throat worked. Had he heard her barely audible words correctly? *Forget it, Ramsey.*

It's not your turn for miracles. A flush of heat crept up his face and stung the puckered seam of scars that divided his cheek. He removed his hat, fiddled with the brim of it, raked his nervous fingers through his hair and settled the Stetson back on his head. He shifted his position, bit his lip when he moved his bum leg to stand. *Antsy* didn't begin to describe the twitchy sensation in his gut.

"Well, I'm glad for that," he managed to croak after he cleared his throat. He didn't dare look at Abby any longer, afraid of finding the glimmer of an invitation there. Afraid he wouldn't.

He focused on the boy. Safer territory. "I've got this bum leg, see?" He tapped it with one finger. "And I can't be a cowboy if I can't ride a horse."

Teddie studied his rescuer thoughtfully. "Does that mean I can't be a cowboy, either?"

A boulder lodged in Bo's chest, so damn close to his heart he could barely breathe. He crooked a finger under the neckband of his T-shirt, stretched it away from his throat. *Not safer territory, after all.*

"Do you want to be?" He forced out the raspy words.

"Yup, more than anything," the boy answered and pointed to Star. "That's my very favorite pony over there." Sudden shiny tears welled in his hopeful eyes. "But I got bum legs, too, so I can't ride her." He stuck out one leg, pulled up his pants leg to expose a small, fragile limb. "Guess I'll never be a real cowboy, either, will I?"

Bo's heart constricted painfully at Teddie's droopy little shoulders and sigh of defeat. *Awww, hell.* Bitter regret for all the things in his life he couldn't change clogged his throat, stifled his breathing. Right now, he'd give anything he owned to be able to change this youngster's situation. No kid should have his dreams destroyed. But how could he make a difference when his own life wasn't worth spit?

But he couldn't seem to get past Teddie's expectant gaze, the tentative wobble of his mouth in an almost smile. Shoot, even Abby and the child's mom looked at him like they expected him to perform some sort of miracle—something that would transform the sad little boy into a happy, confident kid again. Cryin' out loud, he wasn't God.

And he definitely wasn't prepared for the idea that slammed into his brain with the force of a well-aimed sledgehammer. Cold-cocked him right where he stood. He refused to even consider it. No way was he gonna get tangled up in this boy's life when he couldn't even untangle his own.

But he hadn't counted on how tightly a young child's hopes and dreams could wind around his heart. Hadn't counted on the sudden realization that he'd been hoping all along for a reason to stay in Sweet River—near Abby.

Well, Ramsey, what're you gonna do about it?

Abby stood in the kitchen with her back to her dinner guest, but she knew he was there. His presence filled the room with an electric charge that made her pulse race and her toes curl. She didn't need to turn around to see him. His image was permanently etched in her mind.

Pop's surprise supper invitation to Bo and Shorty had caught her unprepared. She'd had to hurriedly revise her meal plan. That, along with the disturbing incidents earlier in the day, had her in a snit of megaproportions.

She'd been simmering over the fact that Pop hadn't bothered to consult her—just assumed she would be overjoyed for the extra company—when Bo walked in and offered to help. Now she was simmering for a different reason.

The roomy old-fashioned kitchen suddenly grew smaller than a teacup. Much too small to accommodate the whopping amount of sexual tension generated by their close confinement. Bo's physical closeness was difficult enough to deal with, but the mental gymnastics going on in her mind had Abby grinding her teeth in frustration. Great, her day just kept getting better and better.

"You shouldn't have made a promise you don't intend to keep," she said and kept right on with what she was doing. Adding salt to boiling water took a great deal of concentration.

"But I do intend to keep it," Bo said. "What makes you think I don't?"

The way he took plates out of the cabinet with such at-home familiarity, forced Abby to recall past times when they'd set the table together. What was he was thinking right now? Did he remember those intimate times, too, when they'd shared meals—and more?

She stirred the breaded okra sizzling in the heavy iron skillet, put it in a serving dish and stared at the pot of boiling water on the stove. What had she intended to do with that?

"Abby?" Bo finished setting the table, walked over and turned off the burner under the pot. He picked up the bowl of okra. "You didn't answer my question."

She faced him. "You promised Teddie you'd help him be a cowboy. Do you think it's fair to build his hopes up like that? He's just a little boy, Bo. How do you plan to get him to ride Star, when I've been trying to accomplish that very thing ever since he joined the class? He's much too frightened of falling off to chance getting in the saddle. You haven't seen him try. You don't know how that fear nearly paralyzes him." She took the bowl out of his hands, walked to the table and set it down, keeping her back to him. "And broken promises can break hearts. I won't let you hurt Teddie."

"But you don't know..." He followed her with the pitcher of iced tea and began filling the glasses.

She spun around, took the pitcher from him and set it down on the table so hard the tea sloshed over the rim.

"What is it that I don't know? Tell me." Hands on her hips, she tried not to shout. It wasn't easy. His evasiveness irritated her. His moodiness bordered on self-pity when she knew darn well he was capable of doing anything he set his mind to. His injuries had nothing to do with the man behind them. She wanted to shake that *poor me* attitude right out of him.

But it was his concern for Teddie that confused her. His promise to the boy came from out of the blue—almost too easily to be believed.

Bo's eyes turned the color of a stormy sky. Dark and brooding, they smoldered with more than simple annoyance at Abby's persistence in making him reveal the real reason he'd left. Passion flared in their inky blackness, diamond-hard and bright, lasting only a brief second.

It was enough for now. Enough to spark the memory of their shared passion only hours before. Enough to twist her insides into a tight knot of apprehension—and leave her wondering if their relationship would ever be more.

"I'd never do anything to hurt the boy. Don't you know that, Abby?"

His words were quiet. And deep inside her aching heart, she grudgingly acknowledged his sincerity. But her pain lingered, a bittersweet reminder of the past. She was afraid of being hurt again.

"You didn't think twice about hurting me." She should've enjoyed the anguish that sliced across his face. She didn't. What on earth had made her say that? She sounded like a shrew.

Then he took her hands and placed them on his shoulders. She let him, because she couldn't help herself. Because his closeness took some of her tenseness away. Seeped into her pores and filled her with warmth and longing—and need. Oh, God, the need. Wanting him hurt so much.

"I explained about that," Bo said.

She sighed. "I know, but I'm having a hard time believing you. I want to, but even if I did, I still don't understand why you waited so long to admit Marla wasn't carrying your child. It's been nearly two years, Bo. You didn't even tell Shorty the truth." Her hands slipped from his shoulders to rest on his chest. The heat from his body felt good.

She tipped her head back for a clearer view of his incredible eyes. To search for the honesty she hoped—wanted—to see there. Anything to convince her that his preposterous story was true.

"I was ashamed of being a failure. Ashamed of being duped by a woman who only wanted a one-way ticket out of Sweet River. I was a damn stupid cowboy who honestly thought he was doing the honorable thing by walking away from you. I was a total screwup, Abby. You deserved a better man than me." His voice dropped to a husky whisper. "After the divorce, I thought I could redeem myself by making it to the top in the rodeo circuit, maybe even be someone you'd want to see again, but that didn't last long. Marla, lawyers and that damned bull made sure of that." He stroked her cheek, his fingers gliding down the curve of her throat to linger in the valley below.

She let them stay, felt the familiar warm sensation pool low in her belly, and knew she couldn't fight it. Didn't want to. Being honest about the way Bo made her feel would be so much easier than living with the bitterness that kept eating away at her.

"Failure's an ugly word, Ramsey." *I should move away.* She touched his face instead.

"How else would you describe making a mistake that cost me the most thing important in my life?" Bo placed his hand over hers, pressed it to his cheek. "Losing my career was nothing compared to losing you, Abby."

Oh, dear God. Tears stung her eyes. Her throat burned. Hearing him say those things, her heart couldn't help but believe him. Did she dare? When her nose started to run, she pulled away to search for a tissue. Of all the rotten timing.

When she returned from the bathroom, Bo was leaning against the counter next to the stove, waiting for her with dark eyes that invited, tempted. She knew she should be putting the finishing touches on the meal that was fast becoming a cold disaster, but she wasn't ready for their discussion to end. She'd waited a long time to reach this point. She wanted—needed—to hear more. If only the icy knot in her stomach would go away.

"Did you honestly believe Marla carried your child?" She stared at the pot of water left cooling on the stove, reluctant to face the cause of her out-of-control heart rate.

He pushed away from the counter, and gently took her hands in his. "What will it take to make you believe me?"

His hypnotically quiet words danced along her nerve endings. Sent a shiver up her spine. She lifted her shoulders. "As I remember, Marla was very convincing when she spread her news around before you left. No one doubted her."

Bo frowned, his face grim. "Oh, she was a mighty convincing gal, all right. Played me for a fool, and it's a sorry fact that I knew there was a onetime possibility she could be telling the truth."

His hands wandered in an erotic journey up and down the length of her arms, igniting tiny sparks of pleasure along the way, making her aware that she was still susceptible to his touch. A weakness she didn't want to fight anymore.

"But I believed things were over between us, Abby. You refused to go with me, remember? No guarantees in a rodeo, you said."

He was right. She'd accused him of being selfish for wanting a rodeo career. She wanted stability, and thought that staying in Sweet River was the only way to have it. But she had been selfish, as well. Expecting him to give up his dream because she was afraid to take a chance was wrong. They had both been wrong. She knew that now.

Bo tugged her closer. "I guess it's difficult for you to understand, but I felt I owed it to Shorty to do right by Marla. She was his niece, and he kept blaming himself for letting her run wild. Like he could've stopped her. Marla and trouble were a matched pair. Hell, Abby, I admit I was no saint back then, either." His eyes begged her forgiveness.

Did he have to look at her that way? Her

resolve was slowly turning to mush. She searched for inner strength.

"Are you saying what you did was for the sake of the child you believed was yours?"

She held his gaze. Waited. Thought he would never answer.

He nodded. "Yeah, it was. I didn't want the kid to grow up never knowing his father. Like I did."

She drew a shaky breath, slowly released it. If her heart felt any more pain, it would likely splinter into a million pieces. "Then you didn't fail by doing the responsible thing. The wrong thing was leaving without saying goodbye. Without giving me the explanation I deserved. That's where you failed, Bo." She waited a second for the hitch in her voice to go away. "I was the loser, not you."

He reached up with his thumb and caught a tear sliding down her cheek.

"But you've moved on, Abby. Made something of your life. My losses haven't stopped. These," he put her hand on his face and slid it along the rough ridge of scar tissue, "keep reminding me." He stuck out his crooked leg. "And this makes me realize I'm not indestructible. No future to speak of, either."

Misery darkened his eyes. "Both give me nightmares."

His hands slipped around her waist, barely touching her, yet creating a circle of heat under her shirt.

She was torn. Forgive him, or send him away forever? Her heart and her head were at cross-points.

The first solution was, quite possibly, hormone-driven. She acknowledged that without apology. Denying it would have been useless. Sex with Bo had always been a sumptuous feast for the senses. A giving of body and soul, a sharing of minds and spirits that lifted them both beyond the realm of reality to an astonishing level of sensuality. A gift she had offered to no one else. A gift she believed he had accepted for always. She wanted that incredible magic again, and if she forgave him, she could have it back. Couldn't she?

Sending him away was the sensible solution, of course. One she couldn't bear to make, but knew she should. To allow him back into her life would be opening herself up to the possibility of hurt. Could she trust him not to shatter her heart again? Could she bear it if he did?

She needed to resolve this gnawing doubt

before she could make an honest decision. Having him so close made it difficult to think rationally. With his hands touching her now, warm and familiar, and his face so tantalizingly close, she could see the faint redness along the scars that marred his incredibly tempting mouth. All she could think about was kissing him. Her heart didn't recognize imperfections.

For as long as she lived, Abby would always remember this moment. Just when she'd thought her heart was safe, Bo had returned and managed to find a gaping hole in the tightly woven safety net she'd cast around it. Walked straight through to the center of her well-guarded emotions and opened the door to her dreams. Nothing would ever be the same again.

She strained to keep her voice calm, but her words still faltered. "You have…nightmares?"

"Mmm-hmm. Every night. In fact, some nights I can't get to sleep at all."

"Because of the pain?" There must have been pain, but she didn't know how much he still experienced.

"There'll always be pain, Abby, but not just

from the accident. Believe me, I don't want your pity."

His hands still circled her waist, almost as if he was afraid to let her go.

"I've never pitied you, Bo. Pity is a waste of time. But I am sorry you were hurt so badly." Her voice softened. "Sorry about your injuries." She leaned back against the comforting warmth of his hands. "They're not insurmountable, you know."

"That's debatable." He shrugged, kept his touch loose. "You always were a strong-minded woman. I admired that about you right from the first. But you never gave me any reason to think you really needed me. You were so damned self-sufficient. You never seemed to need anyone."

Abby couldn't stop the breakneck speed of her pulse. "Are you joking? Where did you ever get the idea I never needed you? I was self-sufficient because I had to be. Pop and I had a ranch to run, the only security we had. He depended on me. You knew that."

Being stiff-spined and determined had helped her face the barrage of questions from the community after Bo left, too, but she wasn't about to reveal that. Her true emotions remained carefully hidden from friends and family. She'd made certain of that.

During their time together, Abby had cherished the sweet luxury of having someone to love. Being loved in return had been a dream come true. Hadn't she made that clear to him? Yet it appeared that without meaning to, she'd kept her need for him hidden. Hadn't dared to admit the intensity of that need for fear of losing her dream. With a sinking feeling in the pit of her stomach, she realized that not completely trusting him with her heart hadn't protected it, after all.

"Yeah, I knew," Bo said. "You had a ranch and the security of knowing you were part of something important. All I had was an extra pair of jeans, a good hat and the ability to father a child. Not an impressive list of assets, especially since the hat and jeans turned out to be the only actual items on the list." He grinned wryly. "And the damn jeans wore out. So, now you know why I thought it would be easy for you to forget about me."

Abby's knees turned watery. She slid her hands around his neck, laid her cheek against his chest. "You were wrong," she whispered. "So very wrong."

Chapter Eleven

"Supper 'bout ready in there?"

Buck's gruff voice reached the kitchen about a half step ahead of the man himself. Shorty followed close behind. Their boot heels clicked an off-beat duet on the wooden floor as they entered the large, airy room.

Abby untangled herself from Bo's embrace. Embarrassed at having been caught in a moment of weakness, she tried not to look guilty as she hurried past them. She knew her face was flaming. Buck's raised eyebrows confirmed her suspicions. She wished desperately she could disappear.

"I'm just finishing up. Go ahead and sit

down." Not trusting her voice to any further explanation, she turned her back to them, grabbed the platter of sliced ham that had been sitting on the counter so long it had dried out, and hoped it was still warm enough not to draw any smart-mouthed remarks from Pop or Shorty.

Buck shot an inquisitive look her way as he motioned for the others to sit down. That didn't help her jittery nerves, so she ignored it.

Bo made himself useful without being asked by carrying two bowls of food to the table. As soon as he placed them in front of Buck, Abby felt the tension crackle between the two men. She was grateful Bo let it pass. He returned to the stove to grab the plate of biscuits, but if he noticed they were cold, he didn't say a word. Abby sent him a silent thank-you as he passed her, but received only a terse nod in return. Apparently, Bo was as flustered as she was.

It was the meal from Hell, and Bo couldn't wait for it to end. The prickly looks from Abby and the unsettling thoughts that occupied him to the point of distraction were giving him a major headache. Not to mention the way Buck and Shorty eyed him like some sort of bug on a pin. And there was the food—not that he thought the disaster was Abby's fault. Shoot, he'd eaten dried up ham and overcooked potatoes before and lived. He didn't even mind the cold okra and hard biscuits, since he really wasn't paying attention to what he ate. He knew the reason for the meal's mess was as much his fault as hers.

Remembering Abby's earlier admission had his insides tied up in knots and kept him from tasting the food he put in his mouth. Might as well have been sawdust. He wouldn't have noticed.

He'd turned her words over in his mind all through the meal. She'd told him he was wrong. Said she *had* needed him. Those words had sucker punched him, nearly put him on his knees.

From somewhere deep inside his gut, he knew she'd called it right, too, about the way he used his injuries as an excuse to keep from getting on with his life. He'd become slogged down in self-pity simply because it had been easier than facing the truth. He'd never ride again. His scars weren't going to go away. Facts were facts.

Then Teddie came along, and Bo was done for. Seeing that kid give up—admit defeat be-

fore he ever tried to actually ride a horse—
had stirred up a whole passel of unfamiliar
feelings. Gave him crazy notions like trying
to help the boy overcome his fear of riding.
Maybe even redesigning the safety strap to
give the kid a stronger feeling of security.
Something. Anything. Hell, he couldn't believe he was actually thinking of getting involved.

"No way," he mumbled under his breath.

"What's that?" Shorty said, looking up
from his plate. "No way what, Bo?"

"Nothing. Just thinking out loud. Sorry."
Bo dared a glance at Abby. She gave him one
of those soft, knowing smiles that made him
wonder if she could read his mind.

Buck pushed his empty plate back, gave
Bo his full attention. "So, what do you think
of Abby's riding program, Ramsey, now that
you've seen a class go through the routine?
She's done a helluva job. But of course, I'm
prejudiced."

Bo heard the pride in the man's voice,
saw the swell of his chest as he spoke of his
daughter's accomplishments.

"She's doing a first-class job. Must be great
to know you're helping so many kids have fun
learning to ride."

Abby leaned forward, her expression serious. "It's a lot more than just having fun. It's knowing you've made a difference in their lives by giving them the opportunity to achieve a new skill. To strengthen their self-confidence."

"You done a fine thing, too, Bo, when you grabbed Teddie out of the way of ol' Lucky. Saved 'em both from getting hurt." Shorty grinned around his mouthful of food. "That leg of yours didn't seem to slow you down none."

Bo shrugged off the comment. *Like hell, it didn't.* He'd be paying for his superhero action the rest of the evening—probably longer. He hadn't given his leg or his own safety a second thought when he'd bolted into the arena toward the boy.

"Thing is," Buck tipped his chair back on its rear legs, immediately straightening it when Abby frowned at him, "it takes a heap of money to keep the program going. Abby's been trying to get more local sponsors involved, but there's not much big money in Sweet River, you know. She was passed over for a grant this spring." He covered a nervous cough with his hand. "So, well, uh, Shorty and me, we had this idea and we'd sorta like to hear your take on it."

"Yeah," Shorty joined in with an eager nod that had his long gray braid bouncing up and down. "Wait'll you hear. It's bound to be the biggest thing ever to hit Sweet River." He forked the last bite of ham in his mouth, then washed it down with a gulp of tea. "Might even get you a spot on some big TV show." He grinned.

Abby's navy blue eyes widened right before she sat back in her chair and shot a skeptical look at Pop and his friend. "Okay, what have you two been plotting now?"

Bo nearly laughed out loud at the sheepish expressions on the faces of the pair. They looked as guilty as he'd felt when they'd walked in on him with Abby tonight.

"A rodeo," Buck said. "Right here on the ranch."

"Yep." Shorty's head bobbed in agreement. "With Bo here headlining the show, we're bound to draw a good crowd. Bring in a bundle of money for the school."

"Not a chance." Bo shot up from his chair so fast it clattered to the floor. "I'm not getting on a horse in front of a bunch of people who just want to see me fall off. No way." He headed for the back door. "Get somebody else to be your clown."

The screen door slammed behind him. He stomped awkwardly down the back porch steps, out into the yard.

"Well, what's eatin' him?"

Buck's question hung in the air, unanswered, as Shorty grabbed the last cold biscuit.

Abby set the toppled chair to rights, then picked up the empty plates. "Maybe the two of you ought to quit meddling in something that doesn't concern you," she said. "Did it ever occur to you to ask before you jump right in and make decisions for everyone?"

She loaded the hardworking dishwasher while she argued. "Which one of you had this bright idea, anyway? Think of all the time and work involved in putting on an event that large. I don't have that kind of extra time to spend coordinating it, Pop. Neither do the volunteers. And what about the initial expense? Permits to apply for. Food booths to set up and stock to arrange for." She shook her head. "We can't afford it, plain and simple."

The liquid soap glub-glubbed as she filled the detergent cups, closed the door and pushed the on switch. The appliance groaned, clunked and finally hummed to life with a loud protest.

"But, Shorty here, he's offered to bankroll part of it. Even contact the proper authorities about the permits and all."

Abby sighed. Pop just wasn't going to give up. "That's very generous," she said, "but there's no way we could line up enough entries. The best riders have their itinerary planned way ahead of time. And a rodeo without real crowd-pleasing events wouldn't attract anyone. Sorry. But thanks for the thought anyway, Shorty."

Shorty stood, retrieved his hat from the wall peg and turned to Abby with that ever-present look of optimism on his face. "Well, how about this for another idea, then? Let your students perform. Be the stars."

The two men headed out the door. Shorty looked at Abby over his shoulder. "You think about it while your daddy and me do some neighborin' down at the Rawhide, okay?" He winked and butted Buck's arm with his fist. "Don't wait up for us."

"We could do it," Buck said. "I'm sure we could."

The screen door banged shut and the truck's gears ground as the men left the ranch.

Abby stood motionless, listening to the fading noise of the truck. The whole idea was preposterous. Wasn't it?

By the time the sun washed the twilight sky with soft, rosy shadows and disappeared below the horizon, Abby had finished up in the kitchen, knowing Buck and Shorty were safely ensconced at the local bar with their old cronies, well out of range of her scolding.

They should be ashamed, she thought, as she dried her hands and hung the towel on the rack next to the sink. I should've made them do the dishes before they scooted out of here. Serves them right. She loved them dearly, but a rodeo? With her students? Preposterous! Where had they ever gotten that ridiculous idea? Sometimes those two could stir up more trouble than a pair of imaginative five-year-olds. Honestly!

She wandered out on the back porch and sat down on the steps. The peace and quiet was just what she needed to ease the knot of tension between her shoulders. The day had been a killer. The hot and heavy episode with Bo had unnerved her more than she cared to admit. She'd be better off ignoring the longings that curled inside her. Shouldn't even consider them. But she couldn't help wondering, what if...?

Ditch meandered over from his spot under the pecan tree to lay at her feet. She scratched behind his ears, rubbed his belly when he rolled over and serenaded her with a mournful whine all about being left behind.

"He'll never make it in Nashville." Bo strolled over from somewhere in the shadows.

Abby looked up at the sound and her nerve ends prickled at his approach. "I agree," she said, her voice wobbly and low.

How did he do that? Make her go all soft and warm inside. She should be thinking about the sorry state of her finances. Needed to be making some major money decisions if she wanted to stay in business. Instead she couldn't keep her thoughts from focusing on Bo and his kisses. Bo and his roughed-up face that made him uncharacteristically self-conscious and so very vulnerable. Bo and his admission that he still cared about her.

She scooted over when he eased his lanky frame down on the step beside her. Her heart danced when he slid one arm behind her, providing a natural, intimate support for her shoulders. Ditch made room for him by ambling off to sprawl under the pecan tree again.

"How come old Ditch didn't go with Shorty and Buck?"

Abby shrugged. "I don't know. Maybe he's getting too old for carousing." She laughed softly.

"And they aren't?" Bo's chuckle mingled with hers. She loved their blended sound—his, warm and suggestive, hers, soft and slightly breathy. Made her remember the sweet sounds of the sultry nights in the past. Made her want so much more than she should.

"I've been thinking," Bo said, settling closer.

"About Pop and Shorty's suggestion to hold a rodeo?" The warmth of his arm across her back was becoming a major distraction.

"Oh, no. That's the last thing I'd be a part of." He inclined his head, cracked a half grin. "Those two should never be left alone for very long. Their devious minds come up with the damndest notions."

"You shouldn't blame them, though. They're only trying to help." *Leaning against him feels so natural—so good.*

"Yeah, guess you're right, but Shorty oughta know I don't figure on riding again, especially in front of a crowd."

Abby looked into his eyes. The shadow of

subdued pain lingering there made her want to cradle him like a child and love the hurt away.

"You could, you know." Her words were whispered, but she knew he heard her.

"Not a possibility." He grew still. "Not anymore." His hand slid from her shoulder to trail lightly up and down her arm.

She shivered at the delicious sensation warming her blood.

"Anything is possible, if you want it bad enough, Ramsey. Look at what the kids who come here have accomplished. Do you think they learned to ride on their very first lesson? Nope. But they keep coming back. Keep trying until they get it right and they know they've done the best they can. Besides, you were injured by a bull, not a horse."

She watched him struggle with his thoughts. Watched his brow furrow as questions filled his eyes. "Do you know what puts those smiles on their faces, Ramsey?" She touched his arm. "It's learning to live with their limitations but never giving up trying to improve on their achievements—their hard-earned accomplishments."

His hand came to rest against the curve of

her hip. "Teddie wasn't smiling. Why won't he ride?"

"He did—once. Oh, not here," Abby said quickly. "He was at a summer camp up in the Hill Country. Something spooked his pony. When it reared, Teddie fell off and the animal landed on his legs. Broke both of them and did some muscle damage. He's been through a lot of physical therapy, but the doctors still aren't certain he'll ever walk normally. His fear of falling again has him scared to death. Afraid to try any new challenges." She paused, searched Bo's face and was encouraged by the concern she saw in his eyes.

"Teddie needs someone to help him find his courage again," she said quietly. "Is that what you plan to do?" Her gaze held his. "Don't make promises you don't intend to keep."

"Like I said, I'd never hurt the boy. Just forget about it. It was a stupid idea, anyway. I'm the last person to give advice about riding."

Abby huffed out an impatient sigh. "You're right. If you don't believe in yourself, you can't expect anyone else to. Trust is important to these kids, Bo. They have to trust the helpers, the horses. They even have to learn to trust each other, but most importantly, they have to trust themselves."

Bo remained silent, his pensive gaze moving over her in a look so poignant, it plucked at her heartstrings. A look that told her his next words weren't going to have anything to do with Teddie. She was right.

"About what happened today…" he said.

"It doesn't matter."

The lie didn't come easy for her. Bo and his kisses mattered more than she wanted to admit. She leaned away from the enticing warmth of his arm. Better just try and forget the whole incident. *As if I could.*

Bo turned to her, placed his hands around her waist. "Maybe it doesn't matter to you, but it's pretty damned important to me."

Bingo. Straight to the big stuff. How was she supposed to answer that?

The suggestion in Bo's heavy-lidded gaze was as obvious as if he had spoken it aloud. Abby's breath caught in her throat.

"Is it?" she murmured when her breathing finally leveled. "How can I be sure?"

The question had barely left her lips when he leaned forward and whispered against her mouth. "Let this convince you."

And she did.

On a scale of one to ten, the kiss was a fifteen. Abby knew it the minute her toes curled inside her boots and the world rocked beneath her. Knew, too, that the feeling didn't have to end there unless she wanted it to. Bo was leaving the decision to her, even though his own preference was extremely obvious. No fair.

With his seductive mouth on hers promising a trip to paradise with slow, sweet thrusts of his tongue, the temptation to let her heart rule was truly impossible to resist. Emotions hiding deep within her very core struggled to the surface, demanding her immediate attention.

This is way too much for one woman's yearning heart to handle.

"We shouldn't…" Her lips moved against his. "I want…"

He nipped her bottom lip, his mouth only a whisper away from hers. "Go ahead, tell me what you want. I need to know."

"Why?" She held her breath, closed her eyes.

"Because… I…need you, Abby." His words whispered across her eyelids as he kissed each one…and she was lost.

Chapter Twelve

How they got from sitting on the steps to standing by the back door would remain one of life's little mysteries, but Abby knew the minute they crossed the threshold, there'd be no turning back.

The urgency of their kisses had escalated until they practically fell through the door. The wooden frame dug into her back when his lean, hard body pressed into hers, connecting perfectly. The sensation was like finding the prize in a treasure hunt that had lasted for years. She wanted to shout Hooray! at the discovery. She fumbled behind her for the elusive door handle.

He reached around her and his hand quickly covered hers. Together they tugged until the screen door squeaked on its hinges and swung open. Tangled like a knot of wet rope, they stumbled into the kitchen while Bo continued to rain hot, wet kisses on her face. He plundered her open mouth with his tongue, then kissed a trail to her ear.

"Last chance to back out," he murmured. His lips nibbled along the curve of the sensitive shell and his hot breath sent electric currents shooting through her veins.

Had he lost his mind? Backing out was definitely not an option anymore.

Even though there'd been no mention of the word love, Bo had said he needed her. Abby's heart was so full, she feared it would explode. She wanted desperately to believe him. Wanted to believe she could wait for love. At least for awhile. She'd always been good at waiting. But not right now. Not at this precise moment—their moment.

"Forget it, Ramsey," she said, her voice husky and low. "No one is backing out."

She loved the way he grinned at her then. Every scar on his rugged face vanished with that single, deliciously crooked smile. Her heart saw him perfectly, lovingly. And right now he was hers. If that made her shameless, then so be it. She wasn't going to let the past rob her of the present. Not when he was so close.

She all but dragged him through the kitchen—or was he leading her?—and down the hall to her bedroom. She kept forgetting that he knew the way. *Hurry. Please, just hurry.*

They fell on the bed, and she tugged at his shirt, pulled it over his head.

"Whoa, darlin', slow down. Buck and Shorty won't be back for hours." Bo's words, thick with emotion, were muffled in one tangled sleeve. He sat up, yanked the stubborn garment the rest of the way off and tossed it on the floor.

"Are you sure, Abby? Because once this starts, I don't know if I'll be able to stop, if you change your mind." His eyes were dark and smoky. Intense. Filled with desire.

Sitting up on her knees, she took his face in her hands and leaned into him, opening her mouth over his and giving him her answer in a soul kiss that came from the innermost depth of her being.

He pulled her onto his lap so she could wrap her legs around him and settle against his growing hardness while they rocked together, their need for closeness consuming them. Their kisses deepened while their hands caressed, stroked, remembered. And then there was just the two of them—and a pair of hearts that overflowed with memories.

"Oh, Abby, I've missed you so much." His voice cracked. His hands shook.

Tears leaked from the corners of her eyes. Her heart ached unbearably at the tenderness of his touch, skittered crazily when he unbuttoned her shirt and kissed her through the soft cotton of her bra. His mouth was hot, needy, and her nipples grew hard. With a deft flick of his fingers, he released the clasp. She gasped when her throbbing breasts filled his waiting hands. Whimpered when he kneaded them.

"Yes, pleeease," she moaned as they struggled out of the last of their confining clothing.

With each stroke of his exploring fingers, erotic spears of heat surged through her body. Low in her belly, between her thighs, in her heavy, sensitive breasts. No place was safe from his magic touch. Or his mouth. Sanity help me, she thought and squeezed her eyes shut when he slid from the bed to kneel before her.

Bo was determined to pleasure her like he'd never done before. Not only because he hadn't brought any protection with him, but because for once, this moment wasn't about him. It was about Abby. Her wants, her needs. Even though he wasn't worthy of her love, at least he could give her this. His own pleasure would come from the giving. They had never shared this expression of love in the past. This would be his ultimate gift to her, if she'd let him.

He led the way slowly, giving his undivided attention to every curve and hollow of her body. He tasted, teased, savored. Caressed, kissed, enticed. But as he trailed his mouth lower, pressing hot kisses across the softness of her abdomen, he felt her shiver and grow still.

He waited. Her whispers encouraged him. Excited him when she didn't pull away. Tempted him to throw caution to the wind. He steeled his self-control, instead murmured, "Let me love you, darlin'."

She gasped at the first stroke of his tongue, and he paused to let her catch her breath, increasing the pace only when she dug her fingers into his shoulders, urging him on. Her soft sighs escalated from throaty purrs to insistent moans, nearly catapulting him to his own satisfaction. But not yet. Not before Abby. He grasped her hips and brought her hot, sweet center closer.

"Please… Bo…now." She clung to him. Moved urgently with the pulsing tempo he set.

But he wanted to give her more. Shifting his position, he rolled his mouth over hers and kissed her openly, wetly. His tongue stroked in sensual thrusts while his fingers pleasured her. She tangled her fingers in his hair, clutched at him and wept softly as she shattered in complete, uninhibited release.

Cradling her close, he sipped the tears from her face and whispered secret love words until she quieted in his arms. He longed to tell her that his heart had always belonged to her. But he couldn't.

Instead, he'd given her the only thing he had left to offer, hoping to erase some of the hurt he'd caused her. The pain in his own heart would never go away. His body was still rigid with wanting her, but for the first time in his life, he felt satisfied and complete in a whole new way.

Abby lay in his embrace and listened to her heartbeat struggle to return to its regular pace. How could it possibly be normal again after what she had just experienced? Would *she* ever be the same again? Her body still thrummed with heat. Deliciously warm aftershocks rippled through her. Her nerves danced on the surface of her skin, sensitized by Bo's incredible touch. She turned in his arms and burrowed against him. When their bodies met, she suddenly realized that his needs were still unfulfilled.

"Bo...?"

"Aw, darlin'," he murmured. "Just give me a minute. It's my own damn fault I didn't have any protection with me. Besides, this time was for you."

Tears of understanding welled in her eyes. Knowing Bo had set his own needs aside in order to fulfill hers made the moment that much sweeter. She'd never experienced the kind of unselfish loving she'd just received. And now that she had, she wanted to give him the same pleasure. The same gratification.

"Let me share it with you," she whispered.

She trailed kisses down his chest and across his taut stomach, hesitating only slightly, when her mouth encountered the rigid length of his desire.

He groaned at the touch of her lips. Cried

her name as she made certain his satisfaction was complete.

The afterglow didn't last nearly long enough to satisfy Abby. She knew the minute Bo sat up in bed that he wasn't going to stay.

"You're an amazing woman, Abby," he said, his voice tinged with sadness. "You deserve a lot more than a no-account cowboy with no money or future."

"Shouldn't that be my decision?" Her heart was already sinking back to its old hiding place. Bo's words hurried it along.

"I'll never be the man you need."

"You could be," she whispered. "If you really wanted to."

"You don't know what you're asking, darlin'. I'd stay right here with you all night long, but…" He leaned over and kissed her forehead. "I don't want to wake up with Buck's shotgun pointing at me." He pulled on his jeans and shirt. "I'll wait on the back porch for Shorty."

Abby sat up, wrapping the sheet around her. "Are you saying this was a mistake?"

Bo shook his head. "Not a mistake, just a situation we should have avoided," he said. He lowered his voice. "But I'm glad we didn't."

Abby tried to convince herself that Bo really did need to leave her room before Pop came home. She didn't allow any other reason to crowd her thoughts.

Much later, she was still awake when she heard Ditch bark at the rattle of Shorty's truck coming up the lane. Knowing Bo was outside didn't make her feel any easier, since Pop and Shorty would have no problem figuring out what had transpired in the last two hours. She knew the men had expected her to drive Bo home right after she'd finished the supper dishes. How would he explain the reason he was still there? She should have spread the Monopoly game out. Or a deck of cards. Right, like they'd believe she and Bo had spent the evening playing games.

Abby didn't close her eyes until she heard her father's bedroom door shut. She fell asleep dreading Pop's inquisition at breakfast.

"G'mornin'." Bo's greeting, when he entered the barn the next morning, startled Abby from her deep concentration.

She had just begun the morning chores in preparation for the first group of students and was attempting to keep her wayward thoughts on what she was doing. Ha! No such luck.

And now, the main attraction of those

steamy thoughts was walking toward her, albeit with a labored gait. Low-slung jeans, tight enough to reveal every sinewy muscle of his legs, made her heart skip as her gaze lingered on the bulge along the length of his zipper. She smiled, remembering the night before and the fact that Bo's injuries hadn't hampered his ability for lovemaking.

"Hi. I didn't think you'd be back today." She couldn't quite read the expression on his face. Didn't know what to expect after last night. The shadows cast by the flickering fluorescent lights above the stalls kept her from seeing him clearly. *I have to remember to buy replacement bulbs the next time I'm in town.* Doing chores in such dim light made it difficult to check the equipment properly.

"Shorty let me use his old Bronco today. He needed his truck to go to the feed mill. Guess he figures I can haul myself around now." He lifted a pitchfork from a hook on the wall and went into the first stall. "Hey, Cloud, how about movin' over so I can do some housecleaning for you?" The horse whinnied, but did as Bo asked.

Abby thought it uncanny, the way the animals all responded to his voice. But then, he had a way of coaxing a response from her, too, and not just with his voice, sexy as it was. She felt a silly grin tug at her mouth.

Bo picked up the feed bucket and set it out of his way without really seeing it. Doing chores was so automatic, some days he didn't even think about what he was doing. Today was one of those days.

He was angry at himself for being here this morning. After he'd left Abby last night, he'd decided that he wasn't coming back today. Wasn't going to see her again. He knew if he stayed around any longer, he wouldn't be satisfied until he'd made love to her totally, without reservation. He wanted to be inside her. It was that simple. And it couldn't have been more complicated.

His decision had lasted all of five minutes after Shorty'd told him, on the way home last night, about Buck's financial mess and how a big event like a rodeo would sure help him if they held it as a fund-raiser for Abby's riding program. Shoot, by the time they'd gotten back to Shorty's ranch, Bo had agreed to help with the whole damn show.

For cryin' out loud, he couldn't believe he'd done that. Especially knowing how much Abby was against the idea. But Shorty'd had a helluva sales pitch. He'd convinced Bo that a rodeo was the best way to fix things.

This morning, however, Bo had serious second thoughts. He'd come here early to talk things over with Abby before Shorty and her father got their heads together again. He just didn't quite know how to go about it. Last night they definitely hadn't talked about fund-raising.

He needed to settle *that* with Abby, too. How the hell could he possibly work with her every day and not think about what they'd shared? He knew she expected him to make a commitment after he'd loved her so thoroughly, but he couldn't. He wasn't about to tie her to a down-and-out cowboy when she could do so much better for herself. His heart would always be hers, but that would forever remain his secret.

So if helping Shorty plan a rodeo would raise money for her ranch, then the least he could do to prove he wasn't a total jackass would be to agree to help wherever he could. It wasn't like he'd promised to perform or anything. Nope, he'd made that clear to Shorty from the very first. He would make some phone calls. Maybe try contacting some of the riders he knew. That was all.

He looked up just as Abby swung the stall door open.

"You didn't have to come over so early," she said. "Pop will be coming out to help pretty soon."

Bo detected a faint blush on her cheeks and smiled. He wondered if seeing him had brought that glow to her skin. Her soft voice evoked memories of the night before, stirred his blood and he grew hard. Damn it, he couldn't keep on like this or he'd become permanently three-legged. Embarrassed by his instant arousal, he moved to the far side of the stall, putting the horse between him and Abby and hoped he looked sufficiently interested in his chores. Old Cloud snorted his impatience at being kept inside.

"Yeah, well, I thought maybe Buck needed a day off. He seemed kinda tired when Shorty brought him home last night. 'Course, maybe that was just from spending the evening down at the Rawhide." He kept his back to her, moved some more straw around and adjusted his jeans for the third time. Damn.

Abby sensed his uneasiness right away, and her stomach tightened. Was he regretting last night? If he'd meant all those wonderful things he'd said and done, shouldn't he be kissing her hello right now, instead of turning his back on her and mumbling stupid remarks about Pop looking tired? How could he possibly be immune to the incredible things they'd shared? That had to mean something.

He'd shown such tenderness and caring, giving her incredible pleasure in ways she'd only dreamed of without considering his own needs. The whole experience had made her realize just how unselfish and caring Bo could be, even though he tried to hide his emotions behind a gruff exterior.

When she'd loved him equally well and just as enthusiastically, he'd cried out her name in the heat of his explosive deliverance. The wonder of that—of knowing she had the ability to grant him such intense pleasure—increased her own sexual delight. How could you share that ecstasy and not care?

She refused to believe him when he said he'd never marry again. Even though his marriage to Marla had been a sham, and she understood why after he'd explained, his reason for not making a commitment now didn't ring true. Not after the way he'd acted toward her. Clearly, he wanted her, and after last night,

Abby was certain he still loved her even if he refused to admit it.

Well, this time she wasn't giving up. She was going to fight for what she wanted. And she wanted him. All she had to do was convince him.

She looked forward to the challenge.

Chapter Thirteen

"I could use some help with the children today." Abby leaned against the wall of Cloud's stall and watched with amused interest as Bo spread the clean straw. Cloud had moved over, affording her a clear view of the man responsible for her sleepless night.

If he thought she hadn't noticed his condition, he was wrong, but she certainly wasn't going to mention it. Her smile remained in her heart instead and she struggled to keep it from showing. "So, how about it? Want to take a turn around the arena with the class?"

"I'll be more useful right here in the barn."

He strode past her and hung the pitchfork back in place.

She followed him, stopped directly behind him and waited for him to turn around. Determined not to be ignored any longer, she stood perfectly still until he faced her.

"Teddie will be here this morning. I thought maybe you would want to work with him. After all, you did promise him."

Bo shot his hat to the back of his head with one finger, arched an eyebrow and gave her a speculative look. "You thought so, huh?"

The child was her ace in the hole, her best shot at actively involving Bo with the kids. She knew about his promise to spend some time with the little boy and counted on his sense of honor to follow through, even though he clearly regretted the promise. She crossed her fingers behind her back, silently rejoicing at the flicker of interest in his eyes.

Bo reached for her hands, tugged them so that she was forced to take a quick step toward him. "What's it worth to you?"

His unexpected question caught her off guard. *Another night like the last one?* No, she definitely couldn't give him the first answer that popped into her head, though she was tempted, just to see what kind of reaction it would bring.

There was something exciting in the way his gaze held hers; in the taut, expectant position of their bodies, so close yet not quite touching. Then he gave another tug on her hands, and she teetered into him, unbalanced on shaky legs.

His hands circled her waist to steady her, and she looped her arms around his neck, pulled his head down and whispered in his ear. "Are we talking business or pleasure here, Ramsey?"

She thought it was a reasonably legitimate question, especially since the gleam in his eyes grew brighter. A thrill raced through her when she heard him suck in his breath.

"You're not playing fair." He angled his head so that his lips brushed her cheek. His words were warm. Inviting. Downright bonemelting.

"Speaking of fair…" She leaned closer.

He nuzzled her neck. Nibbled the soft hollow at her shoulder. "Like this, do you?"

She nodded eagerly. His hand cradled the back of her head and brought her mouth to meet his.

Her entire body liquefied. *And he expects*

me to answer now? She closed her eyes and fell into the moment.

Not forceful or demanding, the kiss was sweeter for its tenderness and the gentle way his tongue glided over her lips. Tears gathered behind her eyelids as the sheer beauty and simplicity of his touch rocked her soul. Restored her hope.

"I forgot the question," she murmured with a weak laugh against his chest when the kiss ended.

"Mmmmm…as a matter of fact, so did I," he drawled. "But the distraction was worth it." He looked deep into her eyes, huffed out a ragged breath. "Abby, Abby, what are we gonna do?"

"About what?"

He kissed the tip of her nose. "About us, of course."

Us. The word swirled through her mind. *Us.* A tiny word that held a world of meaning. Did she still want to be an *us* with Bo after two years? Her heart shouted an emphatic yes, even as she questioned her own emotions. Tried to picture a future that included him. Wondered if he was willing to accept his limitations and move ahead with his life. Was she?

"Do we have to deal with this right now?" She needed more time. This was not a decision to be made lightly, and practical thinking was impossible with the thrill of Bo's kisses still warming her body.

He dropped his hands and backed away. "Not if you have a problem with it."

His chilly words stung. "Wait, you don't understand," she said, anxious to explain. "Class starts in a few minutes, and the students are already arriving."

She gestured toward the cars beginning to line the drive in front of the barn. "There's Teddie and his mom now, getting out of that gray car." She placed her hand on his arm. "Please, at least talk with him this morning."

"Well, hell," Bo muttered under his breath, knowing she was right. This was not the time or place for intimate discussions. He wasn't going to refuse her, and she knew it. Besides, he'd promised to show Teddie how to be a cowboy. What a damn fool thing for someone like him to do.

"Let's go," he said and followed her out of the barn, hoping the tension in his body would eventually disappear. He made a mental note to steer clear of any close contact with her tempting body as long as the kids were around. But he wasn't making any promises beyond that. There were too many unresolved feelings between the two of them to ignore. And his patience was in short supply lately.

His edginess evaporated quickly when Teddie called his name and waved his stick-thin arm in an enthusiastic greeting. A warmth spread through Bo's heart and an unusual feeling of joy settled there. Strangely enough, he liked it.

When he knelt beside Teddie and the boy hugged his neck, he kinda liked the way that felt, too.

Abby was talking to Teddie's mother, but Bo saw her glance his way and knew she was watching to see if he would back out of his promise. He'd already decided he would keep it, even though he'd rather eat worms than pretend to be something he no longer could claim to be—a proficient cowboy.

"Are we gonna do cowboy stuff today, Bo?" The absence of one front tooth caused a slight lisp, but the wide smile on the child's face was easy to interpret.

Bo looked Teddie straight in the eye. "You bet, pardner. We'll start by taking Star out of her stall so you can learn to groom her. She'll like that."

Without waiting for the child to argue, Bo stood, took the small hand in his and walked with Teddie toward the corral. He glanced back only once to see if Abby was watching. She was.

Kids and horses mingled in the arena ready to begin the class. Abby always felt a surge of happiness and pride when she saw the eager faces of her students. Nothing warmed her heart more than this. She'd already checked each child's saddle and tack, making certain everything was secure, even though she knew the volunteers had already seen to it. She took her place beside the mounting block and gave a wave for the first rider to begin. This morning, IdaJoy helped Laura walk her horse to the mounting block, and the girl chattered happily with the fashionably dressed café owner. The two had hit it off right away and both were progressing—Laura in her riding confidence, and IdaJoy in her ability to make the girl forget her problems.

Abby noted that this morning the woman wore a subdued plum-colored jumpsuit and gray Stetson. Quite a change from her usual, peacock-bright garb. Even her shiny black boots were unadorned. Could it be the gregarious blonde was having a fashion change-of-heart?

Abby was almost sorry to see the change. IdaJoy brought a certain spark of fun wherever she was, and the Sweet River Riders loved having her around. She could always be counted on to make the children laugh, no matter how difficult their challenge. A welcome addition to Abby's list of volunteers, IdaJoy quickly learned to cope with the different types of situations arising when special needs kids were involved. Abby was deeply grateful for her help.

Laura and IdaJoy reached the mounting block and the girl managed the ordeal of getting into the saddle without much difficulty. IdaJoy's soft words of encouragement were just what the girl needed. They began the circuit, and Abby watched them carefully until she was assured IdaJoy was handling Lucky and his rider just fine. She hadn't meant to let her attention wander to the far side where Bo stood talking with Teddie.

Her heart kicked against her ribs when she saw them disappear into the barn. She was certain Bo intended to coax the boy to work with Star. If he could persuade Teddie to groom the mare, even a little, it would be a wonderful step forward. For them both.

By the time the other four students had completed the workout in the arena and their horses were lined up ready to dismount, the sun was burning high in the sky and everyone was ready for a well-deserved break. Abby gave the call that ended the session.

After the riders dismounted and their horses were led to the posts, the volunteers secured them and helped the students collect their grooming equipment. Before they started the final rubdown, Abby spoke to each student, praising their progress. Even though she was anxious to hear what had happened with Teddie and Star, she focused on the students who had been performing so diligently all morning.

"Rory, you did so much better today," she said, giving the teen's shoulder a squeeze. "Next time, you can have an extra turn."

She walked to the next horse and rider. "Susie, don't forget to hang up the bridle."

The child waved. "I won't, Miss Abby."

She would never cut short her time with a student for her own selfish wishes. But as soon as the last child was gone and the horses had been taken care of, she planned to corner

Ramsey. They needed to talk—about a lot of things, including the possibility of holding a rodeo.

Abby approached the area where Caroline North stood waiting for her son. The woman's anxious expression changed to one of relief the minute she spotted Teddie and Bo coming out of the barn wearing matching ear-to-ear smiles.

"Mommy, guess what?"

The youngster's excitement nearly toppled him over when his legs wobbled, but Bo reached out to steady him. A look of pure hero worship lit the boy's face.

Caroline knelt and hugged him. "What, sweetheart? Tell me what's got you so excited."

"Star let me brush her. I did it exactly like Bo showed me." His little voice rose higher. "And Star stood really, really still. She really likes me. Bo said so."

Bo shrugged his shoulders. "You did it just right, buddy. Star knew you wouldn't hurt her." He ruffed Teddie's hair. "Next time, you can put the blanket and saddle on, and I'll bet she'll even let you sit on her. How about it?"

"Well…" Teddie's eyes grew wide. "I don't

know...." He clutched his mother's hand. "What about my legs? What if I fall off?"

Bo glanced at Abby before he spoke softly, more to the boy than the two women standing close by. "Remember what we talked about while you were brushing Star? You think about that when you get home and let me know what you decide when you come back tomorrow. Deal?"

The youngster squared his shoulders and nodded. "Deal, Bo. Just like we said." But his eyes still held a look of panic.

Abby's curiosity ballooned to epic proportions. What deal had Bo concocted now? She'd more or less insisted that he keep his promise to Teddie the way he thought best, but after all, this was her program. Shouldn't he at least consult her before making any major decisions that concerned one of her students?

Suddenly she felt as if she was losing control over something she'd worked hard to build. Pretty ridiculous, when you thought about it. He'd made it clear that he didn't plan on helping with her program indefinitely. So what was it between him and the boy?

Puzzled by the uncomfortable left-out feeling growing in her chest, she resolved not to let petty jealousy rule her actions. With a quick goodbye to Teddie and his mom, Abby left them talking to Bo, and made her way to the parking lot to speak with some of the other parents. There'd be time enough for examining her feelings later.

There were always questions after each class. Every parent wanted assurance that their child was improving in some small way. She hoped to set aside more time to spend with the individual families in the near future—if the program even had a future. Worry churned in the pit of her stomach. Why did money always have to be such a problem?

Hiding her distress with an encouraging smile for Laura, she listened patiently while the girl's parents gave their reasons for wanting to take their daughter out of the riding sessions.

"But, Laura's doing so well," Abby said, her heart sinking at the thought of losing a student, especially one who was making such great progress. "Won't you reconsider?"

"No, I really don't see that it's making a difference with her. She'll always have the problem of her prosthesis. It's not like there's a cure." Mrs. McBride gave Laura a sympathetic pat on the shoulder and *tsk-tsked*. Mr.

McBride remained silent, his expression unemotional.

Laura's face crumpled in disappointment and Abby had half a notion to ask them if they honestly cared about their daughter's feelings at all. Of course, she wouldn't, but she wanted to so badly, she had to bite her tongue.

Just then, IdaJoy sashayed up to the little group and joined in the conversation, totally oblivious of the tension that hovered.

"If there's one thing I know," she said, interrupting without so much as a blink of her false eyelashes, "it's a natural rider when I see one. Your daughter sits like a born horsewoman. Why, I declare, she could ride Lucky without any help from me or anyone. You must be mighty proud of her. If she tackles all her challenges as well as this, shoot, she'll be out on her own before you know it." She winked at Laura and gave her a hug. "I could use someone like you down at the café, hon. What do you say? Think you'd like to give waitressing a try?"

Laura beamed with pride and nodded enthusiastically. "Oh, yes. I know I could do it."

Abby bit her lip. Leave it to IdaJoy. Her enthusiasm was as contagious as a case of measles, but sometimes it was a bit over the top. Laura's parents had had difficulty agreeing to let her participate in a program of this type. Abby doubted they'd ever agree for her to go off on her own. Not for a good long time, anyway. Laura was seventeen, but they treated her like a seven-year-old.

Still, Abby understood what IdaJoy was trying to say. Laura was determined to deal with her physical challenge and get on with her life. She hoped the parents would eventually come to understand and give their daughter a chance to try. Since starting this program, Abby had learned that maturity didn't always belong solely to the adults. But she understood, also, that parents of special children often needed to hold on to them far more than the kids needed their clinging. Letting go of someone you love always hurt.

Mrs. McBride shuddered at IdaJoy's suggestion that Laura work at the Blue Moon. "Oh my, no," she said, pressing a hand to her ample bosom. "Why, that would never do."

Abby and IdaJoy exchanged a knowing glance. Nola McBride was the biggest worrier in town. And her husband, Claude, made a marshmallow look tough. The pair didn't appreciate what a terrific young woman Laura had become. Laura had been a toddler when Nola and Claude adopted her. They were almost too old to qualify, and their announcement had set the town gossips on their ears. Abby remembered the event very well.

She also remembered that Nola McBride had a great deal of influence at the bank, so she discreetly gave IdaJoy a nudge in the ribs to make her hush. It didn't work.

"Well, if you ask me—" IdaJoy stopped right in the middle of her sentence and pointed toward the barn. "My Gawd! Fire! Fire in the barn!" She jumped up and down, waving her arms. "Someone call 9-1-1!"

Abby spun around just in time to see orange flames spurt out of the hayloft. Caroline North ran toward them, shouting hysterically. "Teddie went back into the barn, and Bo went after him. Please, someone help them!"

The almost-human screams of the trapped horses sent chills racing down Abby's spine. *This can't be happening!* She raced toward the barn, but young Karl Kelly grabbed her arm and pulled her back.

"No, Miss Abby, you can't go in there. It's too dangerous."

Fear and hysteria bubbled inside her chest. "I have to," she cried, fighting against his hold. "Bo and Teddie are in there. And the horses."

Karl shook his head. "No, ma'am, I can't let you do that." He clung to her arm, held on tight against her struggle.

Buck rushed from the house, shouting and waving his arms. "Get back, Abby! The fire department is on the way. Karl, make sure there's no one else in the arena. And tell the others to clear the drive so the trucks can get in."

When Karl hesitated and looked questioningly at Abby, Buck said, "I'll take care of her. You go on." The boy hurried off, calling out directions as he went.

"Pop, we have to get them out!" She looked around helplessly.

Shouts of warning broke through the thick layers of smoke filling the air. Crying children and screaming mothers scrambled to get away from the area. To safety.

The enormity of what was happening spurred Abby into action. She jerked free from Buck's hand and dashed over to where the volunteers, with the help of some of the parents, already had water hoses hooked up and were running back and forth with buckets. In the distance, the wail of sirens grew stronger, along with the roar of the approaching vehicles belonging to fire department volunteers coming from surrounding areas.

High-pitched whinnies pierced the air and the pounding of hooves shook the ground.

"Look, there they are!" Abby cried.

Buck looked back just as some of the horses surged through the barn door, heads up and tails flying.

Before Abby could shout directions, Karl ran to open the pasture gate. The animals raced through, never stopping until they reached the safety of the distant fence line.

Abby counted them, thankful for Karl's quick thinking.

"Where are the others?" she called to him.

"I don't see no more, Miss Abby. I'm afraid the fire's too far gone." Karl hurried off to check on the surviving animals.

"Where are they?" Abby screamed, her frantic gaze sweeping the smoke-filled arena. She turned to her father. "Where are Bo and Teddie. And Star?"

Her heart lodged in her throat. Terror gripped her, froze her to the spot. The barn was a scorching inferno. There was no sign of the man or the little boy.

Chapter Fourteen

This must be what hell feels like. Smoke. Thick, black, choking. Heat so intense his whole body vibrated. The stench of scorched horseflesh, combined with burning straw and charring lumber filled Bo's lungs and stole his breath. He staggered back from the door after the last horse had fled to safety.

Fumbling, he pulled his bandana back in place over his nose and mouth. His eyes were two hot coals lodged in their sockets. Tears scalded his face, impairing his vision as much as the acrid smoke hanging in the air.

When a knifelike pain sliced upwards through his knee, he prayed his leg wouldn't give out. Where was the boy? Teddie and Star were still somewhere in the blaze.

"Teddie? Answer me, buddy!" Panic crowded his chest. Bile rose in his throat, bitter and gagging. This was all his fault. Making stupid promises to the kid.

"Teddie! C'mon, pardner, yell so I can find you." He flung his arms out in front of his face and struggled farther into the center of the building, shouting, cussing, searching. Hoping.

A spark-laden beam fell from overhead with a crash, barely missing him. "Damn." He staggered around it when a shower of sparks peppered his shirt, searing his skin through the thin cotton. He slapped at them, running awkwardly, dodging the falling timbers and burning piles of straw.

"Teddie, dammit, answer me!"

What was that? Bo jerked to a stop and listened, but all he heard was the hiss and pop of aging lumber burning. He strained to listen again, scarcely breathed. There it was again. A tiny voice, barely audible through the suffocating blanket of smoke.

"Bo."

"Teddie! Teddie, where are you?"

"Help, Bo. We're back here."

"Hang on, buddy, I'm coming." He tried to pinpoint the direction of the faint voice. *Where the hell were they?*

"Keep yelling so I can find you. Talk to me." His heart swelled right up into his scorched throat. He fought his way to the rear of the building, past flaming piles of fallen rafters and smoking timbers. Twice, he had to beat the sparks from his clothes with his hat. Flames shot out from every stall. Heat singed every exposed part of his body. His eyes blurred.

Teddie's frantic voice sounded closer. "Hurry, Bo. I'm scared."

Dragging his aching leg, Bo strained to see through the thick smoke. Even with his bandana over his mouth, his lungs were filling fast. He tried shallow breathing. Dizziness was only a heartbeat away, but he had to stay conscious—had to find Teddie and Star.

A nervous whinny came from somewhere on his left. He turned when a soft muzzle nudged his arm. Star! He hadn't even seen her. Almost walked right past her. She stood next to where Teddie lay curled up on the floor. Her eyes were glazed with fear, but she kept her small, sturdy body close to Teddie.

My God! She was shielding him from a

fallen beam. Bo couldn't believe it. He moved closer, not wanting to startle her. The weight of the heavy timber was on her back. The slightest move could send it sliding right on top of the boy.

"Whoa, girl, easy." He talked softly with a false calm while he worked to shove the log away, careful not to let it hit the boy. Some of the hair on Star's back was singed. He hoped she could do what he was about to ask of her. Star bobbed her head and whinnied, then sidestepped away from Teddie, allowing Bo access to her little companion.

Teddie looked up with hero worship in his tear-filled eyes. "I knew you'd find us, Bo. I just knew it."

The boy's ragged whisper tore at Bo's heart. He dropped to his knees, ignoring the sharp pain shooting to his thigh when he bent his leg.

"Hey, buddy, let's get outta here, okay?" He glanced around, saw the flames getting closer. In minutes they'd be trapped inside the inferno. Minutes he couldn't waste.

A harsh cough rattled up from Teddie's chest.

"Keep that handkerchief over your nose and mouth. It'll help you breathe easier."

"Awright, but...my arm hurts something awful, too." He pointed to his left arm, laying like a scrawny mesquite branch across his stomach. "I think I broke it when I fell."

Fire licked its way down the center of the barn, shifting directions when a gust of wind whipped through the crumbling doorway. Crackling flames threatened to completely cut off their escape.

Bo jerked off his singed leather gloves and fumbled to fashion a crude sling from his bandana. He eased Teddie's arm into it, swearing at his clumsiness, apologizing when the boy whimpered. His right hand was blistered and raw where his glove was burned away, making his efforts take forever. *Hurry up, Ramsey. Time's running out.*

"I'll be careful," he assured the frightened child, "but we've gotta get out of here, so hold your arm real tight like this while I put you on Star's back. She'll get you out of here." He patted the mare's neck, murmured softly in her ear.

With the smoke thickening around them like dense fog, Bo worried the horse might bolt before he could secure Teddie on her back. But Star stood still. Only her eyes reflected her nervousness.

"This might hurt a little. Keep your hand tucked inside the waistband of your jeans." Bo gave him a careful hug. "You're being mighty brave, buddy."

Lifting Teddie up on Star's back took every bit of strength Bo could muster. He tried to be as gentle as possible to spare the little animal any extra pain, wishing he had something to protect her injured back. Star never wavered while Teddie wiggled to a sitting position and grabbed her mane with his good hand.

"Am I a cowboy yet?" The boy looked at him with such naked devotion, Bo's heart dropped clear to his stomach.

Aw, hell. He swiped a hand across his eyes. The tears stinging them weren't entirely from the damned smoke. Neither was the tightness in his chest.

"Anybody as brave as you are is a real cowboy, Teddie," he said, his voice so raspy and full of emotion it hurt to talk. He squeezed Teddie's hand and choked back the urge to grab him in a bear hug. Now wasn't the time for sloppy sentiments.

The child's unflinching courage and refusal to cry gave Bo's own dwindling courage a powerful booster shot. He could do this. He *would* do this. Teddie was depending on him, and so was the boy's mother. Abby, too. He vowed not to disappoint her this time.

Her sweet image flashed across his mind. She was everything, and he was nothing without her. If he got out of here in one piece, he was going to tell her exactly that.

The heat from the flames intensified. The window of time for escape narrowed. The entire top floor was only minutes away from collapsing. Through blurred eyes, Bo spied the service door on the back wall, and hope surged through him.

He jerked his shirt off and flung it across Star's eyes. She tossed her head nervously, but he ran a soothing hand along her side.

"All right, girl," he said with more calm than he felt. "It's up to you to get Teddie out of here. You can do it."

With one hand bracing Teddie securely on the pony's back, and the other on her mane, he limped toward the door. The latch opened with a tug of his bleeding hands.

"Hang on tight, Teddie. She'll take care of you." He used the last of his remaining strength to throw open the door, and with a strangled shout, slapped his hat across Star's rump. As he tried to follow them through the door the smoke overcame him and he collapsed inside the burning barn.

Abby pushed her way through the hysterical crowd. Buck scurried right behind her. Star raced past from behind the barn with Teddie struggling to stay on her back.

"Help! Somebody! Help!" the boy cried.

"Hang on, Teddie!" Abby ran after them, stumbling and shouting, her heart in her throat.

Karl rushed forward, grabbed the shirt from Star's head and threw his arms around her neck. Digging his heels in the dirt, he brought her to a halt a safe distance from the chaos of the arena. With help from one of the other volunteers, they eased the boy to the ground. Others hurried to assist, shouting instructions.

"He's hurt, be careful," one of them yelled.

"Get back and let the medics through." A fireman held back the swarming crowd.

"Somebody see to that pony. And call Doc Wilcox," another volunteer shouted.

"Mom…meee?" Teddie's small voice quavered.

Caroline North rushed to where her son lay. She knelt beside him, crooning softly while she caressed his face.

After a bit, Abby urged her to move away. "Come on, Caroline, let the medics take care of Teddie. Stand over here, where he can still see you." She led the frantic mother aside, keeping a comforting arm around the woman's shoulder. "He's going to be all right."

"Is Bo okay?" Teddie looked from his mother to Abby. "Is he? He got out, didn't he?" A sob escaped from the boy's throat.

"I'm sure he did," Abby said, uncertainty gnawing its way to the pit of her stomach. "Where was he when you and Star escaped?"

She scanned the smoldering building. Firemen kept running back and forth, shouting and aiming huge fire hoses at the blaze. They were volunteers, but as professional as any big city organization. And every man there knew Buck and Abby Houston personally.

"He put me on Star's back. Then he shooed us out," Teddie said between shuddering breaths. "It was scary in there, Mommy. I could hardly see, and I fell down, but Star stayed with me so I wouldn't be afraid. I'm sure glad Bo found us."

"You were very brave, Teddie," Abby said, moving aside so the paramedic could splint the child's arm for transporting to the hospital in nearby Granite City.

"That's what Bo told me. He said I was a real cowboy, being so brave." Teddie's smile blossomed across his soot-covered face like a ray of sunshine through a dark cloud.

A surge of tenderness warmed Abby's heart. There was no doubt in her mind that Bo was the brave one. He'd proved that by putting his life on the line to save a child. She understood now. He'd done the same thing when he married Marla. He'd altered his life to give his name to a child he believed he'd fathered. It was the honorable thing to do. He'd been a hero then, too. A misjudged one in the eyes of the community. This time an actual child was involved. And Abby was here instead of Marla. But where was Bo?

As soon as she was certain the boy was being cared for, Abby gave his mother a quick hug, then turned to Buck. "Have they found Bo?"

Buck shook his head. "Not yet."

"I'm going to find him." She darted around him and headed for the area behind the barn.

"You can't…" Her father grabbed her arm, tried to pull her back.

"No, Pop. Don't you understand? He could be unconscious in there, or badly injured. I have to find him. He needs me." She jerked free and ran past him, past the shouting firemen, ignoring their warnings.

Fallen timbers, scorched and smoking, lay in her path, but she jumped over them, paying no mind to the danger they presented. All she could think about was Bo. She had to get to him. *Please God, let him be all right.*

She found him sprawled on the ground just outside the rear of the barn. Despite his dirt-smudged face and blackened clothes, he was the most beautiful sight she'd ever seen.

Scrambling over smoldering debris to reach him, she knelt beside him. "Bo, oh Bo," she whispered. "Thank God you made it out."

Through tear-filled eyes, she gazed at him longingly, eager to reassure herself he was really alive. She wanted to hold him close, touch him all over, smother his face with kisses, but she didn't dare. Instead, she brushed her lips lightly across his. Her tears of joy landed on his cheek and left a shiny trail on his soot-blackened face.

His eyes opened slowly. He reached for her hand and lifted it to his lips. "Well, darlin'," he breathed against her palm, "I...figured...we had some...unfinished business to take care of." A harsh cough tore loose from his chest. His eyelids fluttered, and his hand dropped to his side.

"Oh, Bo!" Abby jumped up and shouted toward the emergency crew. "Help! Please! He needs oxygen! Over here!" She waved her arms in the air, frantically trying to catch the attention of someone in the crowd.

A young paramedic rushed to her side, quickly clamping an oxygen mask on Bo's face while another checked his vital signs. "Step back, ma'am, and we'll take care of him."

She knew they would, but she couldn't bear to let him go. She hung on to his hand and ran alongside as they carried him out of the area of danger, her mind spinning with myriad thoughts. What if he hadn't managed to escape? What if…? The sudden realization that he could have died because she had goaded him into helping Teddie was almost more than she could stand. *Dear God, hadn't he endured enough?* A wave of bitter nausea swept over her, and she stopped to lean her head down until the dizziness passed.

"Abby-girl, are you all right?" Buck appeared out of the crowd, tucked his arm around her waist and led her away. "Sit." He gently eased her to the ground, then knelt beside her.

"Oh, Pop, everything is gone." She buried her face in his comforting shoulder. "All of it." The magnitude of the disaster hit her full force, and her whole body trembled with shock. Buck held her close and let her cry. "We'll get through it, Abby. We'll find a way."

"But…what am I going to do about Bo?"

Banner Medical Center bustled with overly eager interns making rounds with overworked doctors, and harried nurses doing their best to efficiently carry out too many orders in too little time. Typical procedure on any given day in Granite City's only hospital.

Lying on the gurney in the emergency room, Bo watched through a haze of pain-killers as the nurse on duty finished treating his hands. He remembered the last time he'd been a guest in an E.R. cubicle. Admittedly, he didn't remember a lot about that episode except the pain—too much of it. The team attending him back then hadn't had the luxury of extra time to practice gentleness. Their job had been to put him back together and they'd done it expertly, with confidence. Thankfully, the sweet release of sleep-inducing drugs had kept him from remembering the worst part of the ordeal.

Today his injuries weren't life-threatening. Plenty of time for the nurse to practice her skill. Her smile was genuinely reassuring— her touch gentle and compassionate. No unnecessary motions, just quiet confidence. She reminded him of someone from his past, but he couldn't quite clear the fuzz from his brain enough to snag the image and bring it to the surface of his mind.

Though his eyes were treated with drops to prevent further inflamation, he was still able to watch the nurse move about the small area. The shot of painkiller he'd received when he first arrived was taking effect with amazing speed. He drifted in a soft, cloudy haze, only half-aware of his surroundings. Not really caring.

He turned his head at the scraping sound of a curtain being drawn back along a metal rod. Through a fog of wavering consciousness, he thought he saw an angel wearing soot-covered jeans and a baseball cap. He squinted, tried to focus. Nope. Not a wing in sight.

"Miss, you'll have to wait outside until we're finished here." The nurse's quiet, yet stern directive was clearly being ignored as the angel strode past the woman without so much as a nod. "Miss, you can't stay in here."

Abby wasn't about to be scooted out. She moved closer to the bed. "I'm not leaving."

She needed to touch him. Her hand shook as she reached out to stroke his face.

The crooked grin lifting the corner of his mouth triggered an ache deep inside her chest. A tightness that made it difficult to breathe, yet calmed her with an immense sensation of relief. *Thank you, God.*

"You look…" his hoarse voice broke as his intense gaze swept over her, "damned beautiful."

She laughed softly as she pulled her cap off and ran a hand through her tangled hair. "Seriously, how are you feeling?"

"Right now, pretty scuzzy."

He coughed harshly and raised up on one elbow. "What about Teddie? And Star? Did they make it out okay?" Anxiousness furrowed his brow.

"Yes, thanks to you. They're both going to be fine. Teddie's arm had a clean break. He wants you to sign his cast." She sat down carefully on the edge of the bed. "You're a hero, you know."

She trailed her fingers along his arm, rested

them lightly on his bandaged hand. Watched with a heart brimming with unshed tears as his soot-darkened fingers curled around hers.

"No, I'm not. Not even close." He looked straight at her, his eyes dark, his mood suddenly somber. "So don't be telling Teddie any different, you hear?"

"You'll never convince him otherwise." She leaned over and brushed his lips with hers. "Me, either."

He grasped her arm with his good hand, drew her down and growled deep in his throat. "Get me out of here, darlin' and I'll convince you of a helluva lot more." One dark eyebrow quirked suggestively.

"I'm working on it, Ramsey. I'm definitely working on it."

Chapter Fifteen

"You're going to bed, so no arguments."
They'd only just returned to Bo's cabin from
the hospital, and Abby was well aware that
he was exhausted and weak.

She folded back the well-worn quilt and
plumped the feather pillows on his bed, before helping him from the chair where he'd
been sitting. His skin still appeared ashen,
and she wanted to get him into bed before
he collapsed.

The doctors had been reluctant to discharge
him, doing so only when she promised to stay
with him and see to his care. Now it was up

to her to keep that promise, even if Bo didn't think he needed her help. Stubborn cowboy.

He'd been quiet on the way back from the hospital, and no wonder. The fire that destroyed her barn hours earlier had nearly claimed him, as well. His superhuman effort to rescue Teddie and Star had proved his strength to anyone who might have doubted his competence.

She hadn't pressed him for details, just let him talk when he felt like it. She'd explained that Buck and Shorty were still at the site, along with the fire inspector. The horses had been trucked over to Shorty's for the time being. Hopefully, the cause of the blaze would be found soon. Then the monumental cleanup process would begin.

She still trembled at the vivid memory of seeing Bo lying motionless on the ground. Of flames racing through the building and black smoke engulfing the entire area. The sickening feeling that she'd lost him forever had sent her in search of the nearest bush. So much for her strong constitution.

She snapped her attention back to the job at hand. Caring for Bo was her priority now.

"While you get settled, I'll fix some soup.

Or would you like something more substantial?"

He made a face when she eased him onto the bed and gently worked his grimy T-shirt over his head. "Soup'll do," he said and leaned over to toe his boots off. Abby knelt to help, then unzipped his jeans and slid them off.

With a weak "Thanks," he flopped back on the bed and closed his eyes. His bandaged hand rested on his bare abdomen, the other lay unmoving at his side. He never stirred when she pulled the sheet up and tucked it around his shoulders.

She started out of the room carrying his charred boots, stopping momentarily to ask if he wanted toast with his soup. His soft snores told her he didn't really care. Careful not to make any noise, she closed the door behind her and tiptoed to the kitchen.

The layout of the house was unfamiliar, but it only took a few minutes to explore the small rooms. At one time, it had been the ranch foreman's lodging, but there hadn't been an actual manager on the place for a number of years. Recently, the three-room cabin located behind the main house had been restored to use as guest quarters for the occasional out-of-state cattle buyers. Shorty had offered it to Bo as a temporary place to stay after he was able to take care of himself.

Abby looked around. The kitchen was tiny, but efficiently arranged. The small pantry was well stocked, but she doubted Bo had done much of his own cooking. It didn't take long for her to heat a can of vegetable soup. Not exactly steak and potatoes, but probably easier to digest in his weakened condition. Deciding on a soothing cup of herbal tea for her patient instead of coffee, she filled a blue-speckled teakettle and put it on to boil.

When she carried the tray into the bedroom half an hour later, the sun had already slipped behind the horizon. Pink and gold shadows filtered through the bedroom window and played across Bo's sleeping figure. Abby put the tray on the bedside table, then pulled the rocker closer and sat down.

He had to be exhausted. She decided to let him sleep. The hot tea tempted her, so she helped herself to the cup and settled back to wait. No point in letting it get cold, she thought, inhaling the fragrant brew before taking a sip.

Weariness seeped through her. She sat there in the darkening room, quietly rocking and sipping her tea, mesmerized by the rhythmic rise and fall of his chest. Images drifted in and out of her mind's eye. Images of the first time they'd met. Of the two of them as their relationship had grown from that sudden, make-your-toes-tingle awareness to a total surrender of body and soul. Then Marla's face appeared, intruding in Abby's private reverie, and she felt a familiar ache return to her heart.

She placed her empty cup on the tray and leaned back with her eyes closed, trying to dispel those painful memories. She needed to remember the reason she'd fallen in love with Bo. The reason she'd trusted him with her heart. Maybe then, she could reconcile the way she felt toward him now.

He'd been easy to fall in love with. Treated her as if she was special. Someone who mattered. No one but Pop had ever done that. She'd been barely twenty-three at the time, with only one unlucky college relationship for comparison. Pathetic, but true. So, how was she to know that love would show up in the form of a rugged cowboy? One who understood her love for ranching. He thought she looked beautiful even when she was driving a tractor or cleaning out the barn—and told her so over and over again.

It hadn't mattered to him that she didn't own satin and lace. Or that she'd left the university in Austin before finishing her second year, in order to come back and help Pop. Money had been hard to come by, yet Bo had made her feel like a princess. She'd been rich with love, and nothing else had mattered.

She'd given him her heart and trusted him not to break it. It had never been her own again. He'd promised to keep it safe and had offered her his own heart—and his love. They had shared a part of themselves on that special night when they declared their love, and Abby thought her life was complete.

Then Bo told her he was leaving Sweet River to make a career with the rodeo. He wanted her to go with him. Their awful argument had followed, but she'd secretly held out hope for a reconciliation. When Bo left with Marla, Abby's heart felt like a war-torn combat zone.

She looked at the man lying on the bed and wondered if she dared trust him again. Now that he'd told her the truth about Marla, she realized he'd never meant to hurt her back then. But, forgiveness didn't come easy, and she wasn't sure she could ever forget. He still had the power to break her heart. She knew that as sure as she knew her name, because she loved him. Always had, always would. Admitting that scared the living daylights out of her.

The stress of the day settled on her shoulders, a heavy weight she could do without. She rubbed the back of her neck but the tension remained knotted there. Obviously, she couldn't make any competent decisions tonight. *Maybe a shower will help me relax.* Falling asleep was doubtful, but at least she would be clean.

An hour later, with the cool night breeze nipping her skin, she slipped silently across the room. A thick towel and a silver shaft of moonlight were her only garments. She stifled a sudden yawn and gazed longingly at the sleeping man—and the soft bed. If she hadn't been so exhausted, she might have considered going back home and tackling the mountain of decisions waiting for her there, but the long, hot shower had relaxed her to the point of drowsiness, made her so heavy-lidded she couldn't keep her eyes open. She let the towel drop to the floor and crawled quietly into the bed. With a long sigh of contentment, she snuggled her chilled, naked body next to Bo's warm one. And slept.

* * *

He awoke to the surprising realization that his burned hand wasn't the only thing throbbing. Damn. Must be morning, the way the sun was poking its glaring rays through the sheer curtains of the bedroom window. The intrusive brightness made his eyes smart… when he finally managed to get them open.

Something soft and warm was pushing against his personal morning wake-up call. *What the…?* He opened his eyes wider and wondered, in the space of a heartbeat, if he'd died and gone to that magical place where dreams come true. Where else would he find himself in such a fine situation?

He looked under the rumpled sheet for confirmation. Well, well, well. Sure enough, Abby's enticing bare backside was smack up against his rock-hard erection. He didn't know which way to turn, but obviously, his body did. Now, if he could just shift a little bit to the right, he could slide his bandaged hand out of the way. He hitched himself up carefully on one elbow and managed to keep the body contact without waking her. Or so he thought.

"Mmmmmm…" Abby wiggled again and turned over to face him. Sleep-heavy, navy blue eyes opened slowly and gazed at him through lush, gold-tipped lashes. He was lost, with no chance of rescue. *Do not send help*.

"Good morning."

Her throaty purr curled its way through his nervous system, leaving him a long way from calm and a short way from paradise. Her drowsy greeting was accompanied by a languid overhead stretch that pulled her body taut, every mouthwatering inch right out there for his delighted appreciation. He swallowed hard, struggled for control and appreciated like hell.

"Yeah, definitely good," he agreed when he finally untangled his thoughts. The soft curve of her neck was just asking to be tasted. He did, happily. The fresh scent of his Irish Spring bath soap lingered on her skin, and he wondered when she had showered. Wished he had shared it with her. He kissed her left breast. "Absolutely the best." Now the right one. "Oh, yeah." A third kiss landed on her shoulder.

When she reached for him, his gut tightened, his blood pumped hot and headed straight south.

"Have mercy, woman," he groaned, right

before she fitted her mouth on his. "You still take my breath away."

The kiss was sweeter than he'd hoped for—briefer than he'd wanted. The taste of her lingered on his lips. He relished it—wanted more—but she moved away and eased over him, bracing her hands on either side of his head. *Oh, man.* He gulped air, closed his eyes, and counted his blessings. To his everlasting delight, she leaned forward just enough for her breasts to brush his chest. When her tight nipples nudged his, the contact sent a jolt of electricity zigzagging through his body.

"Slow down, darlin', or the show'll be over before the curtain even goes up."

He had to make it perfect this time. For both of them. Clenching his jaw, he slowed his pulse by sheer force of determination, and scooted out from under her.

She rolled to her side, eyed him warily. "Problem?"

He slanted a crooked grin, pulled open the drawer of the nightstand and latched on to one of two foil packets he'd tossed in there when he'd moved his gear from the main house. "Not anymore, but I might need some help." He held up his bandaged hand.

Her eyes sparkled in anticipation as she

tugged off his shorts. "My pleasure to assist," she said, her smile matching his.

The touch of her hand nearly set him off. He sucked in his breath, which he seemed to be doing a lot of lately, grabbed her hand, and held it away from his body until he could bring his eyes back into focus. "Sweet mercy, not yet, honey. Not just yet."

The unopened packet slipped to the floor when he released her fingers. She walked them up his abdomen, trailed them maddeningly along his ribs, tested his measured control beyond reasonable endurance. His breath *whooshed* from his chest with a shudder.

"Aw, Abby darlin', I want you so much it's killing me, but please, give me a chance to make you want me, too."

He kissed her full lips, her eyelids, the tip of her nose, trying not to miss any delicate part of her face. He curved his arm so that her head cradled against his shoulder and his bulky bandaged hand was out of the way. Useless damned thing.

With his good hand, he stoked the fires within her, felt her dampness. Rockets went off in his brain. He kissed her again, and his heart hammered when she thrust her tongue deep inside his mouth to claim his very soul.

Give me strength. Could a kiss last forever? He hoped so. Reluctantly, he raised his head. His breath jerked hard as if he'd just run a marathon. He caressed her with his gaze and concentrated on the moment at hand. "Darlin', you are one fine kisser."

He had to slow down or risk losing the chance to make love with the one woman who would always own his heart. And she deserved more than a quick shuffle between the sheets. This was Abby—his heart's own life. He wanted to give her loving like she'd never had before. Loving her made him a whole man, in his soul, if not in his body. Was he selfish to want her? Could she love him in spite of his busted-up body? Ah, hell, did he even deserve her?

Abby felt the world shift beneath her. She clung to him when he started to move away, not ready to relinquish the wonderful sensation thrumming through her. That heady feeling of being on the brink of flying into space without wings. Her fingers dug into his shoulders and she held on.

"Stay," she whispered, pulling him back. She wrapped her arms around his waist, placed a moist kiss on his chest, tasted his salty skin.

"Darlin', I need a shower. I'm sweaty and smell like a side of barbecued beef." He brushed her forehead with a tender kiss.

"I don't care." And she didn't. All she wanted was for him to be inside her. Now. Not later. Not after a shower. Right now. She wanted the smell of him on her own skin, in her own pores. Nothing was going to change her mind. However...

She smiled, put her lips close to his ear and whispered. "If you promise to let me help you shower, I might reconsider." She shivered at her own suggestive words.

Bo's eyes lit up. She loved that about him— the fact that he didn't try to hide his pleasure—and that she was the one who pleased him. Slowly, she eased her legs over the side of the bed and held out her hand to him.

With his good hand in hers, she led him down the hall to the bathroom. When she had the shower turned on and the temperature adjusted, she helped him in, and they stood facing each other under the pelting spray.

"I don't think I'm supposed to get this bandage wet," Bo said as streams of water soaked his head and ran down his face.

She licked at a rivulet glistening near the corner of his mouth. "Probably not." She caught another one as it dripped off his chin. "Hold your arm out away from the spray and I'll take care of the rest of you."

"Yes, ma'am," he said, pleasure shining in his eyes.

She grinned at him, grabbed the soap and began to swirl foamy soap circles down his shoulders, across his chest. His abdomen tightened beneath the slow, seductive journey of her fingers.

Following the path of his rib cage, her hands wandered lower, exploring the muscles that twitched on the inside of his thighs. Her knuckles brushed his throbbing hardness, wrenching a whispered oath from him and a sigh from her. Soap had never been so stimulating—or so much fun.

A groan came from somewhere deep in his throat, an emotional admission of desire. The pure sensuality of the heartfelt sound excited her, made her knees wobble. That she had the ability to elicit such raw emotion from him filled her with unexpected pride in her own femininity.

"You do realize you're latherin' up a lot more than soap, don't you?" He looked at her through dark eyes filled with yearning. And oh, the promise they held.

"The shower was your idea, Ramsey," she answered and blew away the soap bubbles coating his rigid erection. "I only offered to help. You wanted clean. I'll give you clean."

His undisguised eagerness made her own body quiver with need, yet she wanted to savor this opportunity to control his pleasure, to draw it out until they both had no control at all. A fine plan if she could hold out long enough.

She scooted around to stand behind him. His buttocks were hard and tight when she pulled him against her. Desire gripped her, pooled low and simmered in her belly. For one exquisite moment they stood body to body, slick skin against slick skin, aroused by the warm cascade of water sliding over them. Scarcely breathing.

He was the first to break the silence. "This feeling is way too good to waste in a shower." Glib words, but his voice was thick and emotion-filled. He pulled her hands away from his waist and turned halfway around. "I'm shuttin' the damn water off."

Okay. Absolutely no argument from her. Forget the plan. After all, she'd been ready before he insisted on the shower. She wanted all of him, and her need was stronger than ever before. Because she could finally admit to herself that she loved him.

"Are you sure you're clean enough?" Even as her hands slid over his water-slick skin and hard angles, the chance to tease tempted her.

"Darlin', if I get any more slippery, I won't be able to stay on the bed." He grabbed a towel from the towel bar, slung it around them both and maneuvered their dripping bodies toward the bed.

Laughing, kissing, they fell onto the rumpled sheets, wet hair tangled in their eyes, wet bodies stuck together—wet mouths open and eager.

Suddenly, his laughter stopped, replaced by ragged breathing and urgently whispered words. "Where's the damn condom?"

She clapped a hand over her mouth, bit back a burst of laughter and lifted her shoulders in bewilderment as he raised up from the bed.

"There's nothing funny about this." He scrounged around in a frenzied effort to snatch the last precious packet from the drawer, clutched it tight in his fist and flopped back. Embarrassment flushed his face deep red.

Abby rubbed her cheek against his shoulder. "It's okay, Ramsey," she said softly. "I'm willing to wait."

He sat straight up. "You think I'm not… that I can't…?"

Puzzled, she glanced down. *Well, hello.* "Obviously, I was mistaken. It's just that you looked flustered." She smiled, delighted that she'd been so wrong.

"Hell, yes, I'm flustered. I wanted this to be perfect for you, and what happens? I lose the damned rubber. Like a bumbling fifteen-year-old on his first try."

She slipped the tiny packet from his fingers and looked straight into his dark eyes. "You're definitely not fifteen, Ramsey. And everything will be perfect. If we ever get around to it." She kissed him then, thoroughly, exquisitely.

At the first crackle of foil ripping, Bo's heart rate shot skyward. He felt her sheathe him and silently counted his blessings. *Busy hands, happy man.* The thought filled him with wonder as they shared another soul-deep kiss. *As long as they're Abby's hands.* He was just about the happiest cowboy in the entire Lone Star state. Oh, yeah.

It was his turn now. He rolled on top of her, nudged her legs apart with his knee and settled between them. He could barely contain his exuberance. Could anything be sweeter than being with her?

"Much obliged, Miss Abby," he teased.

He nipped the corner of her mouth, traced the outline of her lips with his tongue. Roamed her lush curves with his good hand while he invaded her mouth, savored her delicate taste on his tongue. A rush of painful need hit his gut. Blindsided him. He wanted to be inside her. Needed to feel her tight around him. He'd reached his limit of endurance.

She must have read his mind. "I aim to please, Ramsey. Now, shut up and make love to me."

Thank you. Thank you. Thank you. There was absolutely no need to ask him twice. He positioned himself above her, anticipation and need driving him quietly, exquisitely out of his mind. Without any further preliminaries, she was there, ready for him. Hot and wet, she throbbed around him the instant he entered her.

He didn't move. Didn't dare. Just let the feeling of their intimate joining suspend them in ecstasy. Aware of nothing but the heat of being buried deep inside her, his intense need accelerated as he felt her soften, welcome him. Her tiny whimpers sent his mind reeling. His body was so sensitized, it responded instantly to her slightest quiver. He increased his tempo, driving deeper until he lost all track of time and place. The upward thrusts of her hips matched the rhythm of his strokes. Sent him racing to the highest peak, left him rocking there while she pulsed and tightened around him.

Her unrestrained passion amazed him. The explosive hunger she exhibited for him was a gift he hadn't expected. He'd never be the same after this. No matter what happened, his love for her would always be there, in the center of his heart—forever in his soul.

And if he had no more days on earth beyond today, he'd always be grateful for this moment Abby had given him.

He soared as their bodies strained to reach that elusive summit. "I…can't…hold on… much longer, darlin'. Are you…?"

"Yes—yes—yessssss!"

Her cry of ecstasy was all he needed. With a final burst of urgency he drove deeper, felt the warm flood of her release surround him. He came hot and hard as they tumbled into the universe—together.

Chapter Sixteen

Horns honked. Men shouted. Sun streamed through the open window of Bo's bedroom.

Abby shot straight up in bed. The cool morning air slapped her bare skin awake, demanding her attention.

She rubbed her eyes, squinted to focus on the clock on the nightstand, and groaned. She must've fallen asleep after they'd made love. A smile started from somewhere in the vicinity of her heart.

Next to her, Bo stirred and flopped over on his stomach. She eased the tangled sheet from under his leg and pulled it up over his naked torso. The urge to run her hands over that hard, sexy body nearly got the best of her. Good thing he'd only had one condom or they wouldn't have gotten any sleep at all. She placed a soft kiss between his shoulder blades and slipped quietly from the bed.

Standing at the window, she had a clear view of the drive in front of the barn. Stuart Wilcox climbed from his Tahoe and began unloading all sorts of boxes and equipment. She watched Shorty hurry from the barn to meet him with Ditch loping along at his heels.

Her horses milled around the fenced in pasture near the barn, cropping the grass and looking quite content. None of them appeared to have any major problems as a result of their close call in the fire. She knew Stuart had inspected them carefully before Pop and Shorty trucked them over here last night while she stayed at the hospital with Teddie and Bo.

The glaring, oversized numerals of the clock reminded her that it was well on to midmorning. She hadn't intended for this to happen. Now she had to go out there and face Stuart and Shorty. *Oh, great.*

She was in and out of the bathroom in record time, tugging on her clothes and wondering how on earth she was going to account for her presence here at this time of day. It wouldn't take much deep thinking for anyone to figure out that she'd spent the entire night with Bo.

The last button on her shirt refused to cooperate. She swore softly and left it open, then gasped when she stopped in front of the mirror to run her fingers through her tangled hair.

There was no mistaking what had occupied her time only a few hours earlier. She looked like the poster girl for The Morning After. Her lips were still kiss-swollen and her cheeks held a pleasure-pink blush. To be perfectly honest, she felt like her whole body glowed. And it probably did. There was nothing to compare with this feeling of having been thoroughly, totally and exquisitely loved.

But all good things must eventually…wake up. She glanced at Bo's sleeping figure and smiled. This particular good thing would be waking up very soon. The temptation to crawl back in bed with him was downright risky. Her body hummed with remembered delight. She only hoped their overenthusiastic activities last night hadn't complicated his injuries. She recalled with satisfaction that he definitely hadn't shown any signs of weakness. None at all.

She should never have gotten into his bed in the first place, but the need to feel the closeness of his body had overruled her good sense. She needed to be reassured that she hadn't lost him. She'd only meant to sleep next to him. *Oh, go ahead, admit you wanted to make love with him and stop dodging the truth.* The smile spreading across her face felt like it reached from ear to ear.

She sat on the chair to tug on her boots, but one slipped out of her hands with a *thunk*. She glanced toward the bed. Darn.

He was propped up on his elbow, watching her with a slow, sleepy scrutiny that tripped her heartbeat. Loaded her senses with such a warm, liquid heaviness, her limbs felt floaty and disconnected to her body.

"Goin' somewhere without telling me?" One dark eyebrow lifted.

She could hardly get her other boot on. "Not really. I, uh, heard Stuart drive up and thought I should be there when he checks out the horses. I was going to wake you before I went out. Honest." She walked to the side of the bed. Couldn't keep herself from touching his face.

He snagged her hand and pulled her close for a mind-boggling kiss. "Can't that wait till later? Much later?" His mouth was on hers and his words were warm on her lips, too tempting to be safe.

She tipped her head back a fraction. "Huh-uh. Gotta go now, Ramsey." She kissed him lightly. Darn, she just couldn't keep her mouth off of his. Addicted to kissing him. Lovely.

Bo sat up, eased his legs over the side of the bed and snatched his jeans from the floor. "Then, I'll go with you," he said, zipping up. "Some of those horses might still be spooked. You'll need all the help you can get if they get out of hand."

Shaking her head, Abby put a hand out to keep him from following her. "Wait a few minutes, will you?" She looked deep in his eyes for understanding. "I'd better speak to Stuart alone first. I should have done it sooner."

He took her hand, brought the palm to his mouth and planted a soft kiss there before sliding his fingers inside her half-buttoned shirtfront. "Yeah, I guess you're right, darlin'. It's pretty obvious how mooney-eyed you've got him."

Abby swatted halfheartedly at Bo's wandering hand and wiggled to straighten her clothing back to a respectable order. Feeble efforts that weren't working at all. "I don't think Stuart's ever been mooney-eyed over anything, Ramsey. But he happens to be a very nice man. And he's a friend." She took a backward step toward the door. "Give me some time before you come out. Please?"

His grumbled agreement wasn't exactly cheerful. Especially after he'd spotted the lost foil packet on the floor next to his boots.

The screen door slammed and her boots tattooed on the wooden steps as she hurried from the porch to the gravel drive. Stuart and Shorty both glanced up when she approached the Tahoe.

"Well, this is a surprise, Abby." Stuart's strained expression didn't fool anyone. His effort to hide his shock as he watched her walk out of Bo's cabin was far from convincing and Abby deeply regretted the hurt she'd caused him.

"Hello, Stuart. Shorty." She nodded to both men, then quickly averted her eyes to hide any remnants of her night with Bo that might still be apparent.

From Shorty's frown, she was sure her face gave her away and she tried to straighten out her smile to something less giddy. After all, she had a disaster to deal with. A loss of property that may well put Pop and her in the poorhouse, if such a place still existed. And there were her special kids to think about.

"Mornin'." Shorty's brief greeting came with his own brand of knowing smile. "How long you been here, missy?"

Darn him. She'd been hoping to avoid that particular question. She swallowed, fiddled with the buttons on her shirt. "Awhile." Turning to Stuart, she motioned to his medical bag. "Do any of the horses need attention?"

"I just got here. I haven't had a chance to look at them this morning." He stood ramrod stiff, shoulders squared, arms at his side. His face was solemn and unreadable. Well, not quite.

Abby knew she couldn't put it off. She turned to Shorty. "Would you give Stuart and I a few minutes alone? I need to speak with him privately. Please?"

Without a word, which was unusual enough to worry her, Shorty gave her a slow wink and retreated. "I'll be in the barn, if you need me."

She could've hugged him for not demanding any further explanation.

Taking a deep breath for courage, she said softly, "Stuart, I'm sorry."

He shook his head. "Don't be. I should've

known. All the signs were there, even before your cowboy came back to town."

He took her hands in his, looked at her with a longing, a sadness, that made tears sting her eyes.

"Oh, Stuart. I never meant to hurt you. I've always enjoyed being with you. You're a wonderful person and a dear friend." *I absolutely hate doing this.*

"And you've been sending those 'dear friend' signals all along," he said. "I just chose to ignore them, hoping they'd eventually change from *stop* to *go.*"

He tipped her chin up, thumbed the single tear from her cheek. "Hey, it's all right. You were never anything but honest with me. Call me a hopeless optimist. Or a hopeless dreamer. Either way, you're not to blame. Life goes on. I wish you happiness, Abby. Always." He dropped his hand, shoved it in his pocket.

"Thank you, Stuart. I'd like very much to still be your friend." The lump in her throat burned like the dickens. She reached out to touch his arm, but he stepped back. She understood. Their friendship would never be the same. She'd have to remember that. She had hurt him, and though it was unintentional, he needed time to forgive her. If he could. Hurt and forgiveness were two words she knew quite well.

Stuart cleared his throat. "By the way, I'll just keep those saddles and blankets I'd ordered for the kids at my place until you're back on your feet again. And you'll need the helmets replaced. I'll take care of that, too."

The kindness in his eyes told her she was already forgiven—a little. Stuart was a special man. Abby hoped someday he'd find a woman who would appreciate him the way he deserved.

"I don't know what to say. 'Thank you' seems insignificant, in light of all you've done. But, it'll have to do for now, I guess." She offered him a smile of gratitude. "Why don't we get busy checking on those horses of mine?"

Stuart inclined his head toward the house. "What about him? Your cowboy."

Your cowboy. The possessive term tipped her composure off-kilter. She paused to regroup. "Oh, he'll be along in a bit. He wants to help, but he's not a hundred percent recovered from last night."

Stuart raised an eyebrow, glanced from her crookedly buttoned shirt placket, to the cottage and back again. "You mean from the fire, don't you?" His mouth curved in amusement.

A blush warmed Abby's face. "Of course, what else?" She couldn't conceal her own smile, though. Didn't even try. Just fell in step beside him as he walked to the barn.

A week had passed since the fire. Abby had been too involved to help at the café, but today she made a point of stopping by to see IdaJoy and get her opinion on the fund-raiser.

IdaJoy set a glass of iced tea in front of Abby. "You've been mighty busy these last few days, hon. Is everything okay?" She glanced beyond the lunch counter to check on the last of the customers enjoying the noon special of chicken-fried steak, then turned her attention back to her favorite friend.

Abby shrugged. The past week had seemed longer than a lifetime, and she was bone-weary. The stress of dealing with the million and one problems caused by the fire had given her a nagging headache. She dug in her shirt pocket for the antacid tablets she'd begun to carry with her.

"A rodeo seems to be the best solution to our money problems. I was against having one, but I was overruled. Shorty's going to help us get the publicity out to the media and distribute the posters around. The only thing left to do is confirm the lineup of contestants. Bo's contacting some of his rodeo buddies to see if they're available. I'm keeping my fingers crossed. We want to have it as soon as we can." She tossed the pills in her mouth, followed them with a swallow of tea.

"What about the kids? You gonna give them a chance to be in the show?" The waitress rested one hip against the counter. "Some of them ride real good now. You know, Laura would love to be a part of it."

"That's the big question right now," Abby said. "I'd like to have some opinions from you and the rest of the volunteers. I know the students would be thrilled to show off their skills. Most of them, anyway." She rubbed her forehead, smoothed the worry lines there. "I'm just not certain it's wise. Safety has to be considered. I couldn't stand it if we had any more accidents."

"But, I thought the fire started from a bad electrical connection or something," IdaJoy said, unwrapping a stick of gum from the stash she kept under the counter. "A faulty light fixture, wasn't it? That's what Shorty told me, other day." She had the gum in her mouth, cracking it between her molars in the space of a second.

Abby nodded. "Yes, and I meant to replace the defective bulbs, but hadn't gotten around to it, so I am to blame." Her shoulders sagged.

"Oh, fiddlesticks," IdaJoy said. "Just quit tryin' to carry the world's worry on your bitty shoulders, hon. Nobody blames you, at all." She patted Abby's hand. "What we need to do now is get this show organized. Fast. You've got plenty of friends to help you, so stop fretting. And for goodness sake, put those dog-gone pills away."

Abby studied a drop of condensation forming on the outside of her glass of tea, wiped it with one finger, then looked up with a sigh. "The fact is, Teddie and Bo were injured and I could've prevented it. They were lucky they weren't hurt more seriously."

IdaJoy shook her head vigorously and leaned forward, getting right in Abby's face. "Yes, they were. So you should be thankful and just get on with what has to be done. Sugar, if I'd let all my shoulduv's and coulduv's get me down, why, I'd never have stuck my neck out to buy this café. All I had to start with was my cussed stubbornness and a big mortgage." She flashed a wide satisfied smile. "And I did mighty fine. Got me more customers than I can feed on a good day." She cracked her gum again. "You know I'm right."

Abby wasn't about to disagree. She knew IdaJoy had worked for the Clancys until their retirement four years ago. When they announced the sale of the café to their number one waitress, the entire community was happy for both the seller and the buyer. And IdaJoy didn't exaggerate when she said she started with next to nothing. Hard work and determination had made her business pay off. Of course, her optimism hadn't hurt, either.

Something about the other woman's fierce pride settled Abby's indecision. She finished her tea and slid off the stool.

"Thanks, IdaJoy, you've just given me the answer I've been looking for. If we work hard, I'll guarantee this will be the best darned show ever. Our kids will have everyone stomping and whistling. Are you game?"

IdaJoy rubbed her hands together. "You know me, hon, I'm game for anything. Whatever it takes." Her eyes sparkled with excitement, her voice reaching nails-on-chalkboard quality. "Is Bo gonna ride, too?"

Abby hesitated. "Mmm, I don't know. He hasn't agreed to anything more than helping out with the contestants, so far." She turned to go. "I'll let you know when our next session will be. Shorty's letting us use his place until we get our barn rebuilt and inspected."

"Having Bo's name on the posters and ads ought to make people sit up and take notice. I'm gonna put two of 'em up in here." IdaJoy continued talking even though Abby was already opening the door. "I've got an idea for costumes for the kids, too." Her escalating voice followed Abby out to the parking lot. "I'll even help sew 'em up. I've got a sewing machine, you know."

Abby waved and got in her car. Costumes? Oh, Lordy. She pulled a frown as she drove off. Knowing IdaJoy's eclectic taste in fashion, that idea could prove to be a colorful subject for discussion with the parents of the students. Still, IdaJoy was a big hit with the students, and her offer of help was appreciated.

The knot of tension between her shoulders tightened. One more thing to think about. And she hadn't even resolved the issue with Bo yet. There had to be a way to convince him to participate in the rodeo. He didn't have to enter any competition. She would never expect that of him. Just lead the opening parade, that's all. His reluctance to ride a horse puzzled her, since she knew he'd recovered sufficiently enough to engage in other activities.

An inner smile warmed her heart, as she remembered the past days they'd spent together. She'd been reluctant to stay every night at the cottage, knowing there were so many issues to deal with regarding the devastation left by the fire. Too many for Pop to handle alone.

She'd managed to spend a portion of each day there until she was certain Bo could manage on his own. And she was more than certain of that, especially after their last night together. It had been two in the morning before she crept into her own bedroom, trying her darndest not to wake Pop. Oh, yes, Bo was well recovered and she could hardly wait to see him this afternoon.

Chapter Seventeen

Bo stood on the steps of his cottage after breakfast and watched the gray sedan bump down the drive toward the main house of the Packer ranch. He tugged at the brim of his hat. What the hell was Caroline North doing here so early?

He took two awkward steps down to the ground and walked slowly across the small bit of yard that fronted the place where he'd been staying, thanks to Shorty's generosity. After the fire, he'd been grateful for the privacy the small cottage afforded him.

Privacy was something he appreciated after all the time he'd spent in rehab after the rodeo accident being dependent on everyone from doctors to physical therapists and nurse's aides. Well-meaning people had swarmed around him day and night, and privacy had been nonexistent. Not that he'd cared at first. His depression, along with the excruciating pain of his injuries, made him sullen and his disposition had bordered on nasty. The nurses hadn't failed to inform him of that.

Shorty'd hovered over him like a mother hen during the time he'd stayed in the main house when he first came back to Sweet River because he still needed help getting around. Made him feel like a helpless child. At least, here in the cottage, if he stumbled or his leg gave out and he landed on his ass, there was no one around to witness his clumsiness.

The shout of a young voice broke his reverie and he turned in its direction. Teddie. His heart got all mushy around the edges at the sight of the youngster struggling on wobbly legs and sporting a bright blue cast on his left arm that was clearly covered with autographs.

"Hi, Bo. I came to see if Star is all right. Did you hear Miss Abby's gonna have a rodeo? She needs to build a new place for the Sweet River Riders."

The boy managed the uneven terrain of

the gravel drive without his mother's help, a sunny disposition and exuberance lighting his face with a hopeful smile that went straight to Bo's defensive heart. He didn't want to acknowledge the feelings that were stirring around in his insides like a high-speed mixer. He knew his own attitude needed a major adjustment, but he wasn't ready to deal with that just yet.

"Hey there, Teddie." He waved to the boy and nodded to Caroline as she made her way behind her son. She had a smile for Bo, too, and he just wished to hell they'd quit acting like he was some sort of hero. Anyone would have done what he did. He just happened to be there.

"Yeah, I heard about the rodeo, all right." He took his hat off, fingered a path through his hair and resettled it. Waited to see if the child would pursue the subject further. Hoped he wouldn't.

"How would you like to see Star? She sure missed you." Bo caught the curious look from Teddie's mom at the sudden change of subject. Too bad.

"Can I, really?" Teddie eagerly grabbed Bo's hand and pulled him toward the corral. "Let's go."

"Teddie, don't pester. We only came to thank Mr. Ramsey for helping you and to get him to sign your cast. Remember?" Caroline touched her son's shoulder. "You have to be careful not to fall again."

"Aw, Mom…"

The disappointment on the child's face was too much for Bo.

"I'll see that he doesn't get hurt, ma'am. Why don't you come along, too?" *Okay, so I might be a tad bit attached to the kid.*

"Well, I don't know…" Caroline hesitated.

"Mom, pleeeeeeze," Teddie coaxed. "Bo said Star missed me. She wants to see me, I just know it."

His mother relented with a sigh.

Nothing is more convincing than a six-year-old with a heart-tugging smile and a determined mind. Bo took the boy's small hand in his and led the way to the gate. Their shuffling gait made a *shusshing* duet along the gravel path. When Bo turned around and saw Caroline following them, her quiet smile told him this was a good thing. Actually, he already knew that.

The little mare recognized her friend and trotted over to greet him with a whinny. Her rump still showed signs of where her coat had been singed, but the immediate treatment she'd received had prevented any serious injury.

Bo reached in his shirt pocket for a sugar cube. He'd taken to carrying some every day, just in case. He handed it to Teddie.

"How'd you like to give her the treat? She's been waiting for one and now you can be the one to hand it to her."

Teddie held his good arm outstretched and let Star sniff his open palm before she lipped the sugar cube into her mouth. She twitched her ears at the boy's giggle, then nudged his chest in a friendly hello. It was plain to both Bo and Caroline that the two were enamored of each other.

"You know, Miss Abby said some of the kids are gonna ride in her rodeo." Teddie stroked the little mare's nose, laid his cheek against her, then looked up at Bo. "She said maybe you'd ride, too. Are you, Bo?"

Sucker punched, that's what the youngster's question felt like. Bo could almost feel the fist slamming into his gut. He needed two tries before he could swallow around the prickly lump in his throat and speak.

"Ah…no, buddy. I won't be doing any riding." He averted his gaze from Teddie's inquisitive look. "But I am gonna help Abby get the riders ready."

"Oh." The boy's disappointment was evident in that single, heart-wrenching word. His frail shoulders drooped, but he kept his attention focused on Star. "I thought maybe..."

Caroline smoothed her son's hair, her anxious words soft. "You know, honey, we've already discussed this. You can't ride with a cast on your arm. Not without help. Besides, you haven't even tried to ride all summer."

Bo looked from Teddie's crestfallen face to Caroline and back to the boy. Oh no, huh-uh, he wasn't even gonna think about it. Not a chance. Why did Abby keep raising the boy's hopes? *She knows I can't ride, dammit.*

But Teddie persisted with a quiet challenge. "We could both be cowboys, couldn't we, if we tried real hard?" His small shoulders lifted as he tried to stand tall and straight. "I will, if you will."

The lump in Bo's throat swelled to choking proportions and a strange phenomenon was making his eyes damp. Didn't the boy understand? He was washed-up, a loser. Riding a horse again was out of the question. Hell, he doubted he could even stay in the saddle. You needed two good legs for that.

"He's been asking about this ever since Abby told him the Sweet River Riders were going to participate," Caroline said in her soft-spoken way. "It would mean so much." Her gaze held him frozen to the spot.

Could a crippled cowboy survive being sucker punched by a kid twice in the space of minutes? Hell, no. The big question was, could he and Teddie manage to actually put their imperfect bodies in harm's way again and survive? God, he wasn't sure. Was too scared to even think about trying.

Teddie'd been handed enough disappointments in his young life. He deserved a chance at his dream. Bo swallowed hard. Could he make it happen? Could he put aside his own fear of failure in order to help the boy conquer his own anxieties?

Bo's insides churned at the thought, but deep down, he wanted the opportunity to prove himself as a worthwhile human being again. He needed this chance as much as Teddie did.

A cold wash of apprehension sluiced through his veins—an icy fear of disappointing the people who were counting on him. Teddie and his mom. Shorty. And Abby. Always Abby.

He looked down when the youngster's hand found its way into his, and a powerful surge of warmth washed away the coldness that he'd lived with for so long. Determination replaced fear and all at once, he knew what he had to do if he ever wanted to redeem himself in Abby's eyes.

He knelt to bring himself to eye-level with the child, stifling the groan brought about by the painful position. "Is riding Star what you really want to do?"

The small hand gripped his tighter. "Yep," Teddie whispered. "I wanna be a real cowboy, just like you."

Bo's heart melted right there on the spot. "Then that's what we'll do, partner. We'll ride in the rodeo together."

Teddie whooped with delight and flung his right arm around Bo's neck, bumping the blue-casted one into his chest and nearly toppling them both to the ground. "I knew you would. I just knew it," he cried. "Mom said I shouldn't count on it, but I told her you wanted to be a cowboy again, just like me."

Bo shifted for balance and accepted the child-sized bear hug, blinking hard to hold back stinging tears as he spoke around the gigantic lump in his throat. "Yeah, kiddo, just like you."

What a helluva stupid thing to do, Bo concluded later that afternoon. He swung open the heavy, wooden gate to the area of Shorty's corral that had been designated for the Sweet River Riders practice. The arena buzzed with enthusiastic activity. High-pitched sounds of excited young voices mingled with grown-up laughter.

Standing just inside the gate, he briefly wondered if a person could get seasick on dry land because that's exactly how he felt. He tasted fear like a bitter pill stuck in his throat. Cold sweat popped out on his face, dampened his armpits and trickled down his chest.

He admitted his pride was the reason he couldn't return to the circuit. His rise to rodeo star status was a rush he hadn't expected and he had been relentless in his effort to deliver a perfect, crowd-pleasing performance every time. He'd done it, too, until his luck ran out on a bull that had never been ridden to the buzzer. Bo never intended to enter the arena again unless he could be the best. It was a matter of pride.

Now, here in Sweet River where it all

started, he had a chance to redeem himself. The challenge was there for the taking. Did he believe in himself enough to take it? The spunky determination he saw in Abby's students made him want to try.

It's only a horse, not a damn bull. You've ridden hundreds of them. You can't back out now. He dug deep inside his heart, looking for some kind of inner strength and there it was… Abby's expectant, smiling face right in the center of his soul.

After he'd made that crazy, impulsive promise to Caroline and her son to meet them at the regular afternoon class time and begin working with Teddie and Star, he'd spent the rest of the morning pacing his bedroom, arguing with himself. How could he have even considered such an absurd idea? He could handle helping the boy, but the thought of getting on a horse himself made his stomach spin. *You sure landed in the deep stuff this time, Ramsey.*

He searched the group of people and horses gathered near the entrance to the big barn. *There she is.* His pulse sped up, his whole body energized at the sight of her.

With her pale gold ponytail bobbing from the back of her baseball cap, Abby rushed from student to student, issuing instructions to faithful volunteers, making certain everyone knew what was expected of them. A bundle of energy and efficiency, she was taking charge and getting results. He felt damned inadequate, watching her.

When she reached Laura McBride and IdaJoy, she lingered a bit. Bo observed their serious expressions and guessed Abby was discussing their part in the rodeo exhibition. She'd told him about her decision to have Laura perform first, since the young woman and her horse, Lucky, worked so well together. He also knew that Laura's parents continued to give Abby a hard time. They weren't convinced their daughter's venture into independence by working part-time with IdaJoy was a sensible thing. They held Abby responsible for bringing the two together.

Watching while Laura finished saddling Lucky, Bo saw how animated and cheerful the young woman was around IdaJoy. The two had become close friends in the past few weeks. Abby had told him about IdaJoy spending time with Laura outside the class too, taking her shopping and treating her to "girl things." Laura's new hairdo and bit of makeup made Bo suspect they might have been experimenting with that stuff, too. She'd blossomed as a result of IdaJoy's friendship and kindness. Working at the Blue Moon helped boost Laura's self-confidence, too.

He thought about the other close attachments made between volunteers and students, between students and their horses. Between Abby and the entire group. Because of the extraordinary love she shared with these special kids, she'd found a place for her heart after he'd gone away. A place that didn't include him. He longed for his heart to make its home with hers, but that wouldn't be possible unless he could offer her some kind of security—and a reason to trust him. Something he should have done two years ago. Now, he had to make her believe in him again. He knew what he wanted and what he had to do to get it. And that wasn't gonna happen by standing here like a scared kid.

He shoved aside his growing case of jitters with a deep breath and clenched his jaw. There had to be some way to build a future that didn't require him to be in a saddle. Didn't require being in the public eye.

Abby caught sight of him as he moved away from the gate toward the approaching figures of Caroline and Teddie. She hung back, watched him, and savored the rush of love that swept over her. Waited, instead of running over to embrace him like she wanted to. Keeping her emotions in check when she was near him was no easy task lately. Waiting until they were alone definitely heightened her anticipation of their time together.

So far, they'd managed to keep the status of their renewed relationship fairly private. They weren't ready to reveal their feelings to the public just yet.

Of course, IdaJoy had caught on right away, but solemnly promised to keep their secret. It was anyone's guess how long that would last, though.

Pop and Shorty were aware of the situation, too, since Abby had been spending so much time at the cabin. In fact, she'd been relieved when Pop confronted her and she finally admitted her feelings for Bo.

And then, there was Stuart. *Hmm, maybe their relationship wasn't so private, after all.* Her smile couldn't be contained any longer.

Life kept getting better and better, in spite of all the interfering factors they'd been dealing with since the fire. She and Pop were still in the midst of inventorying their losses for the insurance company. Replacing everything was a gigantic endeavor, even with Stuart's generous donations.

Spending every spare minute in Bo's loving arms made her problems easier to cope with. Made her glad he'd come back to Sweet River, even if it hadn't been for her sake at first. Made her almost thankful for the accident that brought him back to her even though she would have spared him the pain.

"Miss Abby…" A small voice interrupted her thoughts and a small hand tugged her arm.

She looked down to see Teddie grinning up at her, his big, brown eyes shining. This was a surprise. She hadn't expected to see him today, although Caroline had mentioned she would be stopping by later with cookies for the students. Teddie's recovery from the trauma of the fire had been unusually quick, but his family still kept a protective watch over him.

The boy's difficulty walking on uneven ground kept him from being in the arena without assistance. With his arm in a cast, his balance was even more off center. Today, Abby noticed he seemed more excitable than usual.

"Hey, there, Teddie," she said. "Have you

come to get my autograph?" She pointed to his cast.

"Huh-uh, you already signed it, remember? Guess what? Bo and me are gonna practice our riding stuff for the rodeo today," Teddie declared, puffing his chest out proudly. If smiles could be measured by their brightness, his would qualify as megawatts.

"Bo will have you riding like a true cowboy in no time, I'm sure." Abby was glad Bo had decided to keep his promise.

"I'm gonna ride Star. Which one are you gonna let Bo ride?"

For a second, Abby thought she'd heard wrong. Bo was riding? When had that decision been made? Her heart thumped. Could it be he was actually going to try?

"Why, I...don't know. Are you sure he's planning to ride?" She looked at Caroline for confirmation.

"That's what the two of them decided this morning, Abby," the boy's mother said, a warm smile on her face. "I thought Bo would have told you already. He's going to start Teddie's practice session this afternoon."

Bo strolled over to stand behind the pair and favored Abby with a slow, I-know-what-you-did-last-night smile that caused her blood to sing in her veins. She hugged her arms to her chest to keep from throwing them around his neck. Just knowing he was willing to attempt riding again made her love him all the more. She knew he had to somehow find the courage he needed to face his body's weakness. To admit fear was the first step to conquering it. She hoped he believed that.

Now if she could deal with her own niggling fear that he might walk away with her heart again. During their passion-filled nights, Bo had never mentioned the subject of a future together, but she wanted—no, she needed—to believe that he wanted the commitment as much as she did. Trust. She had to trust him. Why was that so hard?

"I'm ready to learn cowboyin'," Teddie piped up, drawing the adults' attention back to his eagerness. "Let's go get Star." He pulled away from his mother's hand and latched on to Bo. "And pick out one for you to ride."

A flicker of uneasiness passed across Bo's face right before he answered. "Uh, why don't we start with your lessons first, partner?" He inclined his head to Caroline, seeking permission.

"Go ahead, Teddie," she said. "I'll be right out here helping Abby." Her hands were clasped together in a nervous attempt to appear calm.

Abby knew the young mother was trying to dispel the fear she held for her precious child's safety and appear confident for her son's sake. She put her hand on Caroline's shoulder, smiled reassuringly and said, "Don't worry. Bo will take good care of him. Come on, you can help me set out cookies."

What she really wanted to do was follow Bo and watch him work with Teddie. Instead, she caught the promise in the look he sent her way and held it in her heart.

Chapter Eighteen

"What if I fall off?" Teddie sat stiff and solemn in the pint-sized saddle, holding Star's reins in his good hand. His blue cast rested in a sling fashioned from a red, white and blue bandana, a gift from his hero. "You'll catch me, won't you, Bo?" His scrawny legs dangled on either side of the little mare, barely reaching the stirrups.

"Don't worry, buddy. I'm here for you. I won't let you fall," Bo said as he guided one small, booted foot into its stirrup. "Here, put your foot right here. Now the other one."

Satisfied the child was seated securely, he rechecked Teddie's riding helmet, felt Star's belly for a final check of the cinch. "Can't forget to tighten this."

Big brown eyes, wide with half excitement, half fear, stared into Bo's as Teddie waited for more instructions. "Okay. What do I do next?"

The boy's voice wavered and Bo's own gut tied in a knot at the child's nervous words. Teddie's fear was balled up right alongside of his own and he wished a thousand times over that he'd never promised to get on a horse. He couldn't do it. But if he didn't, he was gonna look like a coward. Look like? Hell, he was one. He'd just been doing a good job of covering it up—until now. Still, he had to stay strong for the boy. Helping Teddie feel like a real cowboy was more important than dealing with his own fear of losing face in front of his peers.

"Remember how you rode Star out of the barn during the fire? You did it then and you can do it now." Bo took the lead rope and gave Star a pat on her rump. "Give her the command," he said.

"Walk on," Teddie said. Bo walked beside the horse and rider, hoping against hope that Teddie's excitement at riding Star would make him forget about the damned promise.

Star couldn't have been more cooperative,

almost as if she knew her rider needed assurance that everything would be all right. The mare walked as evenly and as smoothly as a dancer. Bo wondered if she knew she carried a treasure on her back.

The way Star protected Teddie in the fire was as incredible as the way Bo had been able to find them and get them all to safety. For once, his bum leg hadn't kept him from doing what had to be done. But he hadn't needed to do it on horseback, either.

The churning started up in his stomach again. *Think about something else, Ramsey.* He directed his attention to Teddie and the happy smile on the child's face.

"How'm I doing, Bo? Look at me. Am I riding like a cowboy yet?"

The youngster was laughing and bouncing in the saddle, trying to coax Star into a trot.

"Hey, watch that busted arm, kiddo. You're not a bronc rider yet." Bo had to trot a bit himself, to keep up. Not easy with an off-kilter gait that made him look like a sand crab in cowboy boots, but what the heck? The kid was having a ball. And, surprisingly, so was he. He liked the warm feeling that filled his chest.

Abby joined in the midst of their laughter with her own shouts of encouragement as she came out of the barn. "Good job, Teddie. You're doing great."

When she caught up with them, Bo favored her with his sexiest smile and her heart jumped again like it always did when she got within touching distance of his body. Sweet heaven, was this going to be a permanent condition? She certainly hoped so. The tingly feeling that raised her pulse and elevated her heart rate was one she never wanted to lose.

"Whoa," Teddie called when they reached the fence rail. Both the boy and the horse looked like they'd just won a gold medal. Star kept bobbing her head, and Teddie couldn't stop squealing his excitement.

"I did it! Did you see me, Miss Abby? Where's my mom?"

"Yes, I did and you were wonderful. You'll be a real cowboy when you ride in the rodeo." She pointed toward the barn. "Here comes your mom now."

Caroline North cheered excitedly and fairly flew across the dusty corral to her son's side. "Oh, Teddie, I'm so very proud of you." Her words bubbled with joy, her smile shone bright with hope. She turned to Bo. "How can we ever thank you?"

Bo shrugged off the praise and lifted Teddie from the horse so the boy could dive into a huge bear hug from his mother.

"We're all proud of you, Teddie. You're very brave and a real cowboy now," Abby told him.

"I know, and I can't wait till Bo rides with me in the rodeo." He left his mother's embrace and leaned against Bo's side. He wrapped his good arm around his idol's leg, smiling up in total adoration. "We'll be cowboys together."

An unmistakable flash of panic swept across Bo's face. Abby watched him struggle to maintain his composure, a noticeable sheen of sweat covering his forehead.

"You okay?" She hoped he hadn't overexerted. He was unusually pale and the nerve in his jaw kept twitching. Something wasn't right.

She watched as he drew himself up, squared his shoulders. The invisible chip on his shoulder suddenly became visible and she could almost feel his mood grow somber.

"Yeah, why wouldn't I be?" His clipped answer didn't quite match the forced smile he gave the boy hanging on his leg. What in the world had brought about this sudden withdrawal?

"No reason, I guess." Puzzled, she decided against pursuing the subject. Sometimes you got more answers by not asking the question.

"Which horse are you gonna ride?" Teddie tugged on Bo's arm impatiently.

Bo looked down. The boy wasn't going to be satisfied until he'd gotten an answer, and Bo couldn't come up with a valid excuse without disappointing him. Damn this hero stuff. He didn't qualify—never had and never would.

He hadn't missed Abby's sharp scrutiny and pointed questions, either. He tried deep breathing, but that didn't help to calm his jerky pulse or slow his heart rate. Nothing less than an honest answer would satisfy her, he knew. Okay, he'd go pick out a horse, but he didn't have to get on it today. The rodeo was a week away. He could stall a little longer. Like a year or two.

One more deep breath. "I thought I'd give Cloud a chance to show off in public."

"Cloud?" Abby's eyebrows arched in surprise. "But he's so old."

Bo shoved his hands in his pockets and rocked back and forth on his boot heels. "He'll do just fine," he insisted, thinking Cloud was frisky enough for him.

"I think Dooley would be a better choice," Abby said with a smile.

He smiled right back through clenched teeth. He wasn't about to challenge Shorty's stallion to a duel in the saddle. Not in this lifetime.

"Dooley doesn't like crowds," he said, hoping like hell she wouldn't know he was guessing. "So you can forget that notion right now."

Fool he might be, but crazy he wasn't. Falling off a horse like a greenhorn in front of a crowd that paid good money to see a professional rodeo rider just wasn't gonna happen. Huh-uh. Besides, he wasn't about to expose his weakness to all his rodeo buddies who had agreed to help out.

Much to Bo's relief, Caroline North chose that moment to return from the barn with a paper plate full of the much-anticipated sweet treats.

"Here comes your mom with the cookies, Teddie." And a change of subject, he hoped. He didn't want Abby pressuring him any more today about why he didn't want to ride in the rodeo.

With a quick thank-you to Caroline for the cookies she insisted he take with him, he said goodbye to his little riding buddy and excused himself to Abby, pleading the need to talk with Shorty. *Get the hell outta here, Ramsey, before you run out of excuses.*

The shadow of hurt that flickered in Abby's eyes made him feel like a first-class heel. Acting like a jackass was uncalled-for. Why the hell didn't she just tell him to get lost? Every time she looked at him with that forever kind of gleam in her eyes, he died a little more. There was no future with him. Couldn't be. They were both fooling themselves if they thought it could happen.

Only a fool would believe something worthwhile could be salvaged from his washed-up career. And Abby was no fool. She wanted stability, security and all that other stuff he could never give her. He would cut out his own heart before he kept her from having the happiness she deserved. He'd hurt her once before. This time he'd leave before they reached the ever after stage.

As soon as the rodeo was over and he made certain Abby and Buck had their ranch back on its feet, he would hightail it out of Sweet River before Abby discovered the real reason for his refusal to ride a horse. For now, he'd keep up the pretense, help Teddie get ready for the rodeo, and try to find a way to make the boy get over the notion that he was some kind of damned hero.

The screen door squeaked on its hinges when it slammed behind him and the hollow sound of his boots on the planked floor made his uneven stride echo off the walls like gunshots. Shorty's house was dark and cool as he made his way down the long hall to the kitchen.

Just like Bo had figured, Shorty was sitting with his feet propped up on a chair pulled around in front of him. He was indulging in an afternoon cup of coffee. The rancher nodded as Bo entered the room, held up his cup. "Want some?"

"No, thanks." Bo filled a glass with water from the tap, drank deeply and returned the empty glass to the counter. He stalled for time, pretending to study a tiny ant scurrying along the windowsill over the sink. He turned around and saw Shorty studying him in the same way he'd been studying the ant.

"Take a load off and sit. You look almost as bad as the day I sprung you out of the hospital." The older man swung his feet off the chair and shoved it toward Bo. "Whatever's eatin' at you can't be all that terrible."

Bo hated that his friend could read him so

well. He thought about going back to wearing his sunglasses again, but Abby'd already convinced him they didn't hide anything. And what he had to hide was bigger than any damn pair of dark glasses.

He drew a hand across his face. "Just tired, I reckon. Trying to keep up with those kids is a workout. Teddie's doing good, though. Got over being scared and now he's gonna ride that little mare through the whole routine." He turned the chair and straddled it, folding his arms across the top.

Shorty nodded. "What about you? I hear you ain't picked out your horse yet. Why don't you ride that stallion I got from that rancher down in San Antone last year? The one called Dooley. I showed him to you when you first come back here, remember?"

If ice could form inside your gut, Bo was sure there was a glacier in his. Was there a damned conspiracy to see him in the saddle? On Dooley? What the hell difference did it make whether he rode a horse or not? He'd never be able to do it for a living again.

"Not a good idea, pal," he muttered. "Wouldn't want to embarrass your horse."

"That's the dumbest thing to come outta your mouth in a long time, cowboy. The horse is broke, for cryin' out loud. It ain't no wild bull."

"Wouldn't matter, one way or the other. I'm not riding. End of discussion." Bo got up, shoved the chair away and stumbled over Ditch's sprawled-out body, barely managing to stay upright.

By the time he reached the door, he was blazing mad and almost forgot the reason he'd wanted to see Shorty. He turned back and swore under his breath as he pulled a crumpled sheet of paper out of his shirt pocket. He tossed it on the table.

"Here's the list of riders who've agreed to appear. They're all donating their winnings to the Sweet River Riders program. You can let Abby know."

"Don'cha think you oughta' do that yourself?"

Bo was already outside, pretending he hadn't heard Shorty's question. He was getting pretty good at that lately.

The last of the horses had been stabled and Abby was ready to head for home. She was grateful to have the use of Shorty's corral and barn, but she'd be glad when her own facilities were restored.

When the insurance company balked at settling on what she thought was a fair amount, she'd geared herself for a fight. Then she'd found out Pop hadn't increased the coverage as she'd thought, so there'd been no recourse but to take the figures the insurance agent had offered. It was better than nothing, but didn't begin to cover the losses. She'd had to juggle numbers in order to use black ink instead of red. Which wasn't anything new.

She wished she didn't have to count so heavily on the proceeds from the rodeo, but there was no other way to raise money. Sweet River wasn't exactly Cheyenne or Calgary. There were only so many rodeo fans in the area.

Granted, the local merchants had donated just about anything and everything she needed. She'd accepted Shorty's offer to stage the event on the south section of his ranch. Fencing for the arena was erected by volunteers and local carpenters had fashioned wooden bleachers, as well. IdaJoy's café was donating food for the concession stand, and her waitresses, along with some high school students, had offered their services as workers.

Two wealthy ranchers from a neighboring

county were donating extra feed for the animals. Bo had promised to contact a major rodeo supplier about lending some prime stock for the entrants to ride. She hoped he'd had good luck. Without credible stock, the riders wouldn't be able make a good showing and the rodeo would be a flop. Besides, the posters were already up all over the county. And her kids were counting on her. She wouldn't let them be disappointed after all their hard work. Swallowing her pride hadn't been easy.

The decision to have the show on Saturday only was hers, and she'd held to it even though Shorty and Pop had voted for a two-day event. She had to think of her students first and foremost. One solid performance would exhaust them, since they were determined to be the best they could be. By showing everyone their hard-earned accomplishments, they knew they would be helping the riding program and their Miss Abby.

She reached the red Taurus parked under the shade of one of the old live oaks at the edge of Shorty's driveway and slid behind the wheel. With a deep sigh, she turned the key and headed down the drive, thinking about the dinner she still had to fix for Pop. One that she hadn't even planned yet. Didn't really want to.

She was so darned tired. What she really wanted was a long, hot shower, a tall glass of iced tea and Bo beside her in bed. None of those wishes looked very forthcoming at the moment.

She contemplated a quick stop by the cabin to see if Bo was over his touchiness about riding Dooley, just as Shorty hurried out of his house waving his hat. Ditch plodded close by his side, wagging his long tail and woofing his own personal greeting. No chance to see Bo. At least, for now.

"Hey, Abby, wait up." Shorty waved again, this time with a piece of paper in his hand instead of his hat. That well-worn part of his outfit was back in place atop his head, his familiar graying braid swinging as his stubby legs carried him toward her.

She braked and waited for him to reach the car. "What's the matter?"

"This here's the list of rodeo entrants." He stuck the paper through the open window.

"I thought Bo was taking care of this," she said as she quickly glanced at names on the wrinkled scrap of paper.

"He did. Told me to give this to you awhile

ago. Said you needed it." Shorty took a couple of deep breaths. Even the short distance he'd jogged had winded him.

Why didn't he give it to me himself? She wanted to ask, but with Shorty eyeing her so closely, she kept the question to herself. Just let her gaze wander to the cabin barely visible behind the thick bougainvillea bushes surrounding both sides of its porch.

A shadow moved across the front window. What was he doing now? Waiting for her? Highly doubtful, since her remarks about riding Dooley had apparently ticked him off. But the idea of him choosing Cloud to ride in the parade was ludicrous. He'd been a big-name rodeo star. Still was. Cloud was a sweetheart, but he was sway-backed, slightly asthmatic and too old to even pretend to prance. His slow, rocking gait was exactly right for some of her students, but Bo Ramsey needed a horse with more spirit, like Dooley.

She scanned the paper again, this time with more care. A shocked gasp caught in her throat.

"Oh my gosh, did you read the names here?" She waved the paper at Shorty in disbelief. The names written in Bo's tight, slanted handwriting were well-known celebrities in the rodeo circuit. And two big country-western singers. Almost as big as Garth and Reba.

"There must be some mistake. Look at this." She punched the paper with her finger. "These people don't agree to perform out of the goodness of their hearts for a small-time fund-raiser like ours." She looked at Shorty. "Do they?"

Shorty scratched his chin. "Reckon they do, if they've got a free spot in their schedule. Seems Bo's story about your kids and the riding program got some of them all excited and wanting to help." He chuckled. "Ain't that just like the ol' Bo? He could have asked a few unknown newcomers, but he went for the big stuff right off. I told you he'd come around. Girl, you're gonna have one deee-luxe show. Just you wait and see."

"I should thank him." Yes, she'd do that right now. She wouldn't stay long, but after all, she was right here, so why not? She turned off the ignition and got out of the car.

"Yeah, you should." Shorty winked, did a little dance, and whistled for Ditch to follow him back inside.

Chapter Nineteen

"I don't understand."

Abby stood in the tiny kitchen of Bo's cabin, hurt, confused and downright angry at the man standing with his back to her.

"I thought I'd made it pretty clear." After a long moment Bo turned around. "I won't be riding in the parade after all. I'll be out of here before Saturday."

"How can you break Teddie's heart like that?" *And mine.* She wanted to stamp her foot. Punch him. Anything to get him to see how wrong he was. "You made a promise."

He looked at her with so much remorse, she felt her heart crack as sadness crept in to replace her anger. Only the shadowed pain in his eyes stopped her from moving toward him.

"Isn't that what I do best, Abby? Break hearts?" His voice was hollow, empty of emotion. "You of all people should know that." His shoulders slumped as he tunneled his fingers through his hair. "I'm not a hero. Don't expect me to be one. There was a time when I was proud of what I did for a living because I knew I was the best. And I wanted you with me—wanted you to be proud of me, too. But now, I have nothing to offer you. It's better for everyone if I leave."

His last words were a hoarse whisper, but she heard them with her heart.

"You're right, Ramsey," she said, wrapping her arms around herself to ward off the sudden chill racing through her. "Trust has to be earned. I guess trusting you to stay was too much to ask, wasn't it?"

She didn't dare wait for his answer. Couldn't see his reaction through the blur of tears filling her eyes. Barely made her way out to the car. Her world was crumbling and she was powerless to stop it. If Bo really loved her, he would stay and let her help him face his fears. It was a matter of trust.

The pain in her heart was so acute, she looked down expecting to see it shattered in tiny pieces on the floor. How could she live without her heart? Without Bo?

How could he live without her? He grabbed an empty glass from the counter and hurled it across the room. He watched, satisfied, as it hit the door and splintered across the kitchen floor in a shower of fragmented prisms.

He stared at the mess through a red cloud of anger and disgust. The block of ice lodged in the pit of his stomach had *coward* carved all over it. He had to curl his hands into tight fists to keep from bashing them into the wall. Swallowed hard to keep from choking on the bitter taste of disappointment.

His only chance for happiness had disappeared when Abby walked out the door and, like a fool, he'd let her go. Let his fear of failure control his heart…and their future together. Now he was left with nothing but a yearning so deep, the pain was inescapable. Had she felt this same crushing pain before when *he'd* been the one to leave? How had she managed to survive? How could he not have known the hurt he'd inflicted on her? Her strength amazed him. The need to redeem himself, to make Abby proud of him, was like an albatross around his neck. He'd failed everyone who had ever tried to help him, when all he'd ever wanted was Abby's love.

He dropped into a nearby chair, covered his face with his hands, and gave in to the desolate sense of loss tearing at his insides. A wretchedly pitiful sob escaped his lips as unexpected tears slid down his roughened cheek. Harsh tears of anguish released his misery, emptied him of the self-pity that had fed his fear.

He didn't know how long he'd been sitting there, but when he finally raised his head, the sun had already gone down, leaving behind streaks of pink and gold in the western sky. Shadows played across the room, accentuating its sparse furnishings and the solitary existence he'd begun to accept as his fate. The emptiness in his soul was more than he could endure.

He thought about Teddie and the way the boy had overcome his terror of getting on a horse again. Of his own promise to ride with him, if Teddie would just try. Each time they worked with Star, the boy became more confident. When Teddie finally struggled up in the saddle, it was Bo's neck that he'd hugged first. Bo who was privileged to wipe away the boy's tears of happiness and hug him back.

Teddie conquered his fear because he'd never given up on his dream of becoming a cowboy. "Just like you, Bo," the boy had said.

What would he think now, when his hero didn't show up, like he'd promised? Who would make sure his helmet was fastened securely and his stirrups were shortened to just the right length? What if Teddie needed him?

He remembered a time when Abby had needed him—loved him. But he'd failed miserably at becoming the person she believed him to be. Even though he knew he had no right, he'd accepted the love she'd offered again. What kind of heartless, self-pitying man had he turned into?

Bo walked to the window and stared into the lonely night. Was it too late for him to change now, even if he could?

The day of the much anticipated fund-raiser dawned sunny and hot. Temperatures were expected to hit the nineties, so the Sweet River volunteers had come early to the newly erected arena to begin their long list of chores. Water troughs were filled and horses groomed. The arena was raked and ready.

The new equipment Stuart had donated arrived two days earlier and Abby had to admit the saddles and helmets looked terrific.

Shorty and Buck hustled from one end of the barn to the other, making sure nothing was forgotten. The two men had mounted banners of red, white and blue over the entrance to the ranch. This morning, the flags snapped a salute in the welcome breeze. Of course, Shorty made certain that everyone within hearing distance knew whose idea the banners were.

Abby watched the enthusiastic participants scurry back and forth from the corral to the arena with mixed emotions. The prospect of finally being able to rebuild her own barn and corrals filled her with humble gratitude, but she couldn't dispel the deep ache in her heart that constantly reminded her of Bo.

His refusal to carry out his promise to Teddie was only part of her heartache. What really broke her heart was the fact that nothing had really changed between them. He was leaving, just like before.

She blinked back stinging tears and made a quick swipe of her hand across her eyes, resolving to put Bo out of her mind. At least for the duration of the rodeo. She had just pasted a smile on her face when a kaleidoscope of color swept into the arena and Abby knew the day was about to get better.

IdaJoy rushed up to her with a gleam in her eyes and the shiny, color-splashed uniform of the Sweet River Riders clinging to her sumptuous curves like purple and gold metallic paint. There was definitely no way the crowd was going to miss seeing her group.

"Abby, hon," the woman said, her breasts heaving beneath her satin shirt. "I know you said this shirt didn't need any more fringe, but don't you think this teensy bit right here just adds the final touch?"

IdaJoy shimmied her shoulders, causing gold fringe to swing and sway from the top of her sleeves to the bottom of her satin cuffs, to say nothing of the rest of the fringe undulating down the front of her shirt.

If there'd been any more gold trim available at the fabric shop, Abby shuddered to think what else IdaJoy would have decorated.

"You look…fine," Abby said, biting her lip to keep a straight face. "You've done a wonderful job making all the shirts in such a short time."

She eyed the gold satin pants IdaJoy wore like a coat of paint and silently rejoiced that the students were wearing regular jeans for their performance. The purple and gold satin shirts were flashy enough to make them feel like professional rodeo stars. They had clapped and cheered when IdaJoy brought the finished items to the last practice.

Abby had collected enough cowboy hats from a shop in Austin for the entire group and had fashioned hatbands out of purple ribbon. Each hat sported a gold feather stuck in its band. Since they had to wear the new riding helmets when they performed, Abby wanted them to have the cowboy hats to wear while they watched the rest of the show.

"You know, hon, I would've made you an outfit like mine if you'd let me. Then we could all look the same." IdaJoy gave Abby's less-than-colorful white western shirt with its navy blue embroidered yoke, a *tsk-tsk* and a shake of her head. "You would've looked great in a pair of these pants, too."

Not in this lifetime. The day Abby wore gold satin pants would be the day she dyed her hair red to match the new shade IdaJoy had chosen for this week.

"Thanks, but these jeans will work better

for me. I won't have to be careful of them when I'm in the barn."

"Well, I happen to know that good-lookin' Doctor Wilcox thinks these outfits are real nifty." IdaJoy's cheeks turned even pinker than they already were. "You *are* just friends now, aren't you, hon?"

"Of course. That's all we ever were. Why?" Abby studied IdaJoy's face. The woman was actually blushing. Could it be…?

"I, uh, wanted to be sure before I took him up on his offer of dinner next week. Are you, uh, sure you don't mind?" IdaJoy was actually stammering.

Abby laughed and hugged her. "I'm absolutely positive. Oh, IdaJoy, that's so great. Stuart is a wonderful person." The possibility of these two deserving people enjoying each other's company was an unexpected surprise, and guaranteed to wipe Abby off the local gossip sheet. This was certainly proof that opposites really could attract.

As IdaJoy whirled off in a flurry of swinging gold fringe, Abby caught herself envying the woman's effervescent free spirit. Maybe when the rodeo was over and the rebuilding of her barn and stables was finished, she'd work on her personal life. How would she look as a redhead? Pushing the silly thought aside, she made her way to the hub of excitement, eager to immerse herself in helping her students prepare for the most important day of their lives.

"Ladies and gentlemen, cowboys and cowgirls. Welcome to the biggest little rodeo in Texas." The announcer's voice boomed over the loudspeaker as the crowd cheered. "The Sweet River Riders invite you to stand and turn your attention to the south side of the arena where the Stars and Stripes, carried by IdaJoy Sparks riding Sweet Thing, will pass in review, followed by Laura McBride riding Lucky and carrying the flag of the great Lone Star State of Texas."

Abby deliberately stayed away from the entrants' gate after she helped with the lineup. She hoped her students would be inspired and encouraged, knowing she had enough confidence in their abilities to let them perform without her. Besides, the volunteers had practiced endlessly and weren't about to let anything happen to their charges. This performance was as important to them as it was to the kids. The group was scheduled to enter the arena right after the national anthem was played and the crowd sang "The Eyes of Texas."

Abby craned her neck to see better as Ida-Joy and Laura rode by, their backs straight and their eyes bright. Pride swelled inside her chest and pushed against her ribs so hard, she thought she might just explode right then and there.

During the music, she scanned the crowd and mentally tallied the attendance. The bleachers overflowed, and the standing observers were packed in wherever they could find an empty inch or two of ground to stand on. Things were off to a great start.

The last strains of music faded as IdaJoy and Laura circled the arena to ride toward the back gate. There were a few bright pops from flashbulbs going off, but Abby's gaze was fastened on the riders gathering to enter the arena. Bright purple shirts glistened in the afternoon sun as the students and volunteers got ready to give the performance of their lifetime.

The cheers from the crowd began to swell as, one by one, the riders slowly made their way to the center of the arena, each accompanied by a volunteer. They formed a line, faced the bleachers and waved. Then Teddie rode out on Star shouting, "Yippee!" Every single person stood and waved back as he trotted his horse to the front of the line, giving his helper a good run. The roar of the applause was deafening. The cheers exuberant. Then the noise silenced as suddenly as it had begun, and an expectant gasp rippled through the crowd.

Another rider entered the arena, identically garbed in a purple satin shirt with gold fringe. A few cautious shouts rose from the crowd, when the rider was recognized. Those were quickly followed by cheers from the Sweet River Riders and their helpers.

Abby's knees started to shake, and a thousand creepy-crawlies invaded her stomach. She must be seeing things. *Oh, my God.* Her crazy heartbeat stuttered and stumbled. Tears welled in her eyes and spilled. She couldn't stop them. Didn't try. *Where did he get that ridiculous shirt?*

Bo rode toward her on Dooley, his hands white-knuckled around the reins, his cowboy hat pushed back to give the crowd an unobstructed view of his face.

He halted his horse in front of Abby, and Teddie's little mare walked quietly to stand next to Bo's big stallion. Abby's heart stopped beating altogether. With a sweep of his hand, Bo removed his beloved Stetson and placed it over his heart.

What is going on? Abby couldn't stop shaking.

The crowd stilled, suddenly full of eager anticipation and small-town curiosity. No doubt IdaJoy was taking notes.

"Miss Abby Houston?" Bo's husky voice filled the air with such emotion, the crowd gave a collective sigh.

Abby saw his heart reflected in the dark, smoky depths of his eyes, and when he smiled she dared to hope for the promise it held.

"Will you marry me and let me be a part of your life…and the Sweet River Riders?" The words came out a little shaky just then and Dooley did a side-stepping prance. Bo cleared his throat and locked his gaze with Abby's. "I love you."

IdaJoy raised her hand and the students picked up the signal. "We love you, too, Miss Abby!"

Her tears flowed freely now. Dear God, she didn't know what to do. The whole crowd trained their attention on her as she stumbled over the bleachers and made her way around the fence to stand by Dooley. She could barely see Bo through her tear-filled eyes. Her voice disappeared somewhere inside her heart. This was Bo, and he was riding Dooley. She really did believe in miracles.

"Well? Will you?" His hand was shaking as he held it out to her.

She clung to it and looked up into his endearing face. The face her heart recognized as flawless. The face of the man she loved.

"I thought you were gone." She gulped. "I…don't know what to say." Her heart kicked up its pace. Her blood thrummed in her veins. Could she trust him this time? Oh, she wanted this so much.

"*Yes* would be a good choice." His voice lowered. "I couldn't leave because… I need you. I love you, Abby. And I love these kids. Please give me a chance to prove it."

She searched his face, saw sincerity mixed with anxiousness in his dark eyes and knew if he could take the first step in facing his fears, she could take a step forward also. Her fear of being left again might hover in the background, but she vowed silently to do her best to overcome it. Bo's love would make it possible.

"We're all waiting to hear your answer, Abby." The announcer's voice boomed through the speakers and the crowd cheered. A few old-timers even tossed their hats in the air.

Abby heard Shorty and Pop shouting encouragement and when she glanced toward the back of the arena, her students were all chanting "Yes, yes, yes" and waving their new cowboy hats.

Her heart overflowed with love. She squeezed her eyes to stem a fresh rush of tears. Sucked in a deep breath. She could barely speak.

"Yes, oh yes, I'll marry you, Ramsey, but only if you promise to never leave home without me."

"What did you say?" the announcer called out.

Teddie waved his good arm at the crowd. "She said 'yes.' Whoopee!"

Bo swung Abby up in the saddle in front of him, gave her a kiss on her cheek and whispered, "I also promise that our next kiss will be a helluva lot more satisfying."

He hugged her, then leaned over and gave Teddie a high five. "Way to go, cowboy," he said with a wink.

Teddie puffed out his chest, touched the brim of his helmet and winked back—almost.

"You, too, cowboy. We sure did it, didn't we, Bo? I told you we could, if we tried hard enough."

The lump in Abby's throat nearly stole her voice, but she swallowed around the exquisite ache and leaned back against Bo as they circled the arena on Dooley. "You sure did, pardners," she said. "You absolutely did."

They'd waited to slip away until after the Sweet River Riders had given their heart-warming performance. Up until then, Bo and Abby had been surrounded by well-wishers and slaps on the back and, of course, hoots and hollers from Bo's rodeo buddies.

Crazy as it seemed, Abby enjoyed every minute of it and as she watched Bo's reaction to the public attention, she knew he did, too. The open adoration and acceptance from his peers served to reinforce what she'd tried to tell him all along—that his appearance didn't alter the man he was inside.

There wasn't a dry eye in the crowd after the children went through their routines without a hitch. Abby and every one of the dedicated volunteers cheered loud and long, because they knew just how hard the students had worked and what this day meant to each of them. They were special—no doubt about it.

Bo cheered for Teddie so loud he grew hoarse. And Teddie had whooped with joy when Bo gave him his favorite Stetson and told the boy he'd earned the right to wear it.

The enthusiastic crowd cheered because they knew the performance they'd just witnessed was worth much more than the price of their admission.

The media had picked up on the show earlier and turned out in full force. Flashbulbs popped and TV cameras whirred. The reporters even coaxed a promise from Abby for a full interview later. Thanks to the hard work of the entire community, the show was a huge success—more than she'd ever dreamed possible. Her special kids had won the hearts of everyone there. Their performance had outshone the professional stars by a mile. The country singers were so touched, they promised to give a concert later in the year to benefit the program. And Bo promised to work with Abby and the kids to make the riding program one of the best.

The night was magical, especially when Abby and Bo finally managed to be alone.

"Do you think they missed us?" Bo asked

as he rolled over in bed to gather Abby in his arms. "We did sneak out before the main event, you know."

"Did we?" Abby caressed his face, his chest, his hard, bare abdomen. Her hand rested low on his belly and she felt his need for her rise again. "I thought the main event had taken place right here."

He kissed her once more, slowly and thoroughly, until she thought it couldn't get any better.

"And it's about to happen again. Very soon," he murmured against her mouth.

"I certainly hope so." She kissed the curve of his ear, the hollow of his throat, the solidness of his chest. Raising up on one elbow, she met his gaze with a smile. "But, I still want to know how IdaJoy managed to get you to wear that funky shirt." She quirked an eyebrow at him. "And how did she know your size?"

Bo caught her hand and brought it to his mouth. Kissed each fingertip. "Have you ever tried to argue with a gum-snapping whirlwind wearing tight gold pants and a hairdo right out of a nightmare? One who's hell-bent on getting her own way? Darlin', if there's one thing I know, it's when to hold and when to fold. Believe me, IdaJoy can persuade almost any man to fold."

He nuzzled her neck, nipped the soft flesh there while his hands were busy with other highly aroused areas of her body. He was making her crazy with wanting him again.

"Are you saying it takes a woman like Ida-Joy to make you fold?" Liquid warmth raced through her veins at his continued caresses. She gave in to the sensation and trailed her fingers down his abdomen to that wonderfully masculine part of him so eager for her touch.

He pushed her back onto the bed, groaned low in his throat and moved over her. "Miss Abby, you had me folded and bagged a long time ago. You're the only one I ever want to hold. Just like this. Forever."

"That's a promise I won't let you forget, Ramsey," she murmured against his mouth, then kissed him greedily with a promise of her own. "I love you, cowboy."

She was more than ready when he slid into her. Hot and wet, she welcomed him. Arched to meet his thrust. Celebrated when he filled her, touched the very essence of her.

His words were hoarse and filled with emotion. "You…are…my heart and soul.

My strength. You give my life meaning. And darlin', I promise to love you forever."

"I do like the 'forever' part, Ramsey," Abby whispered, moving against him and wasting no time making it very clear she was in total agreement. "I've heard there are countless fantastic ways to spend a lifetime."

Bo grinned. "One can only hope."

* * * * *

HHBPA17

Get 2 Free Books,
Plus 2 Free Gifts —
just for trying the Reader Service!

Get 2 Free Books,
<u>Plus</u> 2 Free Gifts —
just for trying the Reader Service!